I0604121

IN
THIS
WORLD

SHAWN THORN

First paperback edition March 2024
First hardcover edition March 2024

Book design by Shawn Thorn
Image by Firefly
Author photo by Vincenzo Coia
Title: In This World: The Unbound Stone by Shawn Thorn

ISBN 978-0-9940979-3-4 (paperback)
ISBN 978-0-9940979-2-7 (hardcover)
ISBN 978-0-9940979-4-1 (e-book)

Printed and bound in United States
Published by shawnthornbooks.com

This book is dedicated to my husband, whose unwavering support made it possible for me to carve out the time to bring these pages to life. To Audrey, the muse behind the mythical creatures that dance through these chapters. Watching you grow up reading through an eleven-book series about dragons inspired me. To my son, Elio, who nestled close to me with wide-eyed wonder while I typed away. Your patient and affectionate presence turned each writing session into a truly heartwarming and loving experience. These cherished moments of togetherness added a special touch to the creative process, making it all the more meaningful.

And to you, the one delving into these words: as you explore your cherished books and beloved stories, remember the unwritten tale of your own life awaiting its chapters. Your story, an endless adventure waiting to be penned. Dream fervently, and cling to those dreams for as long as they inspire you.

IN
THIS
WORLD

The Unbound Stone

Chapter 1

The first light of dawn painted the sky with hues of pink and orange as Jack and Kass emerged from their tent at 6:30 a.m. They stood in awe of the breathtaking tropical wilderness surrounding them, a pristine world practically untouched by civilization.

"I can't believe we get to witness this view," Jack exclaimed, a sense of wonder in his voice.

Initially hesitant about the school camping trip, Kass found himself caught up in the magic of the moment. Inhaling the fresh mountain air, he felt a profound sense of connection to the natural world.

"You were right, Jack, this *is* pretty cool." Kass's words were more than just an admission, they represented a newfound appreciation for the adventure unfolding before them.

Kass, with his pretty-boy features and perfectly styled hair, exuded a level of confidence that drew eyes wherever he went. His smooth caramel skin and slender frame added to the allure, and his forest-green eyes held a hint of mischief that kept everyone guessing.

But the sense of wonder wasn't confined to just these two friends. The raw, untamed beauty of the Costa Rican wilderness had cast a spell on all eighteen teens from

Cypress High, a school located more than four-thousand miles to the north in the scenic metropolitan city of Kelowna, British Columbia. The teens awoke and soaked up the majesty of their surroundings. For some, this was their first encounter with such unspoiled nature, and it humbled them with its magnificence. Towering trees, vast landscapes, and the overwhelming glory of the natural world left them speechless, promising that their appreciation would only grow stronger in the three days ahead.

Over the first two days of their trip, the class took gorgeous treks, immersing themselves in the wild beauty of Costa Rica. As the sun dipped below the horizon, they then gathered around a campfire beneath the starry night sky, sharing playful stories of mischief and playing daring games. With laughter echoing through the darkness, they played games of Twenty-One Questions, chased each other in flashlight tag, and shared ghost stories.

But on the third night, a new and true adventure began. Eager to break free from the school's structured activities, Jack, Kass's best friend, and Gab, Jack's longtime girlfriend, initiated a clandestine plan with a shared mischievous glint in their eyes. Jack, 6'5" tall, was a quintessentially handsome athlete with blond hair and hazel eyes. Gab was pretty, petite, and Chinese-American. Together, Gab and Jack made a striking pair, despite their height differences.

Silently, Kass, Jack, Gab, and two other close friends, Harlen and Olivia, slipped out of their tents and followed Gab into the unknown wilderness.

"Let's head this direction," Gab suggested with authority.

"Aye aye, captain, lead the way," Jack teased in a whisper, their flashlights piercing the darkness.

Harlen, a lanky-looking teen with a wonderful sense of humor, incessantly rang his bear bells when they were a fair distance from the camp. "Keeps the bears away," he claimed. The group chuckled softly as they ventured into the jungle, the moon's glow and their phone flashlights guiding their way.

"This is so creepy," Olivia whispered to Kass, who offered a reassuring smile.

"Why are we doing this again?" Gab asked, her voice tinged with unease.

"To get attacked by a damn bear, no doubt," Harlen quipped. He was determined to keep the mood light.

Jack, their intrepid leader, encouraged the group to embrace the experience as they continued deeper into the mysterious jungle. Each step into the darkness heightened their anticipation and trepidation.

"Where's your sense of adventure?" Jack said.

"Back in my tent," Kass chuckled, avoiding the loose dirt and brambles concealed in the underbrush.

"Ah, I have to go pee," Harlen's sudden announcement broke the stillness.

"Well, go pee," Jack replied casually. "No one's stopping you."

"No way, Jack! I'm not getting my junk bitten off by some forest creature. And I do not want to get friendly with a python tonight," Harlen exclaimed. "But I'm desperate. Stop walking, I gotta go!"

The group laughed, waiting for Harlen to take care of his business before they continued their journey into the night. Their laughter filled the silence, temporarily erasing the tension that had been building up.

After nearly an hour of trekking, they arrived at a mound of large boulders adjacent to the edge of a steep cliff overlooking what appeared to be a deep canyon.

"Let's stop here," suggested Olivia, catching her breath. "This looks like the perfect spot to rest and stargaze."

The teens settled down on the boulders, gazing at the moon and the sparkling display of stars above, feeling the magic of the night enveloping them. Despite their initial nervousness, they were grateful for this late-night adventure, forging unforgettable memories under the watchful eye of the moonlit sky.

"This is soooo pretty," Gab exclaimed.

"Definitely worth tromping through this creepy jungle to see," Olivia agreed. "Absolutely magnificent."

Perched on the massive boulders like a group of daring adventurers, Gab dramatically flopped into Jack's arms, pretending to be exhausted and sighing in a sexy, breathy voice, "Oh, Romeo, carry me away like the daring knight in shining armor you are."

Jack chuckled, playing along. "As you wish, my lady. I'm at your command."

Harlen used his jacket as a makeshift pillow and laid his tired body back onto the boulder. Olivia and Kass sat peacefully among their friends, gazing upward and relishing the serene environment.

"Wow, look at all the stars. There must be millions," Harlen said.

"Actually, there are billions," Olivia informed him. "Can you see Orion?"

"He's over there," Kass pointed.

"Alright, gather 'round, everyone. I've got an out-of-this-world story for you about the stars and planets," Olivia said, as her friends gazed above and prepared to listen to her story.

Regarded by some as a science nerd, Olivia took pride in her academic prowess. She had been participating in state science fairs since a young age and had secured the first place prize for the past four years. Her dedication and passion for science were evident as she eagerly anticipated the next science fair, just two months away.

"So, you know how we look up at the night sky and see those twinkling little lights? Those are stars, and they're not merely any stars—they're the rockstars of the universe. Picture this: billions of stars are hanging out in space, just like us hanging out in our school hallway, chatting away and shining bright. But guess what?"

"What?" Gab asked, eagerly.

"They have their own cool cliques up there, too. Some stars like to huddle together in big groups called galaxies, like our friend groups at lunchtime. They're super social and love being around each other. So, while you're looking up at the night sky, remember that you're not just seeing random lights. You're seeing stars and planets putting on the grandest show ever, exclusively for us Earthlings. And if you ever feel lost in the vastness of space, just remember that we're all part of this incredible cosmic party, dancing together in this celestial ballroom of the universe."

After a few moments of reflection, the silence was broken.

"Mommy...please tell us another story. Please, Mommy...pl—" Harlen begged, his tone laced with playful mockery, but he was cut off by a thunderous roar that shattered the tranquility of the night and sent shivers down the group's spines.

Kass shouted in panic and his friends all jumped up with fear etched on their faces. An unknown threat had thrust them into high alert.

"What was that!?" Olivia gasped.

"I don't know," Jack exclaimed.

"A bear?" Kass speculated, his voice quivering.

"That would be one big ass bear," Jack stammered, his bravado fading.

Harlen's hands trembled as he frantically rang his little bells, a behavior that would have been comical under different circumstances.

"Rah! Rah!" Jack bellowed as menacingly as possible.

Another bone-chilling screech of primal fury pierced through the forest.

"Oh, what the hell! He heard you, Jack, and he is not amused," Harlen cried out.

Although the beast remained hidden from sight, its proximity was undeniable. Fear gnawed at their resolve, urging them to flee for their lives.

"I'm getting the heck out of here," Harlen declared.

"Me too," Gab agreed.

"Me three," Olivia echoed.

"Stay together and keep ringing those bells, Harlen!" Jack instructed, trying to keep a sense of control in the chaotic moment.

The five friends dashed away from the direction of the noise, their hearts pounding in sync with their hurried footsteps.

The haunting roar repeated, piercing the night and pushing them to pick up the pace. They ignored the scrapes and scratches from the unforgiving underbrush, driven only by an instinct to survive.

As they raced toward camp, the echoing growls grew fainter. The beast wasn't following them, but their fear lingered like a ghost in the night.

Before long, they reached their tents then huddled next to their tent mates, taking refuge in their sleeping bags. The mysterious encounter had left an indelible mark, reminding them of the untamed dangers lurking in the wilderness.

Chapter 2

Morning arrived way too soon with the friends barely rested.

"Rise and shine!" Mr. Beson shouted as he walked around the campsite banging on a metal pan with a wooden spoon. Kass and Jack awoke and stared at each other from their sleeping bags.

"That was some crazy shit last night. What the heck was that thing?" Kass muttered, still half asleep.

"I have no idea and no interest in finding out," said Jack, crawling out of his sleeping bag.

After just enough time to get dressed, use the latrine, and wash their faces, the five friends gathered for an urgent private rendezvous.

"Alright, I'll say it. That didn't sound like a bear," Gab blurted.

"Oh, so now you're a bear expert?" Harlen said, sarcastically.

"I don't think bears even inhabit Costa Rica," Olivia said.

"Whatever it was, it was scary for sure, but also exciting. I'm still running on adrenaline," Jack commented.

"We have to go back," Harlen surprised everyone by saying.

"Oh, hell no! I am not going back there. Whatever that was, it can stay right there."

"I'm with Olivia. I'm not going back," Gab added.

"We have to. I left my jacket," Harlen said, as a matter of fact.

"You can use my jacket," Kass offered.

"My passport is in my jacket. I gotta have it," Harlen emphasized with desperation.

"Damn, Harlen, Mr. Beson specifically told us to put our passports in our backpacks," Gab said.

"We're going back, guys," Jack declared, his voice firm.

The others looked at him, respecting his natural authority, and nodded in agreement. He was right; they couldn't leave their friend without his passport. Nevertheless, they glanced at each other, concerned. Just contemplating going back to the same location evoked a collective shudder.

"I'm not sure we can get out of here before dusk. The chaperones will be watching us like hawks," Jack said. "But we can try. And let's be sure to take more than just bells and flashlights this time."

"What are you guys up to?" Jessica, the school gossip queen, inquired.

"Oh, nothing, just chatting about the birds," Olivia said casually.

"Yeah...yeah, the birds. Just the birds...and the bees," Harlen cracked, along with his voice. He sounded like he was experiencing puberty all over again.

"Mmhmm...birds, eh?" doubted Jessica.

"And bees, don't forget the bees," added Harlen, raising his eyebrows and hoping to get a laugh.

"Nope. You're definitely up to something," she said with a scowl then walked away, but not without first taking a glaring glance back at the group.

"Why is Martin smiling at us from over there?" Jack asked his buddies. Martin was Jessica's stunningly handsome boyfriend and popular school jock. "I wonder if he could have followed us into the forest last night and was the roaring 'beast'. Ugh...I bet you it was him. And he's got a loud enough mouth to do it, too."

"That makes so much more sense than anything I was imagining," Harlen said. "Just look at him. Yep, it was him."

The group questioned where Harlen was going when he stood up and started walking in Martin's direction. With Harlen's slim, unassuming 5'8" frame, and an appearance that subtly hinted at his Latino heritage, he might be described as rather ordinary. However, what truly distinguished him at school was his long, blue-black hair, always impeccably tied in a ponytail that gracefully cascaded down his back.

Harlen approached Martin, nonchalantly sitting next to him in silence. The two boys exchanged side-eye glances, creating a lighthearted tension until Martin couldn't resist breaking the silence.

"Man, what's up with you? Why are you sitting next to me and saying nothing?" Martin asked, raising an eyebrow.

"Ah, just relaxing, Martin. Just getting a little shade," Harlen replied playfully.

"Dude, there's no shade. I'm literally sitting in the sun," Martin exclaimed with a chuckle.

"A'ight, so I was wondering, how did you sleep last night?" Harlen asked, not so subtly shifting the conversation.

"What do you mean, how did I sleep? Alright, I guess. Why, what are you up to? You're being weird," Martin said.

"Man, I'm just saying, I saw you leave your tent last night and was just wondering if you were okay," Harlen said.

"I went pee if it's any of your business. Has a crime been committed here or what?" Martin replied, playing it cool.

"Okay, so you went pee and then where?" Harlen probed, trying to maintain a playful tone.

"Nowhere. I went back to bed. You're really being weird, Harlen. Go back over there with your Rupaul Drag Race gang and leave me alone," Martin quipped, starting to get annoyed.

"Okay, okay, don't get your undies in a bunch. Just making sure you weren't—"

"What!?" Martin barked in frustration.

"Simmer down, simmer down, young man. You're so testy," Harlen teased. He stood up, smiled, and backed up a few feet before turning around and rejoining his friends.

As Harlen walked away, Martin began wondering what Harlen and his friends were up to.

"What did you say to him?" asked Kass.

"Yeah, what did you two talk about?" Gab asked.

"He looked like he was about to punch you," Jack said, concerned.

"It's all good my friends. He said he only left his tent to go pee and that was that," Harlen explained. "But I'm not convinced. He seemed rather defensive."

"Ah hah! So, he *was* the one who followed us. That would explain why he was staring over here with that mischievous smile and why he 'only' went pee," Olivia said, eyebrows furrowed.

"That wicked boy. He scared the heck out of us," Gab said, wearing her hair pulled back in a bun that framed her delicate face and accentuated her smooth skin and bright smile. Gab was not only pretty, but talented, too. She and Kass often acted in the school plays together. She was confident, agile, and quiet—unlike her laugh, which was loud and infectious.

***

The five friends spent the rest of the day enjoying more of the organized camp activities: a nature scavenger hunt, hiking, and games of charades and stick limbo.

Kass enjoyed himself the least, spending more time trying to stay clean and well-groomed than relaxing and having fun. When his friends noticed him being particularly persnickety, they chortled with amusement. As fastidious as he was, however, they thought he was actually doing better than they had expected. At least he was participating in all the activities. They were impressed. And when Kass leaped into the deep, crystal clear waters of Lake Fortono near their camp, an explosion of excitement and exhilaration engulfed him. He had always been a bit resistant when it came to sports, but swimming and diving were different. They were activities he genuinely enjoyed, despite his aversion to traditional team sports.

The lake, glistening like a vast mirror, reflected the surrounding lush greenery and the vibrant blue sky. The gentle ripples on the water's surface danced playfully. A twenty-five-foot waterfall graced the scene near the swimming hole. It was a magnificent cascade of frothy white water that tumbled majestically over the rocks in a rush of soothing sound. Its sheer power and beauty captured their imagination, leaving them spellbound by nature's grandeur. The misty spray that rose from the waterfall's base carried a refreshing coolness, inviting the teens to come closer and immerse themselves.

With a characteristic glint of joy, Kass discarded the idea of a regular cannonball. Instead, he decided to take it up a notch, going for a front flip with a half-twist off the side of the cliff, about fifteen feet above the surface of the water. The other teens watched with admiration at his daredevil antics.

"Pretty nice, my friend," complimented Harlen. "Now, let me show you how it's supposed to be done." Harlen climbed to the same elevation as Kass and made a grand spectacle of holding out his arms as if ready to take flight. With everyone prepared to be impressed, Harlen plugged his nose and jumped, screaming and kicking his legs all the way to the water.

Following Kass's demonstration, his classmates eagerly took turns showcasing their skills. Yet, most opted for cautious jumps or dives from the nearby boulders, often resulting in belly flops and clumsy splashes—far from graceful or aesthetically pleasing. Despite the lack of finesse, the atmosphere was electric with everyone thoroughly enjoying themselves.

In the high school social scene, a notable clique of 'mean girls' led by Jessica held court. Jessica, with her flair for striking poses, stood out in the midst of the laughter and camaraderie. Water-centric fun was not her scene. She was more focused on keeping her hair flawless and maintaining that ever-ready Instagram look. Her mean-girl squad played the role of vigilant protectors, ensuring she remained untouched by any splashes, all while crafting the perfect social media narrative.

Harlen, with his spirited humor, couldn't resist teasing her. "Hey Jessica, the water's fine. You should give it a try. It might help you find your chill...if that's even possible."

The other teens giggled, trying not to be too obvious about their amusement. But Jessica, with her I'm-too-fabulous-for-this attitude, just rolled her eyes and smirked.

"You're hilarious, Harlen. But I'd rather stay dry and perfect, thank you very much," Jessica replied, flipping her hair with dramatic flair.

"Yeah, more like perfectly boring," Olivia whispered to Harlen, a delightfully snarky comment Harlen was tempted to share with Jessica. Fortunately, he did not.

Chapter 3

F ive teenage hearts were all aflutter, knowing they would once again be traveling through the woods in the dark and heading to the same destination to retrieve Harlen's forgotten jacket and passport. Was that really Martin roaring at the top of his lungs, or was there a ferocious bear or other beast lingering in the woods? It seemed inconceivable Martin could have made such an inhuman sound, but perhaps he used some kind of makeshift megaphone to amplify his voice. To believe that horrible noise was made by something other than Martin was beyond what the teens were prepared to accept. With their phone flashlights in hand and Jack in the lead, they commenced their adventurous mission into the dark, muggy night.

"Look for a heavy stick or fist-sized rocks to use as weapons," Jack instructed. "Just in case."

Suddenly, Gab gasped, "Did you hear that?"

"What?" Olivia squealed with a squeaky exhale.

"That's just the sweat dripping down Harlen's back," joked Jack. "It's hella humid out here."

The group chuckled, which helped ease some of their stress.

"Haha, very funny," said Harlen.

"Ah man, I heard it this time," Kass said. He turned around and flashed his light behind him, then waved it from side to side in hopes of not finding a creature behind them. "This place sure is creepy at night."

"Absolutely," Olivia agreed.

Standing taller than most high school girls, Olivia radiated confidence, with her long ebony hair and graceful features adding to her charm. Her dark brown skin and long eyelashes naturally fit with her outgoing personality.

"I can feel Michael Myers's presence," Harlen said.

"Stop cracking jokes everyone," admonished Gab. "Let's find Harlen's jacket and get back. This is no longer fun or exciting."

They continued on their way but before long a loud, undeniable snap was heard by all.

"*What* the..." Harlen gasped.

They gathered close together fearing an animal might be stalking them. The gentle snap of twigs continued, along with a variety of buzzing and rustling sounds, hopefully coming from only flying insects and crawling rodents.

"Who's there?" Jack tried to shout, but his voice barely carried beyond a whisper.

"Hey, we have guns!" Harlen declared, though the uncertainty in his voice wasn't at all convincing.

The others directed their flashlights at Harlen, their faces displaying confusion and concern.

"Okay, no guns, but they don't know that," Harlen muttered, trying to sound more confident than he felt.

"Oh, so you're all gangster now with your flashlight phone?" Kass remarked, his tone more serious than sarcastic.

"Shut up, everyone," Gab said sharply, attempting to keep her nerves in check.

All was quiet. No movement. No sound.

Then, another twig snapped louder and closer.

Gab gasped, her flashlight slipping from her sweaty grip in the moment of panic.

"Hey, hey, don't shoot," said a deep male voice emerging from the dark.

Olivia and Harlen screamed, instinctively throwing the rocks they had collected earlier.

"Stop! Stop throwing things! It's me, Martin," Martin called out.

"Dude! What the heck? What are you doing here?" Jack hollered, aggravated, yet relieved.

"I knew you all were up to something because Harlen was acting so weird. I was curious, so I followed you."

"Just like you followed us last night?" Olivia said, her eyebrows raised with suspicion.

"Yeah, like, we knew it was you," Gab chimed in, folding her arms.

"Last night?" Martin responded, looking shocked. "I didn't follow anyone last night. You came here last night, too?"

After a beat, Jack interjected, "Hmm...I think he's telling the truth, guys."

"Seriously," Martin assured them. "I would have made it known if I was following you last night. Instead, I was super bored in my tent. Mr. Beson cock-blocked my groove. I could barely leave my tent to go pee, let alone hang out with Jessica. Where are you heading, anyway?"

"We were hanging out by a cliff last night and Harlen left his jacket. If you weren't following us, then what was that noise?" Kass gasped.

"What noise?" Martin asked, genuinely perplexed.

Harlen exclaimed, "I've changed my mind. We're not going back to get my jacket if Martin wasn't the one roaring last night. No way."

"We heard a terrifying roar near the cliff," Gab explained with wide eyes. "It scared the crap out of us."

"We can come back tomorrow morning with one of the teachers. Let's head back," Harlen said.

"Come on," said Jack with a level of calmness that helped the group relax. "I'm sure whatever it was is long gone by now. Let's just grab Harlen's jacket and head back."

"Come with us, Martin. We need all the muscle we can get to fight off...whatever it is," Olivia implored, only half joking.

"All right. You don't mind, Kass, do you?" Martin asked, turning his attention to Kass with a rather bashful look.

"No, why would I mind?" Kass replied, puzzled by Martin's question.

Martin, characterized by his sandy blonde hair, long neatly-styled bangs, and striking blue eyes, was the definitive jock on the sports field. However, beneath this exterior, his egocentric demeanor proved to be draining to those around him. Even Harlen, known for his ability to find the best in people, was put off by Martin's overwhelming arrogance and air of superiority.

As they continued their trek toward the cliff, with Martin included in the adventure, they wondered about the ominous noise from the previous night. The forest seemed to hold its secrets close and the group couldn't shake the feeling they were in for more surprises.

The moon cast a gentle gleam upon the forest. And in its soft light the woods were quiet except for twigs snapping under their feet and the tiny noises of small critters hunting or being hunted. No matter how quiet, the forest was obviously alive.

Gab walked next to Jack as they led the group. Harlen trailed behind them and Olivia followed him. Several feet back was Kass and last was Martin, who, prior to this evening, wouldn't have been caught dead hanging out with this group. But, he seemed genuinely interested in doing so.

"This is it. This is the spot," Gab said after they had hiked for an hour.

"Man, this is cool. Wow, look at all those stars," Martin remarked upon seeing the expansive, unobstructed view for the first time.

"Here's my jacket," Harlen said, delighted and relieved. "And my passport is now in hand."

"Yay! Mission accomplished. Let's go," said Kass.

"Wait, let's chill here for a bit. This is amazing," Martin requested.

"Well, I guess we could," Gab said. "All is quiet, so maybe we should take advantage of the opportunity and stay a few minutes."

They each found a comfortable spot near the cliff's edge where they could relax into the moment and relish the view of the sweeping star-filled sky. Gab sat in front of Jack and snuggled into his arms with her back pressed against his torso.

The night felt incredibly peaceful compared to the night before. And even though their remote location and the dead silence of the forest imposed a rather unnerving feeling, the teens were in admiration of the glorious beauty.

ROAR!!

"What the heck was that?" Martin shrieked, leaping up and backing away from the sound, which had emanated from the deep ravine below the cliff.

"That's what we heard last night," Jack said, alarmed. "But we thought it was you."

"Me? That sound did not come from a human," Martin yelped.

"Yeah, then why were you smiling over at us this morning?" Kass demanded rather sharply from a place of fear, realizing Martin really wasn't the source of the roar.

Martin looked embarrassed. "I was smiling at..."

Another roar echoed, closer than before. Panic gripped Gab and Harlen who reacted by seeking refuge behind Jack, as if his size could shield them from the creature making that horrible sound. Clouds had rolled in and the moonlight had become pale, barely illuminating the surroundings and making it impossible for the teens to get even a glimpse of the looming danger.

Kass and Martin stepped closer to one another and exchanged a concerned glance. They too felt the weight of fear bearing down. Meanwhile, Olivia gripped a stick in her trembling hands, her face contorted with terror as if preparing to defend herself against the unseen perpetrator. Each moment felt like an eternity as they strained their ears, desperate for any clue that could reveal the source behind that blood-curdling roar.

"Do you think that's a *bear*?" Gab whispered, her voice barely audible.

"It's too loud for a bear," Martin replied, his eyes darting around, searching for signs of movement.

"I hope it's not something worse," Kass added.

Jack, the epitome of bravery, tried to reassure them, but even his voice wavered. "Stay close, everyone. Stick together."

"I say it's time to get the hell out of here," Harlen said, tying his jacket around his waist. The others didn't argue and were cautiously making their way back to the trail when a blood-curdling howl, much closer than the previous roars, pierced through the dense forest. Its disturbing echo seemed to come from all directions, filling the air with an ominous presence. In the near-black darkness behind them, they heard the heavy shuffling of something massive. They quickened their pace; it was clearly approaching, although still out of sight.

Suddenly, from over the cliff, an enormous shadowy figure leapt skyward and soared over the heads of the stunned teens. Its landing, which blocked the path back to camp, shook the ground and filled them with terror. Their flashlights quivered as they aimed them in the direction of the menacing yet unidentifiable beast. Instinctively, they stepped back, putting distance between themselves and whatever lurked in the darkness just ahead. Yet each step backwards took them closer to the treacherous cliff's edge.

"Watch out!" Jack yelled, trying to steady his flashlight. "Don't get too close to the cliff...and stay alert. Whatever that is, it's fast and dangerous."

"Quick! Hide back there behind the boulders," Kass said with urgency, shining his flashlight onto the cluster of large rocks they had been sitting on the night before.

The forest seemed to hold its breath, its shadows closing in around them. Against the backdrop of the night, the looming silhouette of the creature became visible. It was at least three times taller than Jack with eyes that glowed with an intense grim radiance, like red-hot coals in the darkness. Its massive form blended seamlessly with the shadows until the dim light of the moon gradually exposed its monstrous presence.

It was an abomination of horror. Its upper body, partially concealed by the darkness, revealed mammoth proportions, sinewy muscles pulsating beneath a patchy shroud of fur. Elongated arms, cloaked in obscurity, revealed an overwhelming power. Its head, a malevolent blend of twisted features, remained mostly hidden, adding to its enigmatic presence. The upper part of the creature bore a chilling resemblance to something prehistoric.

Fear paralyzed the teens as they faced this appalling entity, like a hallucination becoming real or a creature crawling out of their darkest nightmares. Its gargantuan presence darkened the night and sent tremors through the earth with each stomp of its powerful legs.

The creature let out a guttural growl, a sound that reverberated through every cell of the teens' bodies. Any last attempts to remain calm were shattered in the face of their primal terror.

Olivia's voice quivered as she whispered, "What is that thing?"

Trapped between the threatening beast and the treacherous cliff, the teens' stifled breaths became shallow gasps as the creature crept closer.

"Hide deeper between the boulders," Jack whispered. "Down in the crevices."

From their hiding spots, they peered out cautiously, no longer using their flashlights in hopes of remaining undetected. The dim shine of the moon and the close proximity of the creature allowed the teens to see it more clearly. Its dark leathery skin seemed to absorb the light around it and ooze a sense of primal strength and agility. It moved with captivating grace and predatory poise, its gait calculated and deliberate.

With each step closer, a few more intricate details came into view. Gleaming fangs protruded from its snarling mouth while its elongated snout bore rows of mangled teeth, each one jagged and razor-sharp, honed to deadly precision through countless eons of predatory existence. Its neck, robust and powerful, supported the weight of its menacing head. Its face bore a mesmerizing fusion of features reminiscent of both a primordial monkey and a fearsome dinosaur. Between its gnarled and misshapen horns, its eyes, piercing and fiery, locked onto the pile of boulders, sensing or perhaps smelling the humans who hid there. A low, guttural growl escaped as its claws scraped against the rocky ground, leaving deep furrows in the surface. Then, for a moment, the creature froze, and time stood still.

The teens held their breath, desperately hoping the creature hadn't spotted them or was no longer interested. They remained silent and still.

Olivia's hands trembled around her makeshift weapon, her bravado crumbling under the creature's malevolent gaze. Jack's eyes darted around in desperation, searching for any glimmer of hope, any chance of surviving this abomination.

In that moment, they found a grain of strength in each other's presence. A silent understanding passed among them, a determination to face this nightmare together, no matter the cost.

They looked to Jack who gestured for them to stay still and slowly lower their weapons. He hoped the monster wouldn't attack if it didn't feel threatened.

However, in the very next moment, the creature let out a bone-chilling growl as if responding to Jack's suggestion. They knew they had no choice but to fight for their lives. Their primal instincts kicked in. Using the boulders as a shield, they prepared to defend themselves against this ancient evil that had awakened from the shadows.

The creature slowly crouched and leaned forward, preparing to attack. What was to come? Death by burly beast or a sickening suicide plunge over the nearby cliff?

Jack, Martin, and Harlen placed their bodies in front of Kass, Gab, and Olivia. Gab had never wanted a boy to rescue her, always feeling confident and secure. But in this moment of terror, she accepted her powerlessness and loved Jack for putting his life on the line for her.

The creature lunged. The boys swung their sticks with all their might and struck the beast on the snout. Having done little if any damage, they crouched down with the others, waiting for the worst to come.

But before the beast could strike again, another creature, drastically different in appearance and almost twice the size, bellowed greatly and charged into the clearing. The distraction caused the first creature to pivot and prepare to protect itself.

The clearing erupted into chaos as the two fierce creatures clashed in a violent and deadly showdown. The larger creature, attempting to overpower its adversary, launched a lethal swipe of its paw, followed by a brutal strike with its long spiked tail.

The gigantic newcomer was adorned with stunning jewels down its spine, displaying an ethereal beauty, even amid the chaos. The shimmering rubies, emeralds, sapphires, and onyx gleamed in the moonlight. The creature possessed both masculine strength and feminine grace, and fought back with equal ferocity. Its long arms and claws were formidable weapons in a deadly dance.

The battle intensified, with the ground trembling under the force of the creatures' mighty blows. The original horrific creature delivered a powerful swipe across the chest of its opponent, eliciting a screech. Undeterred, the jewel-clad beast rose from the ground and charged, head-butting its adversary, causing it to stagger backward.

"Woah, did you see that?" Harlen marveled in a hushed voice.

"Shh, don't make a peep," Olivia whispered.

As the creatures continued their furious clash, a gem the size and shape of a softball detached from the jewel-clad creature's spine. It rolled, then came to a stop eight feet away from Kass, who stared at the jewel, torn between fear and desire.

The group of six watched in terror, uncertain of what would come next. They were mere witnesses to this otherworldly spectacle, where beauty and danger merged in a dance of survival. The moon cast a hazy luster upon the battleground, etching this violent encounter into their memories forever.

The ferocity of the battle showed no signs of abating and the new brute unleashed its fury with unyielding determination. It pummeled the smaller, more creepy looking beast in a vigorous, almost hypnotic, display of power.

In what seemed like an opportune moment, the group swiftly distanced themselves from the battling creatures. However, Kass lagged behind, finding himself caught in a moment of hesitation.

He pivoted and cast a second look at the gem nestled on the ground, its proximity and allure stirring a potent temptation.

With a quick yet calculated glance, confirming the creatures' distraction, he seized the opportunity and sprinted toward the gem. When his fingers wrapped around it, an electrical surge rippled through him, sending a jolting shock through his senses. Nonetheless, he collected his wits, and quickly placed the gem in his backpack before hastily joining the others in their escape.

The six teens dashed through the rainforest, running for their lives. Bushes and thorny branches clawed at their clothing and skin, leaving painful scratches. Overhead, twisting vines threatened to entangle them. In their panic, they wrestled with these natural obstacles, propelled by pure adrenaline. They ducked beneath low-hanging limbs and dodged around scraggy trees, their flashlights briefly illuminating the tangled surroundings.

"You all have some explaining to do," a voice pierced the moment as they entered the campground and a light shone on their faces.

The startled group screamed in unison.

"Mr. Beson!" Gab exclaimed.

"What the heck has gotten into you kids?" Mr. Beson scolded. "What are you doing out of your tents? Never mind, we'll discuss this in the morning. Back to your tents. Now!"

Chapter 4

T he morning sun filtered through the trees, casting a warm glow over the campsite, but for the six who were terrorized by the beasts, the atmosphere remained heavy with a lingering fear. Despite it being time to pack up and head home, Kass and Jack laid in their sleeping bags, their backs turned to each other and eyes wide open, shock and dread evident on their faces.

Neither of them wanted to speak, afraid that uttering a word would bring back the horrors they had faced.

Gab and Olivia were also still trembling with fear inside their tent, unable to shake off the haunting images of the ferocious creatures that had threatened their lives. The night had been a chilling reminder that the darkness held unknown terrors, and they were in no hurry to leave the perceived safety of their tents.

Harlen, alone in the tent after his tent partner Eddie left to eat breakfast, pulled his sleeping bag tightly around him, seeking comfort and shelter from the lingering unease. Sleep had eluded him, as he was too wrapped up in fear of what still skulked in the shadows.

"Hey, what are we going to do, Jack?" asked Kass.

Jack turned over and sat up. He wrapped his arms around his bent legs and pulled his knees closer to his face.

"I don't know, Kass. I just don't know. We can't tell anyone. No one will ever believe us."

"No, they'll lock us up in a crazy house if we tell them what we saw," Kass added.

"Let's talk to the others and see how they are feeling. Come on, we need to pack," Jack said.

It was 6:30 a.m. and the campsite was relatively quiet although students had started shuffling around, packing their belongings, giggling and chattering among themselves.

"I'm scared, Olivia," Gab admitted. "I don't even want to leave the tent."

"Gab, we need to get ourselves together and just get out of here," Olivia responded with as much conviction as she could muster. "Let's talk to the boys and see how they're feeling."

Harlen threw his belongings in his backpack and waited next to the tent for Eddie to help dismantle it. He glanced over at the other guys. Jack flipped his head up and raised his eyebrows as if to say, *What's up, are you okay?*

Harlen shrugged.

An hour later, with everything packed and breakfast eaten, the eighteen Cypress High School students and chaperones were enroute back to civilization. Their two-hour hike down the mountain was the longest part of their four-day journey. Not one of Kass's group mentioned the night before. It was as if they had committed a crime and no one wanted to speak of it.

✳✳✳

After the hike down the mountain and long drive to the airport, the students were finally making their way through security to catch their flight home.

"Sir, is this your bag?" the airport security officer inquired sternly, fixing her gaze on Kass.

"Yes," Kass responded, his voice quivering, well aware he had tucked the creature's precious gemstone in the depths of his backpack. An overwhelming sense of unease gnawed at him, but he summoned every ounce of willpower to maintain his composure and remain steadfastly focused on the pressing matter at hand.

"Can you step over here, please?" she asked.

Kass's face turned red and his palms became sweaty.

Jack and Harlen noticed Kass being questioned by an airport security officer. They were unaware of the jewel Kass had seized, and Kass remained oblivious to the fact that he might be committing a crime. Was it legal to transport a softball-sized jewel through the airport and out of the country? Even if it was legal, how could he ever explain it?

"Sir, you can't bring water through; you'll have to drink it or pour it out," the airport security agent stated.

Relieved, Kass took the bottle from the airport security officer and drank the remaining water in one large gulp. As he did so, a sense of intrigue washed over him, wondering how the gemstone had managed to evade detection during the inspection.

The five friends and Martin sat quietly at the departure gate, waiting for their flight.

"Are you sure you're okay, Gab?" Jack asked for the fifth time.

"Yes, Jack, please stop asking me," she snapped.

"I'm sorry. I just don't know what else to say."

"Nothing to say. Let's just get on the plane and get home. I'm sorry, too. I am just still freaked out right now."

"We're safe, Gab," Jack reassured her. When he hugged her, she sank into his arms and they comforted each other for several minutes before Jack wiped away her tears. "Everything will be fine. We will be home and last night will be thousands of miles away."

Martin sat wordlessly next to Jessica. His eyes repeatedly drifted over to Kass and the others with concern and confusion. Jessica noticed his strange behavior.

"Why do you keep looking over there?" she finally asked.

"What? I'm not," Martin replied hastily, attempting to divert her attention.

Jessica shook her head, unconvinced. "Yes, you literally are. You've been staring over there for the past thirty minutes. You haven't looked at me once."

"Hey, stop badgering me," Martin retorted with surprising terseness. "I just have a lot on my mind, okay?"

Jessica's confusion only grew. She knew Martin well, and this behavior was completely out of character for him. There was definitely something he wasn't telling her. With her arms folded and a pout on her face, Jessica decided to give him some space. But after a few moments of awkward silence, she stood up and walked away, leaving Martin to sit alone with his thoughts.

Olivia sat between Kass and Harlen, their faces incised with concern and introspection. They held hands in silence in an attempt to give each other comfort.

Mr. Beson, a caring and observant teacher, couldn't help but notice the trio's somber demeanor. He approached them with a gentle smile.

"Hello, Kass, Harlen, Olivia," he said warmly. "I hope you all managed to get some rest."

The three friends exchanged glances as if trying to find the right words to convey their emotions. It was evident to Mr. Beson that something significant had happened during the teens' late-night adventure and he wanted to provide a safe space for them to share if they felt ready.

"Last night must have been quite an experience for all of you," he said. "If there's anything you'd like to talk about or share, I want you to know I'm here to listen."

Kass took a deep breath, his mind grappling with how to put their encounter into words.

"We didn't get any rest. We should have never ventured out last night and now we are just extremely tired. Sorry for breaking curfew."

"Well, there was obviously something else happening, but we will let things go for now. Maybe get some rest on the plane," Mr. Beson encouraged them. "If and when you're ready to share more, I'm here to listen and support you."

"*Good afternoon passengers. This is the pre-boarding announcement for flight B157 to Toronto. We are now inviting those passengers with small children, and any passengers requiring special assistance, to begin boarding at this time. Please have your boarding pass and passport ready. General boarding will begin in approximately ten minutes. Thank you.*"

"Hey guys, come with me," Jack said to Gab, Kass, Olivia, and Harlen.

The melancholic teens huddled together against one wall of the departure gate's waiting area. The intensity of their late-night experience weighed heavily on their minds and they knew they had to decide on a course of action.

Their hushed conversation caught the attention of Martin, who, intrigued by their secrecy, stood up and faced their direction. When Jack noticed him, he waved Martin over to join their circle.

"Okay, last night was mental!" Jack began. "But we're okay now, right? We can..."

"I'm not okay," Harlen interrupted, his voice trembling. "This is like something out of a horror movie, not real life. We encountered dragons or maybe dinosaurs with wings that looked like big-ass giant Godzillas!"

"Harlen, I get it. It's hard to wrap our heads around what happened," Olivia chimed in. "But if we tell others about this, I mean, who would believe us? We'll sound crazy."

"She's right. People would never believe us and we'd become a laughing stock," Jack agreed.

Gab nodded. "Yeah, and it could even lead to investigations from the authorities. We don't want to get into any messes."

"How about we all meet tomorrow at my place," Jack proposed. "Let's get as much sleep as possible, then talk about everything. For now, let's keep this between us until we can decide what to do." Everyone nodded in agreement.

With their plan laid out, the five friends and Martin concluded their meeting and proceeded to board the plane for their lengthy journey, first to Toronto and then onward to Kelowna. They knew that facing their mysterious circumstances together was their best chance of understanding what had happened and deciding next steps.

***

"Okay, Martin, what were you all talking about with Jack and those idiots?" Jessica blurted with very little patience, as they sat side by side on the plane, waiting for take-off.

"Jessica, I befriended them during our trip. What's the big deal?"

"For three years you've thought they were all idiots and now you're suddenly buddies?" she grumbled with a snooty tone.

"Yeah, well, things change."

"Well, don't expect me to be friends with them!" Jessica added in a huff, pulling out a fashion magazine.

Martin turned his head and looked out the window—not to watch the airline crew busy at work, but to think about the previous night's events and the upcoming group meeting with his new friends. He smiled.

A second announcement from the cabin crew then followed: "*Ladies and gentlemen, we ask that you please fasten your seatbelts at this time and secure all baggage in the overhead bins or underneath the seat in front of you. Be sure your seat backs and tray tables are in their upright and locked position. Turn off all electronic devices, including laptops and cell phones. Smoking and vaping are prohibited for the duration of the flight. Thank you for choosing NewAir Airlines and enjoy your flight.*"

The plane taxied onto the tarmac and toward the runway. The engines revved.

"Flight attendants, please prepare for takeoff."

In the next moment the plane's engines abruptly fell silent. Wide-eyed passengers and concerned crew then did the same, exchanging glances and looking out the windows in their bewilderment.

"What's going on?" Martin exclaimed.

Above Kass's head, the storage bin popped open, catching everyone's attention. A flight attendant swiftly unbuckled her seatbelt and approached the open bin. With a few deft moves, she rearranged the items and secured the latch before returning to her seat, her expression slightly flustered but composed.

The engines restarted and there was a sigh of relief throughout the plane.

After a few minutes of letting the engines idle, the pilot re-announced, *"Flight attendants, please prepare for takeoff."*

The plane taxied onto the runway and a sense of excitement filled the cabin. Passengers chatted eagerly, discussing their upcoming adventures of the destination ahead.

But then, again, the engines went silent, leaving the aircraft engulfed in an eerie stillness. All power was lost, plunging the cabin into darkness.

"What now!?" several people muttered, incredulous and concerned.

This strange event was unlike anything anyone had ever experienced. Even the seasoned pilots and flight crew were taken aback, unable to explain the sudden power failure. It felt as though the heart of the aircraft had stopped beating, leaving everyone on edge.

And like earlier, the overhead storage bin above Kass swung wide open. He looked up in disbelief and again the flight attendant hastily pushed the bags around, secured the bin, and returned to her seat.

"Passengers, we apologize for the delay. We have technicians looking into the matter and plan to be off the ground shortly," the pilot explained, trying to reassure the passengers.

The abrupt hush in the cabin stirred a wave of anxiety through the passengers. The atmosphere brimmed with murmurs as they voiced their concerns about the plane's safety. Even the flight attendants struggled to conceal their apprehension behind forced smiles that couldn't quite mask their unease.

Among the group of six friends, fear had taken hold, and their desire to return to Canada intensified with each passing moment. They yearned to put as much distance as possible between themselves and the uncertainty that loomed in Costa Rica.

The minutes dragged on; the delay felt like an eternity. Finally, the engines roared back to life and idled for an additional ten minutes. A collective sigh of relief washed over the cabin as everything appeared to be operating fine.

"Thank you, passengers, for your patience. We have been cleared for takeoff and are next in line. Flight attendants, please take your seats."

The plane taxied into position on the runway, the engines began to roar, and the plane rolled forward with increasing acceleration. Gab and Jack held hands, exchanging warm smiles, while Kass and Olivia, palms sweaty and hearts beating fast, breathed deeply and tried to relax.

"You've got to be kidding me!" Harlen shouted when the engines abruptly cut off once more and everything went black. Frustration swept through the cabin. The mood was tense, having shifted from hope to exasperation.

Kass's overhead storage compartment popped open *again.* Reacting quickly, he jumped over the person in the aisle seat and retrieved his backpack from the bin. He clutched the pack tightly and settled back into his seat.

"Sir, you'll have to store your bag under your seat with your seatbelt buckled," the flight attendant instructed with a stern tone while closing the bin and inspecting the cabin to ensure everyone was seated and accounted for.

Kass noticed Olivia looking down at his backpack, which was between his feet. She knew something odd was happening but couldn't figure it out.

"Are you okay?" she asked.

"Yep, all good. Just needed the water out of my bag," he replied.

The engines started and an announcement from the pilot soon followed: "*Passengers, we continue to have a technical situation and need to taxi off the runway. We will have our technicians check things out and hope to be off the ground shortly. Again, we apologize and thank you for your patience.*"

After returning to the gate, another half hour went by. Exterior panels opened and closed as the maintenance crew made their inspections and adjustments.

"Sir, can I get you something to drink?"

"Yes, can I have water, please?" Kass requested.

"I thought you had water in your bag," Olivia said suspiciously.

"Um, I do. I want fresh water," Kass responded with an odd voice.

"All right Kass, what's in the bag? I know you too well," Olivia pressed.

"Nothing...there's nothing in the bag."

"Kass, come on, tell me," Olivia insisted.

Suddenly, the engines started again and the passengers cheered. Hopes were high even though neither the cabin crew nor the pilot had made any announcements.

For another ten minutes the plane's engines idled until, finally, the captain announced, "Thank you, passengers, for your patience. We have been cleared for takeoff. Everything has been resolved. Flight attendants, prepare for takeoff."

Chapter 5

"**W**ell, look who's back from the dead."

"Good morning, Mom," Kass said, entering the dining room.

"Kass, it's after five p.m. You've been asleep all day!"

Kass looked at the clock on the wall with disbelief. He had returned home twenty-four hours prior, entered the house, said hello to his sister, and gone straight to bed for a quick nap before dinner. Needless to say, he didn't know he would sleep until the *next evening*'s dinner. His body felt recharged with an unusual level of energy.

"What's up with all the candles?" Kass asked when he noticed multiple candles scattered around the house.

"The power went out last night, not long after you arrived home. The Campbells' and the Carters' power was also off, and a few other houses around us. Electricians left a few hours ago; they couldn't figure out the problem. But fortunately, the power came on a little bit ago. The weirdest thing," his mom said.

Kass sat down at the table and shared a few camping stories with his mom, while Kallie, Kass's sweet twelve-year-old sister, plopped herself on Kass's lap and twirled his hair with her fingers. Kallie had been diagnosed with autism at age three and struggled with a variety of challenges.

"Okay, those stories sound great, but what about the mischievous ones?" his mom teased with a grin and a twinkle in her eye. "I'm sure you kids got up to no good at least once or twice."

"Mom, you're fishing for stories in an empty pond. Our teen escapades were about as thrilling as watching paint dry," Kass chuckled, downplaying any excitement while also feeling uncomfortable about not telling his mom the truth.

"By the way, you received a ton of texts and phone calls while you were sleeping. Your friends were all looking for you. I heard your phone buzzing through the door all day long. Can't believe you slept through all of that."

"Come on, Kallie, let's go get my phone," Kass said, picking Kallie up and swinging her over his back.

"Piggyback, piggyback ride. Kallie's piggyback ride on Super Kass!" she squealed with a huge smile plastered on her face. The two of them galloped through the house, up the stairs, and into Kass's bedroom.

"You're getting too heavy for piggyback rides," Kass huffed, out of breath. "But I love you, so you have a few more left."

Kass picked up his phone and scrolled through his text messages.

Jack 10:12 a.m.: Hey, what time are we meeting today?

Jack 10:23 a.m.: I spoke to the gang and they are cool with around 4pm.

Harlen 11:30 a.m.: Yo! I just woke up. Are you still sleeping?

Jack 12:15 p.m.: Actually, Gab is going to hang out with her dads today. We are going to meet tomorrow instead.

Jack 12:16 p.m.: But I can come by.

Jack 4:33 p.m.: Hey, what are you doing???

Harlen 4:50 p.m.: Hi Kass. Doing anything tonight?

"Kallie, get out of my backpack!" Kass commanded in no uncertain terms. Kallie's hands were inches away from touching the gem that Kass had confiscated from the mountain. It had sat calmly in his backpack throughout the night and during the day. Kass stopped scrolling through his messages and brought the gem out so Kallie could have a better look at it. Mesmerized by the shimmering red and purplish gem, she became captivated. He tenderly held her hand and caressed the stone.

"Oh, it is hot, Kass. It is hot."

"Is it hot?"

"So pretty, Kass. It is so pretty, Kass. Kass, pretty and soft, Kass, but so hot," Kallie smiled.

"Yes, it is a very special rock and you can't touch it unless I am with you. Okay, Kallie?"

"Okay, Kass. Yes, okay, Kass. Too hot to touch."

Kallie's insistence that the gemstone was hot puzzled Kass because it felt perfectly cool to him.

Kass sent a message to the group thread, "Hi all. I'm good. I literally slept for twenty-four hours. I'm alive!! I'm about to have dinner and will text you later."

With care, Kass placed the gem in the drawer of his nightstand, then galloped with Kallie back to the dining room where his dad waited, having just returned from a round of golf with his buddies.

"Someone joining us for dinner?" Kass asked, when he noticed the table set for six.

"Yes, John and Helen from next door. Their electricity still isn't on. In fact, every electronic and battery-operated thing in their home isn't working. They've changed the batteries in their flashlight, but after a couple of minutes, it dies. It's the weirdest thing."

"Mom, you're starting to sound like Kallie. It's the weirdest thing," Kass said, laughing.

"Yeah, you slept through the whole blackout," Dad said.

"And nobody knows what caused it?" Kass questioned.

"Nope, not a clue," his dad added.

The dinner with the Campbells was filled with bizarre stories as both couples shared their odd experiences during the blackout and their struggles to get by without any electricity or battery-operated devices. John and Helen both had big personalities and together they dominated the dinner conversation with their boisterous anecdotes.

"It was the damndest thing. I kept changing the flashlight batteries, but the thing didn't last but a few minutes," John said, exasperated. "I said, Helen, what did you do to the batteries? You got the old ones mixed in with the new ones."

"I told him I did no such thing. So, we opened a new package and..."

"And the darn thing went out like a light switch," John said, interrupting Helen. "All new batteries. Then we did it again with all new batteries. And, same thing. We wasted at least ten dollars on new batteries."

"New batteries. New batteries for John," Kallie echoed.

"So last night we sat in the dark and drank from a bottle of vodka," he laughed. "We couldn't read, watch TV, or do anything, except, well...drink in the dark."

"By eleven, John was drunker than a cricket in a hubcap!" Helen added.

"Drunker than a cricket in a hubcap? Oh, I am so glad we are not from the Prairies," Kass said with relief. "Who says that, and what does that even mean?"

Everyone at the table giggled. Helen's country dialect always amused Kass. He thought she was very nice, but he also found both Helen and John to be rather odd. Kass's mom and dad, Bailey and Jay, were much younger than their extroverted neighbors.

John and Helen's daughter, Sheila, was twelve years older than Kass, and when Kass was only four years old, Sheila babysat him. It was an almost deadly outcome. When a playful activity of taking turns squirting lemon juice down their throats turned into Kass choking on the nozzle, Sheila had to act fast. She jammed her index finger down his throat, causing Kass to regurgitate the little plastic lid. Sheila had always been thankful for how good Kass's parents had been about the situation when she told them of it later that night.

"Hey, your lights went on next door," Jay announced.

"Oh, fantastic," Helen said.

"Just in time. We had a great meal and now I can go home and watch TV," John added.

***

"Hey, you doing alright?" Kass's dad asked, taking a good look at his son.

"Yeah Dad, just feeling a bit anxious. I'm going to go for a run," Kass said.

"You had a long trip. I'd say get some rest, but you just slept for twenty-four hours. We were about to call the medics," he added with a smile.

Kass prepared for his run and left moments later. He was happy to have his feet in designer sneakers again, and to be wearing clothes that didn't reek of campfire. He also enjoyed not being surrounded by putrid teens with their strong, unpleasant body odor. The sun, still radiating warmth as it set, filled the spring dusk with tranquility.

As Kass began his run down the block, he noticed the street lamps getting dimmer as he ran past each one. He stopped in wonderment, looked up at a lamp, and sure enough, the light flickered, then grew faint.

What the? he thought. Could some electrician be pranking him? Was there a hidden camera somewhere? He scowled, squinted his eyes, and looked around. Nothing. No one.

Again and again, as he continued his run, the lights flickered, then dimmed. In fact, they scintillated, as if giving off sparks. This was too weird. He had to tell someone and there was no one better than his best friend Jack whose house was near.

Kass 7:43 p.m.: What are you doing?

Jack 7:44 p.m.: Nothing. I sent you like a dozen texts, fool. You've been ghostin' me for 24 hours now.

Kass 7:44 p.m.: Come outside, ASAP!

Kass waited outside Jack's house, staring up at the street lamp.

"Hey you," Jack said, embracing Kass in a hip-hop hug. "Dude, I thought you were pissed at me for talking you into going on the camping retreat."

"Nah, well, I was pissed when we first got there, but no, something trippy is happening. Watch this," Kass declared as he ran across the street toward another street lamp.

Jack watched in amazement as the lamp flickered. Kass ran to the next street lamp diagonal to him, and the result was the same.

"Oh man, what's going on? That *is* trippy," Jack exclaimed. "Do it again. Oh, man. Do it again!" His fascination drove Kass zigzagging in a run down the street, with Jack eagerly following behind. "It's like some wild electrical current," Jack observed.

"Should I be scared?" Kass asked, concerned.

"Scared? Nah. Well, maybe. I don't know, but this is cool!" After a moment to think, Jack added, "Have you considered that maybe you're radioactive? I mean, what if you've developed some kind of superpower?"

Kass laughed at the absurd idea. "I highly doubt I'm a walking nuclear reactor or Marvel's next superhero, but hey, who knows? Maybe I'm just in tune with the energy of the universe or something."

"Maybe," Jack laughed but also in awe of the phenomenon he had just witnessed. "Wait, let me see what happens when I do it," he said, running over to the post. "Yep, nothing."

"I need to go home, Jack. I feel like I am going crazy. I'll see you tomorrow morning, okay?"

"Okay, but are you sure? I can keep you company."

"No, I'm, alright. I just need to rest," Kass said, walking toward his house.

"I'll stop by and pick you up in the morning," Jack shouted, as he watched Kass walk down the street with each street light losing luminosity above Kass's head as he passed by.

Kass couldn't shake off the unease that had settled in his mind. As he pondered the chain of events that followed his encounter with the gem in the Costa Rican rainforest, he started to connect the dots. The electrical bonding that he experienced upon first touching the beast's gemstone seemed to have triggered a series of unusual occurrences, from the issues on the plane to the blackout in his neighborhood, and the strange phenomenon with the street lamps.

"I should have known better than to mess with that mysterious gem in the first place," Kass muttered to himself with regret. "But who would have thought it would lead to all of this?"

As much as he was intrigued by the idea of having an extraordinary power, he couldn't deny the discomfort and potential danger it brought. Being at the center of all this drama wasn't his idea of a good time, especially when he realized he might be the cause of it all.

"Hey bud, are you good?" his dad asked again, peeking his head in Kass's room.

"Yeah, Dad, I'm good. I'm just worn out from the trip."

"Okay, get some sleep, so you're ready for school tomorrow."

The gemstone in the drawer of Kass's nightstand beckoned him. He carefully removed it and admired its smooth polished surface. Kass became captivated by its beauty and enigmatic allure. It was unlike anything he had ever seen before. Its colors seemed to shift and dance as he turned it in different directions. Deep shades of emerald green blended with hints of sapphire blue, while fiery streaks of crimson and amber swirled together, creating a captivating array of colors.

Kass felt a sense of reluctance as the prospect of returning to school the next morning loomed. A question gnawed at him: should he bring the jewel along, carefully concealed in his backpack, or leave it at home?

As he scrolled through his text messages and social media chats, his eyes began to slowly close. Open...shut...open...and then finally, closed for the night.

Chapter 6

"Kass, get up. Time for school," Kass's dad Jay said, shaking his son's blanket and bumping the corner of his bed with his leg. "Come on, get up, boy!"

Kass sprang out of bed, showered, and embarked on his daily dressing ritual, treating it like a captivating performance on the Milan fashion runway, even though his destination was just Cypress High School.

In his spotless room, meticulously organized like a high-end boutique, Kass selected his ensemble with utmost care. Each item seemed carefully curated to create a masterpiece of style and charm. His closet, a treasure trove of designer loafers, held the key to unlocking the perfect outfit for the day ahead.

For Kass, school was more than just a place for academics; it was his social playground. As he waltzed through the school's halls, he received high-fives and back-pats from his peers, almost like a celebrity basking in adoration from fans. The less popular students smiled in admiration, though some were too shy or perhaps too intimidated to approach the Hollywood-handsome high school junior.

Beyond his dashing looks, Kass was also a drama club aficionado, bringing his wit and charm to the stage, where he was admired by peers and teachers alike. His humorous banter made him an engaging conversationalist, leaving older teens captivated by his unique blend of style and intelligence. Kass was more than just a pretty face. He was a delightful enigma, charming his way through high school with sophistication and flair.

"Must be excited to get to school," his mom said as she rushed by Kass, guiding Kallie to the bathroom.

"Yep, one-hundred percent," Kass replied with a light-hearted tone.

He couldn't quite explain the sudden shift in his mood, but he suspected the energy from the gemstone had something to do with it.

Their mom, Bailey, was fortunate to be a stay-at-home mother most of the time, focused primarily on Kallie's needs, such as driving her to cognitive and behavioral therapy appointments.

Kass often felt left out of the daily routines of the family, but he approached it with understanding and empathy. He knew his mom's attention was needed for Kallie and he supported her wholeheartedly. Despite occasional moments of annoyance, he cherished his sister deeply, recognizing she was his mom's priority, and that was okay. He had a genuine fondness for Kallie and her bright spirit never failed to bring a smile to his face.

Kallie possessed a petite frame, a bit smaller than the average twelve-year-old. Her long, brown, curly hair cascaded gracefully, framing her face with natural elegance. Her dark brown eyes held a glossy depth, adding a certain charm to her gaze.

Their mom always looked well-groomed and energetic, even though Kallie could be a handful and the source of a lot of stress. But Bailey was also the part-time bookkeeper for her husband Jay, the owner of a specialty boutique featuring rare items only found in Asia and Central and South America.

Bailey's presence commanded respect, not through force, but through the quiet confidence that emanated from her. She carried herself with dignity and a deep sense of pride in her identity. Her radiant complexion, like rich mahogany, seemed to defy time. Her hair, a magnificent crown of tightly coiled curls, was a testament to her roots and spoke of a rich cultural heritage.

People marveled at her ability to defy the visible signs of aging, often asking her for the secret to her ageless appearance. She would simply smile and share stories of her family's long history of youthful looks.

"Whoa, that was quick. You almost beat me down here," his dad said in disbelief as Kass entered the kitchen.

Jay possessed a striking handsomeness. His fair complexion was flawlessly smooth, accentuating his sharp facial features. With a strong, chiseled jawline and piercing blue eyes, he carried an air of rugged masculinity that was hard to ignore.

His chestnut hair was neatly groomed and his tall athletic build was carried with confidence. He dressed sharply, combining style with comfort. His approachable smile was welcoming to all.

"Yep, fired up and ready to go!" Kass repeated. His exuberance was unusual and excessive compared to his typical morning mood.

His parents looked at each other, confused and perhaps a tad concerned. "Hormones," they said simultaneously, then laughed and shrugged their shoulders.

"Do you and Jack want a ride to school?"

"No, we'll walk."

"Okay. I'm leaving today for a quick business trip and your mom might need some help around the house."

"Alright."

Kass could hear Jack walking up the back porch stairs that led to the exterior kitchen door, so he grabbed his backpack off the counter. He could also hear Kallie coming down the stairs from her bedroom, murmuring something repeatedly.

"Hey, say goodbye to your sister," his mom admonished.

Kass waited a few seconds until Kallie entered the kitchen. He then hugged her, kissed her on her forehead, and gave her a high-five before walking out the door to join Jack, who waited on the back porch. Kass had moved through his morning routine at a fast pace. So fast, in fact, his parents looked at each other again and shrugged their shoulders.

"Hormones?" they questioned.

"Whoa, slow down, speed demon," Jack said, laughing and noticing Kass's extra burst of energy. "Are you on espressos now?"

"Man, I don't know what it is. I feel energized," Kass said, effortlessly hurdling over the yard's three-foot fence.

"Dude! When did you become a track star?" Jack exclaimed, impressed. "But I get it. I'm stoked about school, too. Especially after seeing what we saw. Are you okay? Want to talk about it now?"

"Nah man, let's just put all that behind us," Kass suggested.

"Bro, I am not putting it behind me just yet," said Jack with a shake of his head, lips tight, eyebrows furrowed. "That was some serious shit and we should all talk about it. There were huge creatures attacking us and fighting each other. And now you're sucking the electricity out of lamps. Man, I gotta say, you've been acting real weird since we left. Did one of them bite you?" Jack joked, although concerned and half serious.

In stark contrast to Kass's fashion sense, Jack almost always dressed in jeans and hoodies, carrying a duffle bag crammed with shoes, clean and dirty socks, books, and odd scraps of paper—unlike Kass, who kept his designer backpack organized and tidy.

With their backpacks slung over their shoulders, the boys started their short sixteen-minute walk to school, leaving the neighborhood behind.

Visually, Cypress High was a modern architectural marvel that stood proudly atop a gentle hill and overlooked the city of Kelowna. The school was a bustling hub of learning and camaraderie, housing a vibrant community of four-hundred, twenty-three students. Its exterior featured a blend of sleek glass panels and sturdy brick walls, creating an inviting and contemporary facade. Colorful banners adorned the entrance, displaying the school's motto: "Discover, Learn, Thrive."

Cypress High was a collection of cliques, each with its own unique flavor. There were the floaters, effortlessly gliding between groups like social chameleons. The brains were the intellectual powerhouses, their minds sharper than a freshly sharpened pencil. The jocks, of course, were the athletic superheroes who gravitated toward the populars and formed a dynamic duo that rocked the school with charisma. And then, there was the good-arts crowd, whose artistic prowess turned the school into a canvas of creativity. The anime-manga enthusiasts embraced their love for Japanese animation, while the druggies-stoners marched to the beat of their own hazy drum.

Amid the colorful chaos of cliques and groups, the fabulous and fun-loving LGBTQIA+ students broke down barriers with sass and style. And the school's diverse racial and ethnic groups each added their own unique colors to the beautiful tapestry of Cypress High.

"Hi, Gab," Jack said as he gave her a hug and kiss on the lips in front of their shared locker.

"Hi. Hi Kass," Gab said.

"Hi, guys! What's shakin'?" Harlen arrived, his face beaming with excitement.

Despite Harlen's unremarkable grades and occasional bursts of boisterous and rowdy behavior, there simmered beneath the surface a profound yearning for attention and affection.

Harlen's mother, a dedicated surgeon with little time to spare, inadvertently molded him into a self-reliant individual from a young age. The void left by his father, who had departed to Spain to care for his ailing grandmother and never returned, added further emotional intricacies. Harlen's later revelation of his father's romantic affair, culminating in his parents' divorce, weighed heavily on his heart, contributing to their estranged relationship.

Recently, Harlen embarked on a poignant journey to reconnect with his father, aspiring to forge a deeper understanding and a more robust bond as he continued navigating life's unpredictable twists and turns. During this journey, Harlen discovered he had a little brother, adding a layer of complexity to their rekindled relationship.

Nonetheless, amid the intricacies of his life, Harlen's resilience radiated like a beacon. Within his circle of friends, he was the life of the party, armed with a quick wit to brighten even the bleakest of days. His talent for spreading happiness reflected an enduring spirit and an innate ability to find joy in the simplest of life's pleasures. His classmates couldn't resist the magnetic pull of his personality.

Harlen was Kass's prize prodigy. He occasionally dressed Harlen, helped him with his homework assignments, and coached him when studying for tests. While Kass took a mentor role with Harlen, Jack was the friend who often protected Harlen from frustrated or pissed-off classmates when Harlen went too far with his unwanted antics, including making inappropriate jokes or offensive comments. While he never intended to hurt anyone's feelings, Harlen's lack of boundaries and social filters sometimes led to awkward or uncomfortable situations.

"*Students who attended the annual camp this year, please report to the auditorium before their first class,*" Mr. Carter sternly announced over the school's P.A. system.

"Blah, blah, blah. Good thing Mr. Farter didn't come on the camping trip this year," Harlen said, causing his friends to laugh.

"Totes," Olivia said in a cheerful voice, as she walked up behind the group.

"Hi, Olivia," all four said in unison.

"Um, are we still saying 'totes'? That's so last-year," Jessica scoffed as she overheard Olivia's greeting to her friends and decided to butt-in.

Olivia, with her poised demeanor, chose to ignore Jessica's immature behavior.

At home, Olivia embraced a genuine sense of responsibility by shouldering the care of her two younger siblings while her hardworking parents navigated the competitive world of real estate. With her parents often immersed in long days and demanding clients, Olivia willingly stepped into the role of a nurturing guardian for her little brother and sister. She made sure they were well-fed and kept up with their studies, yet still had enough playtime to keep their spirits high. Olivia became adept at managing household chores and ensuring everyone's needs were met, all while juggling her own schoolwork, ambitions, and challenges.

The first bell rang and hundreds of teens scurried to their classes, except for Kass's friends and the dozen other campers who reported to the auditorium. Mr. Carter's voice rang out with purpose. "Thank you all for coming. I trust you've had a memorable experience at this year's camp." Pausing for a moment, he continued, "But before we dive into the school day, I have an important assignment for each of you."

The murmurs in the room quieted as Mr. Carter outlined the task at hand. "I want each of you to reflect on your time at the camp. Write an essay detailing what you learned, the benefits gained, and any personal growth you experienced.

Additionally, I'd like to know if you plan to attend next year's camping trip, wherever it may be."

Mr. Carter's announcement about the assignment was met with a collective groan from the students. Disappointment rippled through the room and many students exchanged dismayed glances with their classmates. Some slouched in their seats, clearly unenthusiastic about writing an essay, while others sighed audibly, already dreading the additional workload.

Kass, Jack, and their friends shared a resigned look, recognizing the sentiment echoed by their peers—although these friends had an experience, a horrific tale, that was sworn to secrecy.

***

Morning classes felt like a boring return to normalcy for the teens and after their much-needed lunch break, they reluctantly shuffled back into their assigned classrooms. They settled into their familiar seats with the early afternoon sunlight streaming through the windows and casting a warm glow on the rows of desks. The whiteboards held remnants of the morning's lessons, showcasing equations, diagrams, and vocabulary.

"Uhh...umm...Mr. Yung?" one of the boys stuttered to get his math teacher's attention. The boy's eyes were focused on something out the window.

"Oh my gosh!" a girl exclaimed in disbelief.

"Shut the front door!" a boy dramatically yelled.

A sudden burst of curiosity swept through the classroom, jolting every teen, including Kass, out of their seats, drawn like magnets to the windows. Hearts raced as they peered outside, fueled by a shared excitement to catch a glimpse of the unexpected spectacle. On the rooftop of the neighboring building, a flock of large black avian creatures had gathered in an otherworldly and menacing formation, like soldiers standing to attention.

Suddenly and in unison, their plumage unfolded like a sinister display, a chilling mix of malevolent crimson and midnight black wings, creating a haunting contrast against the backdrop of a sky filled with cumulus clouds. The birds' beaks were bright orange and the crowns atop their heads were spiked with gems—black onyx, green emeralds, rubies, and sapphires.

"They're eagles!" someone shouted, their voice trembling.

"No, they're hawks," another student insisted, trying to make sense of the horrifying scene.

"Whatever they are, why are they just staring at us? It's like they know something we don't."

"Man, this is freaky."

"There are so many of them."

"Rico, go get Mr. Hanken. Tell him it's urgent," Mr. Yung demanded, his voice shaking.

The students were unable to tear their eyes away from the birds, who stood stone-still glaring into the classroom, their beady eyes filled with an unnerving intelligence. It was as if the birds were waiting for something, something ominous and foreboding.

The classroom grew increasingly tense and suffocating as the seconds ticked by. An invisible darkness descended upon them.

Mr. Hanken, the science teacher, rushed into the classroom, his face pale with dread. He looked over at Mr. Yung and whispered, "What's going on?"

"Look! That's what's going on," Mr. Yung replied, pointing at the birds.

"What the heck!" Mr. Hanken slowly walked to the window to get a better view of the dozens of threatening birds that maintained their military formation.

"What kind of birds are they?" a girl asked.

"They're some type of vulture," Mr. Hanken said, pulling out his phone and scrolling through photos of multiple species. "They most resemble the King Vulture that resides in the Costa Rican rainforests."

The students who had just visited Costa Rica did not miss that point of coincidence. Kass was particularly attentive and not at all surprised to learn the vultures were a Costa Rican breed.

Suddenly, and again in absolute unison, the birds flew directly at the students, their wings flapping with a deafening roar and their eyes leering with an evil blackness, as if possessed by some dark force. The alarming attack seemed unstoppable, and panic spread like wildfire through the classroom. A few students screamed in terror and most took a step or two back, raising their arms to protect their faces, believing the birds were determined to crash through the windows and attack them.

Just as it seemed like the vultures were about to breach the windows, the attack came to an abrupt halt. The birds landed on the lawn, again in perfect military formation, only a few feet from the classroom windows.

With a single, angry voice, the vultures discharged an extremely loud and high-pitched scream, causing the students and teachers to immediately clasp their hands over their ears as if their eardrums were about to burst from the intensity of the shriek. The piercing sound lasted about ten seconds, but it felt like an eternity.

Just as everyone began to lower their hands, the vultures released another ear-splitting scream. The relentless assault of their chilling cries had a paralyzing effect on the students. Fear coursed through their veins like icy tendrils, leaving them trembling and vulnerable.

In the throes of the chaos, Kass remained strangely composed and unaffected by the screams. Locked in a hypnotic-like trance, he maintained eye contact with the vultures. His heart pounded but an unusual calmness washed over him, as if being drawn into a dark pact with the sinister birds.

The vultures' message was clear—Kass had trespassed onto their sacred domain and taken what did not belong to him. They were not programmed to forgive or forget, but instead were following the orders of a higher power, a greater force. Their message was a chilling promise of consequences yet to come.

The vultures finally broke their focused gaze and soared into the sky, circling above the school. The classroom descended into a tense hush. The students were left uneasy and shaken, affected by the alarming presence of the vultures, until they finally dissolved into the distance.

Kass struggled with the growing understanding that he had entered a troubling situation. The gemstone's mysterious power had awakened something within the vultures, unleashing a nightmarish force, and thrusting him into a perilous journey to confront the consequences of meddling with the unknown.

"Okay...okay...kids, calm down," Mr. Yung said. "Get back to your seats, please."

Without having time to follow through with Mr. Yung's request, the bell rang and the students grabbed their backpacks and rushed out the door. Many hurried to the front lawn of the school to see if the birds were on the roof. Mr. Yung and Mr. Hanken also rushed outside, looking up to see if they could spot them. Not a bird was in sight.

Eventually, the crowd dispersed and the lawn was empty. It was time for the last class of the day, so students scurried to their classrooms while discussing what they had just seen. Students who had classes on the opposite side of the school hadn't witnessed the vultures, but news spread fast.

"My dads and I watched an Alfred Hitchcock movie called *The Birds* last year. Maybe the birds are going to attack us," Gab said to Olivia.

"We need a safe house built. A bunker," Olivia added.

"Ohh...we could make it look so cool inside," Gab said.

"Cool inside? I don't care about the inside as long as we keep the birds and creatures outside."

"What creatures?" a classmate questioned.

Ignoring them, Gab took Olivia aside. "We've got to really watch what we say and where we say it."

"I know. Sorry. Hey, have fun with your dads and I'll see you tomorrow," Olivia said.

"Will do. See you then and try to get some rest. We need your brilliant ideas when we meet up with the boys."

***

Dusk approached in Kelowna and the school grounds were empty. The students were home talking to their parents and texting their friends about the events of the day.

On top of the tallest building in town, a thirty-six story high-rise, dozens of vultures gathered in a haunting congregation. Their dark forms blended into the fading light of the day. They sat motionless. Silent. Eyes leering with otherworldly intensity.

Chapter 7

Keith, one of Gab's dads, was known for his slim yet striking appearance. He had a unique sense of style, always dressing with distinct flair and a touch of flamboyance. His wardrobe was a vibrant showcase of colors and statement accessories, reflecting his outgoing personality.

His life journey commenced in Canada, where he was born into a family filled with dreams and aspirations. His parents had faced the challenges of China's one-child policy and longed for a larger family, prompting their immigration to this new land of opportunities. Their adventure began when Keith's older sister was just six months old and the family settled in Canada. In this welcoming and diverse environment, Keith was born, followed by his younger brother two years later.

Keith was the proud owner of *Butter!* bakery, where he mastered the art of pastry-making like a seasoned maestro. The bakery wasn't just a place of business, it was a testament to Keith's boundless passion and artistic flair. Its fame spread far beyond their neighborhood, celebrated for its delectable pastries, and sought after for catering weddings and hosting prestigious community events.

Gab's other dad, Jason, embodied bravery and sacrifice as a firefighter. His career was marked by countless acts of valor, though not without its scars—dark and leathery, they told the tale of a harrowing fire eight years past that forever altered his life. The warehouse inferno had been a living nightmare, claiming the life of a fellow firefighter and leaving many others injured. Whenever Jason thought back to that tragic day, his heart ached, especially for his partner who didn't make it out alive. He had fought valiantly to save both his comrade and himself, but destiny had charted a different course.

After the assistant fire captain ordered the evacuation, Jason had found himself torn between following the order and going back to help his trapped colleagues. His instincts took over, and he rushed back into the inferno, risking his life to save others.

During the horrific event, the merciless inferno swallowed his partner whole, its fiery jaws closing in before he could reach the safety of an exit. The memory of his courageous sacrifice, the way he had braved the roaring flames to save others, was seared into Jason's heart.

Jason's own act of heroism left him with third-degree burns on his arm and shoulder, and his road to recovery was long and grueling. The doctors had doubted whether he would ever fully recover, fearing the nerve damage might be irreparable. But Jason refused to give up, determined to return to the job he loved.

Against all odds, he defied the predictions and slowly but surely regained use of his hand and arm. Though the warehouse fire had left its mark on him, it also strengthened his resolve to continue serving as a firefighter.

Keith admired Jason's courage, but worried about his safety every time he left for duty. The fear of losing him haunted his thoughts, even though he knew he could never stand in the way of Jason's passion, profession, and dedication.

✳✳✳

After Gab proposed meeting at her house instead of going to Jack's, and with Keith's freshly baked pastries as a lure, the group gathered in Gab's brightly lit, contemporary basement. The unusual events at camp had left them feeling apprehensive but also curious, with far more questions than answers and an eagerness to uncover the mystery that had become an essential part of their lives.

They invited Martin to join the meeting, which was a first for them to do anything with him outside of school activities.

"Alright, ladies and gents, welcome to the 'Mystery Makers Club.' We've got ourselves a real-life Scooby Doo mystery to solve," Gab said.

"I hope there's no creepy masked villain with luminous eyes," Olivia said.

"Yeah, and let's hope they don't say, 'I would've gotten away with it if it weren't for you meddling kids,'" Jack laughed.

"Ruh-roh! Raggy, we've got some spooky stuff to solve!" Harlen joined in, doing his best Scooby impression.

The group chuckled.

"Okay, let's do this already," Martin blurted, with surprising intensity.

"Hey, keep your cool. You're lucky to even be invited to the group," Harlen said.

"Well, if it wasn't for me, you would have been eaten alive," Martin sassed back.

"You? How did you become the superhero all of a sudden?" Olivia joined in.

"Hey, I'm just saying, if I wasn't there to protect you five, well, you never know what would have happened," Martin added with false bravado.

The group cracked up, lightening the mood.

Gab grinned. "Alright, enough goofing around. Let's talk about our mysterious and terrifying camp adventures."

"I'll go first," Olivia said. "I think what happened on the mountain was incredibly scary. I never imagined we'd encounter such horrifying and mythical creatures, or whatever those things were."

"Yeah, it was terrifying," Harlen agreed with a grim look.

"It's hard to shake off the fear," Olivia confessed. "I've been having trouble sleeping. It's like those creatures left an indelible mark on my mind."

"I feel the same way," Harlen admitted. "And you're right when you said earlier that no one would believe us. Even our families or friends. It's just too unbelievable."

The atmosphere became subdued as the group acknowledged the gravity of their situation. The memory of those mysterious creatures haunted them, and they knew the experience had taken their lives through an unexpected turn.

"We should be careful not to mention it to anyone else," Olivia said. "Who knows what kind of consequences it might have?"

"How about you, Jack?" Gab asked.

"Man, I totally agree. It was absolutely terrifying. We never had a drill for something like that. I mean, fire drills, earthquake drills, intruder-in-our-school drills, and even a tornado drill, but not flying-creatures-trying-to-kill-us drills."

"No, shizzit," Harlen interrupted.

"I think the best thing we can do is accept that there are things in our world we didn't know actually existed," Jack said with a solemn tone. "But we're all safe now and that's what matters most. Maybe we can keep that adventure between us and move on with our lives."

His words hung in the air, carrying the weight of the extraordinary experience they had shared. The group fell silent, contemplating the profound implications of their encounter with the uncharted.

"Who wants to go next?" Gab asked.

"I'll go next," Martin offered, checking with Harlen.

"Sure," Harlen said.

"Well, I knew you guys were getting up to some kind of mischief, but I had no idea what it was. If I'd known, I would've stayed in my tent," Martin said with a big smile and raised eyebrows. "Well, maybe not, but even though that was some scary stuff, I have to admit, it was also quite the experience. One I don't ever wish to have again but, still, pretty wild. I mean, come on, we only read about stuff like this. And yet we are the people who actually experienced it...and survived."

"I agree," added Harlen. "It was an experience we all shared together and survived. I have no problem keeping it to ourselves. You know, what happens in Vegas, stays in Vegas," Harlen added.

"Well, clearly we were not in Vegas," Gab joked. "But I agree. We experienced something we can't share with anyone else, even though we're safe now."

"I mean, it isn't like we killed someone and next year we're going to get a note saying, 'I know what you did last summer,'" Olivia said.

The group laughed, except Kass. He remained quiet, yet attentive. Only he knew that potential crimes had been committed: stealing from the rainforest and transporting stolen goods through the airport.

Having gone around the circle, expressing their fears and concerns, a sense of camaraderie and understanding enveloped the group. They bonded over their shared secret and an unspoken pact to protect one another from the skepticism and disbelief that would arise if they were to share the truth with others.

Thump.

"What was that?" Martin yelled.

Thump. Thump. Thump. Thump.

Everyone looked up at the ceiling, thinking perhaps one of Gab's dads had dropped something heavy.

Thump. The house shook.

"Hey kids, stay downstairs," Keith shouted from the top of the basement steps.

The teens looked at each other and, ignoring Keith's instruction, ran for the door then up the stairs. Everyone gathered in the foyer where Keith and Jason were already standing.

"I told you kids to stay downstairs," Keith scolded, concerned for their safety.

"Honey, call 911," Jason sputtered to Keith, clearly scared.

"I'm not sure if we need 911 just yet," Keith replied.

THUMP! The tremendous power of whatever was on the house quaked and reverberated at such a terrifying level that Harlen panicked.

"I'm calling 911," he said, pulling out his phone and pushing the speaker button.

"911, what's your emergency?" the operator asked.

They all looked at each other and shrugged their shoulders.

"911, what's your emergency?" the operator repeated.

Jason leaned in closer to Harlen's phone. "We're at 124 Kensington Drive. My name is Jason Collick, I'm with the KFD, Station #2. We're inside the house and something big is on our roof, stomping and making the house shake like there's an earthquake or something."

"Is anyone hurt?" she asked.

"No, not yet, but we're feeling very unsafe and threatened."

"If you look out your window," the dispatch operator continued, "can you see anything? Cars, people, objects?"

"Ah, look over there," Jason interjected.

"Yes, our neighbors are standing in their front yards looking up at the roof of our house. There's obviously something up there."

Suddenly, a loud screech echoed through the neighborhood. People were seen falling to their knees, covering their ears. Keith reported this new information to the operator.

Thump. Thump. Thump.

"What the hell is that?" asked Jason.

"Dad, it's them!" Gab shouted.

"Who's them? The birds from school? Those are the *same birds* on our roof?"

"I think so," Gab said.

Jason scoffed, no longer worried. "I'm going to take a look." He started to open the front door.

"Dad, no!" Gab shouted.

"I am not scared of a bunch of birds," he declared.

Jason, with his firefighter instincts, walked out onto the front lawn, craning his neck for a view of the rooftop.

"What the hell?" Large black vultures with red-tinted wings stood perched in military formation, staring at him. He gasped yet remained fascinated. "What in the hell is going on around here?"

"Dad, I told you they were big and scary!" Gab screamed through the living room window. "Get back in the house!"

The birds let out another piercing cry, even louder than before. Out on the lawn, Jason stood firm, hands pressed over his ears, trying to ward off the intense shriek. The crowd rippled with reactions: hands covering ears, faces showing anguish, and some individuals running to the safety of their homes. Those brave—or perhaps audacious—souls who hung around chatted, snapped selfies, and threw out all sorts of wild guesses about what in the world was happening.

Jack looked over at Kass, who was quiet and didn't seem present.

"Kass, are you okay?" he whispered. "What's happening, man? Talk to me."

"They are here for me," Kass whispered back.

"You?" Jack asked, confused. "Are you serious?"

Kass nodded.

"Dead serious."

Suddenly, one of the vultures dive-bombed from the roof toward Jason. It wrapped its wings around its huge body to form an oval-shape then crashed into Jason with violent force, knocking him over. Gasps and screams could be heard from the neighbors, but the biggest scream came from Gab.

Jason attempted to stand and just when he did, another vulture replicated the dive-bomber position and knocked him down again. The screams got louder as people reacted to Jason's dire circumstance, realizing the vultures intended to injure, if not kill him.

A half dozen good citizens ran out of their houses with bats and brooms, coming to Jason's rescue.

"Jason, get up, get up!" one neighbor shouted, as he stood guard over Jason to prevent yet another vulture from attacking. Soon, Keith and their compassionate neighbors had surrounded Jason so he could stand, at which point he and his rescuers slowly made their way into Keith and Jason's house, where Gab and her friends still remained.

"I gotta get out of here," Kass whispered to Jack. "I need to lure them away from the house."

"Kass, what are you talking about?"

"I'll explain later. But for now, I need to get home."

"Well, I'm coming with you. Let's go out the back," Jack said.

Jack and Kass quietly retreated from the others in the house, who were either engaged in conversation with Keith or keeping their eyes glued out the window. After discreetly exiting the back door, the boys crossed through the yard, silently opened the gate, and jogged down the alley to Kass's home.

"Stay right here. I'm going to get something from my room," Kass said.

"Okay, hurry."

Kass dashed into the house, retrieved the gem from the nightstand's drawer, and secured it in his backpack before exiting his room.

"Hey, where's the fire?" his mom inquired, her voice laced with concern as she comforted Kallie on the living room sofa. Kallie had just experienced a sensory episode, tears streaming as she shielded her ears. Though Kass's mother was puzzled by Kallie's reaction, unable to fathom the cause of her distress, Kass suspected Kallie's heightened senses had enabled her to perceive the distant thumping and screeching of the vultures.

"Jack and I are heading out. I'll be back in a flash," Kass responded, his momentum undeterred by any concern for Kallie or his mom's phone that had begun ringing.

As Kass rushed out of the house to catch up with Jack, the phone continued to ring insistently.

"Hello?" Bailey answered. "Yes, he was just here, Keith. Why? What's going on?"

Keith's urgency was clear as he explained the vulture attack on Jason and the resulting chaos. He was frantically trying to track down Kass and Jack.

Bailey rushed to the front door, her eyes scanning the streets for any sign of the boys, but they were nowhere in sight. Her concern was evident as she tightly gripped the phone.

"I'll call you back if I learn anything, and please call me if you hear from them. Alright?" Her voice trembled with worry as she returned to the sofa to continue comforting Kallie.

"Sure thing," Keith agreed, ending the call with a shared sense of apprehension.

Bailey frantically dialed Jay. No answer. Undeterred, she resorted to sending a text message, but a response remained stubbornly absent. The weight of fear started to close in on her, amplified by the isolation of tending to her other child grappling with painful emotions.

Remarkably, the vultures had ceased their raucous screeches and attacks at Keith and Jason's residence. They had remained gathered on the rooftop, but their aggressive demeanor froze for a tense few minutes. Then, as if guided by an unseen cue, the birds took flight and disappeared into the sky.

The scene at Gab's house, once filled with noise and violence, transformed into a daunting silence. Keith, Jason, and their neighbors sought refuge indoors, retreating from the scene of the bizarre spectacle. Shortly thereafter, with sirens blaring, the sudden-but-late arrival of law enforcement officers shattered that brief moment of tranquility.

Jack and Kass hurried to the school campus with determination. Finding a seat on the bleachers of the sports field, both boys contended with a jumble of emotions. From his vantage point, Kass recognized the mental strain of the decisions ahead, and how the interplay of anxiety with responsibility underscored their importance.

Unable to contain his nervous energy, Jack paced back and forth, his hands rising to shield his head, as if to protect himself from the unreal events of the day.

Kass, with steady hands, unzipped his bag and pulled out the gem.

As tension hung in the air, Jack pivoted to gaze at the precious artifact. "What's that!?" he exclaimed.

"I grabbed it from the mountain. It fell off one of those creatures and I rushed back to pick it up," Kass explained.

"Wait, seriously?"

"Yes, and weird things have been happening ever since."

"That's why all this crazy shit is going down? The birds, those weird lights, your whole dark vibe?" Jack was irritated but also genuinely interested.

"Yeah, this gem's the link, definitely," Kass admitted.

"The plane?"

"Yep," Kass shamefully admitted.

"So, why the secrecy till now? Why not fill me in?" Jack asked.

"I'm not sure, Jack...I wasn't sure how to approach it."

"Come on, man, we're tight. You could've trusted me," Jack said, a touch of understanding in his disappointment.

"I get it, and yeah, I'm sorry. But seriously, what's our next move? Those birds are zeroing in on me, or the stone. And who knows, those big ass creatures might even show up," Kass pondered aloud, his eyes scanning the sky for any sign of the vultures.

"Creatures? Have you seen any?"

"Not yet, just the birds. But with all this weirdness, who knows?" Kass shrugged.

"Maybe we should just ditch it in the ocean or something," Jack suggested, trying to be practical.

"Or we leave it here and bolt," Kass proposed.

Taking the gem from Kass, Jack felt a surge of heat emanating from it. The sensation was so intense that he involuntarily dropped it, cursing, his palm reddening as if scalded. He waved his hand to cool it down but the burning sensation lingered for several moments.

Kass picked up the gem again, finding no change in its temperature. The friends exchanged a puzzled glance, their minds racing to make sense of the strange occurrence.

"There's definitely something going on between you and that thing. This is seriously crazy," Jack remarked.

Kass placed the gemstone on the bleachers then looked up, almost hoping the vultures would appear. More than feeling anxious and upset, he felt responsible for causing the havoc. His impulsive decision to take the gemstone from the rainforest of Costa Rica was threatening his community—his friends, family, classmates, and neighbors. There was no one to blame but himself and he was determined to find a way to clean up the mess he had made. Kass put the stone back into the backpack.

***

While Jack and Kass lingered at the school field mulling over their next move, the police had come and gone on Gab's street, just as they had earlier at the school. By the time they had arrived, the birds had flown away. Fortunately, videos and photos taken by the neighbors enabled the police to understand the nature and magnitude of the emergency. It was soon all over the news and trending on social media. In fact, the attack on Jason went viral, becoming the number one trending incident within minutes.

Chapter 8

"Hi, Mom," Kass said, answering his phone. "Yes, I'm fine. Okay, I'll be home right away. Jack and I are at the school field. Okay. Bye."

"Is she pissed?" Jack asked.

"Just more concerned. Come on, let's get going. We need to talk with the gang and see what they think we should do," Kass said.

"Yeah, good idea."

The boys left the bleachers and began their walk by crossing the field, with the evening sun casting long shadows. Suddenly, a loud familiar screech pierced the air from behind. They froze, then slowly turned around.

There, before their eyes, an ensemble of vultures was lined up on the field—a sinister army of fierce feathered soldiers. The birds stood in perfect formation, their dark eyes fixed on Kass and Jack.

"Ahh shit!" Jack's voice trembled and his eyes widened in terror.

"I second that," Kass murmured, as they took cautious steps backward.

"Nice and slow, Kass. Nice and slow," Jack suggested, trying to keep his composure.

The vultures emitted another unsettling screech, advancing with a strange coordination, their stiff and jerky movement resembling a haunting dance of death. The boys could feel their hostile energy.

The birds inched closer, step by step. With another deafening screech, the vultures opened and closed their orange beaks in creepy unison, as if taunting their prey. Jack covered his ears, desperately trying to block out the perturbing chorus of screeches.

The boys realized the gem held a power beyond their understanding—a power that had drawn these threatening creatures to them.

"Kass, give me the backpack," Jack demanded. "We have to give them the gem."

"No, why would I do that?" Kass replied, clutching the backpack tightly.

"Give it to me."

"Why you?"

"I'm bigger and stronger. Look at you, you're dressed like a model in a Prada fashion show."

"Fine. Just give 'em the damn gem before things get worse."

One of the vultures flew up in the air, its shadow casting a chilling darkness over the boys. With lightning speed, it dove down at them, its beady eyes fixed on its prey. Jack stood in front of Kass, trying to shield him from the impending attack, but it was futile. The vulture wrapped its wings tightly, like a deadly vice, and plowed into Jack. The impact sent him flying several feet back, crashing onto the ground with the wind knocked out of him.

Kass swiftly retrieved the backpack that had been released from Jack's grasp and slung it over his shoulders. Standing firm, his heart racing, Kass braced himself. As expected, another vulture took the same dive-bomb position and headed straight for Kass, its sharp orange beak gleaming with malice. Jack, despite his pain, quickly got up and jumped in front of Kass to once again protect his friend. The bird plowed into Jack. Its razor-sharp talons digging into his flesh and causing him to writhe in agony on the field.

A third vulture swooped into the sky, preparing for yet another attack. Kass's mind clouded with a compulsion to protect Jack and survive himself. An unusual power infiltrated his body, something he couldn't comprehend but knew he must tap into. With newfound strength, Kass became an avenging warrior with astonishing prowess. His actions were not calculated, but pure instinct. One by one, he skillfully countered the onslaught of attacks by the vicious vultures, using his elbows, fists, and any means necessary to immobilize his assailants.

The field became a battleground of chaos and terror as Kass seemed possessed by a primordial force and the gemstone's power had awakened a dormant strength within him.

Despite the horror of the situation, Kass moved with supernatural agility, taking down the attacking vultures with deadly precision. His eyes glinted with an intensity that was both terrifying and hypnotic. He showed no mercy to the creatures that sought to harm them.

The lifeless bodies of the birds lay scattered across the field, a haunting testament to their former vigorous existence. Feathers that once gleamed became muted and disheveled. Wings that once soared through the air were now broken and still. The battleground, charged with energy before, now bore the aftermath of their encounter, with the dead birds serving as a poignant reminder of Kass's formidable power.

Jack remained on the ground, his body trembling in disbelief at the brutal display of strength he had just witnessed. Yet, before he could find his voice to check on his friend, the last bird dived toward Kass. In a swift, graceful movement, Kass reacted with finesse, delivering a final, decisive blow that left the vulture motionless on the ground.

Shocked, Jack looked around to see all the feathered foes scattered about the field.

Kass collapsed to his knees, his body wracked with relief, exhaustion, and despair. Jack hurried over, knelt beside him and tried to offer some comfort in the face of such overwhelming concern.

"Kass?" Jack's voice caught with emotion.

There was no immediate response from his friend. With a gentle touch, Jack brushed the hair from Kass's eyes and pressed a tender kiss onto his forehead, a moment that seemed to linger in time. Drawing him close, Jack held Kass tightly. The ache in his heart mirrored the sight of his dear friend's tear-stained face.

"Kass, are you okay?"

Kass met Jack's gaze, his eyes reflecting a profound emptiness, still brimming with unshed tears. The heaviness of the day's horrors had left him voiceless, his face expressing a shattered vulnerability. Lost and broken, he sought solace in Jack's embrace, yearning for reassurance amid the encroaching shadows that threatened to consume him.

Jack gently helped Kass to his feet, supporting him as they walked across the field, the lifeless bodies of the vultures scattered around them.

"Everything will be okay, Kass. We'll figure this out together," Jack said, though the uncertainty in his own voice betrayed his feeble words of encouragement.

Kass leaned against Jack, seeking comfort in his friend's presence. They made their way to Kass's house and sat on the stoop, feeling the immense tension of the day pressing down on them. The surreal and terrifying experiences of the past seventy-two hours had left scars on their souls that might never heal. In the midst of their silence, they exchanged glances, their eyes communicating their unspoken questions. What had they stumbled upon? What dark forces had been unleashed?

Kass finally broke down and released his pent-up feelings, his heart aching with a profound sense of loss. His once ordinary life no longer existed, replaced by a stark reality he couldn't comprehend.

He clung to Jack's embrace. The future remained uncertain and the road ahead might be fraught with danger, but as long as he had his best friend by his side, he knew he could endure the darkest of days.

Just as the boys were standing to enter the house, the front door opened.

"You're home!" Bailey said, hugging her son, excited and relieved. "What happened to you boys? Were you in a fight?" she asked, noticing their bruises and disheveled look.

"Sorry, Mom, we got distracted on the way home playing tackle football with some of Jack's friends," Kass answered.

"You, playing football? Don't buy it. What happened?"

"I tried something new and it didn't work out for me. I'm tired and dirty. Please let me go shower."

"Well, you both look a mess," she said, still skeptical. "Jack, are you okay to walk home or do you need a ride?"

"No, I'm good with walking two blocks," Jack replied, beginning his walk down the street.

Kass slowly walked up the stairs to his bedroom, looking forward to a hot shower and sleep. As he passed his sister's room, he peeked in to see Kallie sleeping peacefully.

"Kass, are you okay?" his mom asked, trailing behind him.

"Yeah, Mom. I'm fine. I'm just beat-up and tired from the game," he said, continuing the walk to his room.

"All right, but do you want to talk about what happened at Gab's house? The video looks quite frightening."

"It was intense, to say the least. I managed to shoot Gab a message, and it seems like her dad's holding up," Kass recounted, his voice carrying the burden of the night's events.

"Alright, get some rest. I'll whip up a hearty breakfast for you in the morning."

Bailey closed the door behind her and made her way down the hall. Unable to contain the wave of exhaustion and worry crashing over her, tears welled up and cascaded down her cheeks. Balancing the responsibility of looking after Kallie while spending time fretting over Kass had taken its toll. She wiped away the tears, retreating to her bedroom, her heart aching for both her children.

Kass placed his backpack on his desk and let himself collapse onto his bed. He stared up at the ceiling, a whirlwind of thoughts occupying his mind. He stood up and shed his shirt, only to be confronted by a disconcerting sight in the mirror. Bruises marred his arms and shoulders, vivid and striking against his skin. He felt no pain, yet the sight was startling, evidence of having been in a fierce battle. He flopped back onto his bed and let his weariness sweep over him, dragging him, body and soul, into a deep slumber.

***

"Gab, I'm sorry. Kass and I got distracted. We went for a walk to try and lure the birds away," Jack said, calling Gab on his walk home.

"Why did you think you could lure the birds away?"

"We just thought we could. It worked, didn't it?"

"Well, yeah. As soon as you two disappeared, the birds left. Jack, what are you not telling me?"

"Baby..."

"Don't you baby me! That's weird. I know something is up with you two."

"Gab, I'm exhausted. I'll tell you everything I know tomorrow. Please, just trust me."

"All right, I was just worried. I'll see you tomorrow."

"That sounds great. I'm exhausted. I'm going to shower and get some sleep. Good night," he said.

"Good night."

***

The following morning, Kass's eyes fluttered open to the gentle caress of dawn's first light, and a sense of rejuvenation washed over him. He sat up in bed, his fingers tracing the skin of his arms, torso, and back. He couldn't believe what he was seeing. Not a single mark, not even a hint of the deep bruises that had painted his body just the night before.

He raised his arms, flexed his muscles, and twisted his torso, as though testing the reality of his newfound well-being. It was a complete recovery, a transformation that bordered on the miraculous.

Kass's eyes sparkled with astonishment, and he couldn't suppress the grin that spread across his face.

Unbeknownst to Kass, Jack had messaged the gang to convene for an afternoon meeting at Kass's house. Jack's promise to share with Gab about the events of the previous night meant, of course, the entire group, including Martin, couldn't be left in the dark.

Harlen, Olivia, Gab, and Jack, their timing perfectly aligned, bypassed doorbell formalities upon arriving at Kass's house. As they entered the foyer, Kallie hurried over to Harlen, wrapping him in an exuberant hug that infused the room with a tangible warmth and heartfelt connection.

"Harlen is here! Harlen is here!" she announced. Harlen hugged her back and glanced at Olivia with a shrug and a smile, as if to say, *I'm not sure why she loves me so much.*

"Hey, what are you all doing here?" Kass asked, walking into the foyer area.

"Well, good afternoon to you too," Harlen snarked in a humorous way.

"You would have known we were heading over if you had checked your phone," Olivia added.

"Hey, nice to see you, Kass," Martin said, as he bounded up the porch stairs and into the open door of the house.

"Uhh, you too, even though I just saw you yesterday," Kass replied, looking at Martin like he was odd.

"Kass, I didn't know you were having a party," his mom said, walking by the group and picking up Kallie's bag. "Hi, kids. Have fun. Come on, Kallie, we need to go to your appointment."

"Harlen is here. Harlen is here," Kallie echoed.

"Yes, Harlen is here. Say bye to Harlen."

"Bye Harlen. Harlen say bye. Harlen say bye," Kallie said, smiling as she walked out the door.

"Bye Kallie. Have a good time at your appointment," Harlen said, amusing Kallie.

"All right, Kass," Jack said, taking a firm leadership role, "we all need to have a talk about anything and everything. But first, you need to show everyone what's in your backpack and then we need to tell them what happened last night."

"His backpack?" Olivia asked, recalling her suspicions on the airplane.

"What happened last night?" Martin asked, concerned.

"Okay, everyone go sit in the living room and I'll be right back." Kass frowned at Jack, then left to retrieve his bag.

The group got comfortable in the living room, sitting in silence on the velour sofa, the matching high-back wing chairs, and plush carpeted floor. They glanced at each other while waiting anxiously for the mystery to be revealed.

When Kass joined his friends carrying the sling backpack, he sat on the floor next to Jack who was in one of the chairs. The two boys looked at each other and Jack knew it was up to him to get the conversation going.

"So, when we were being attacked by the creatures—"

"The birds?" Harlen interrupted.

"No, the creatures, the beasts, in Costa Rica," Jack explained. "Anyway, when the creatures were battling each other and we were making our escape, Kass noticed one of the gemstones fall off the spine of the big guy. Kass ran back and picked it up." Jack looked to Kass who brought the gem out of his bag.

"Whoa, it's so beautiful," Olivia cooed.

"Like a giant ruby, mixed with other gems," Gab added.

"It must be worth millions!" Harlen remarked, getting excited.

"Its value hadn't actually crossed my mind," Kass said. "But yeah, it's probably worth a lot."

"But that's not the point," Jack said, refocusing the group. "Crazy things are happening because of that gem and something really crazy happened last night," he added.

"Crazy? Like how crazy?" Martin asked.

"So, those vultures that invaded our school? It's looking more and more like they were on a hunt for either Kass or that stone. We're piecing things together and that's the most logical explanation. And guess what? Those same vultures made a dramatic entrance at Gab's place, all in pursuit of Kass. He figured that much out last night, hence the sneaking out. We were aiming to lead them away, and thankfully, it worked. We headed to Kass's house, grabbed the stone, and made a beeline for the field at school, assuming the birds would follow. That's when he finally told me about the gemstone."

Gab's question cut through the air. "Jack, you seriously only found out about this last night?"

Jack nodded his head, a wry smile playing on his lips. "Believe it or not, he kept this whole thing hush-hush."

Confused and concerned, Olivia's inquisitive gaze turned to Kass. "And why, pray tell, would you keep this whole circus a secret, Kass?"

A sigh escaped Kass, his explanation tinged with a hint of frustration. "Honestly, I couldn't quite figure out why. I had intended to share everything once we were safely back home, but something strange came over me. My thoughts started spiraling, and I just felt...off, as if my mind and body were out of sync."

"Your body felt different. Do tell?" Martin joked.

"Last night, the birds appeared on the field, just like we anticipated. In fact, they attacked us. All of them!" Jack continued.

"What?" Gab gasped.

"Are you guys hurt?" Harlen asked.

"That's just it, Kass fought them all off. Knocked the bird poop right out of each and every one of those nasty vultures," Jack explained.

"Hahaha! You two are B-S-ing us now. Kass didn't fight anything off," Harlen snickered.

"Seriously, two of the birds knocked me down," Jack insisted in a stern tone, his face dead serious. "The second one clawed me and nearly knocked me out." Jack pulled up his sleeves and showed the others his wounded arms.

"Jack! Oh no!" Gab shouted.

"That looks painful," Harlen said.

"Those damn birds were strong—and powerful! While I was on the ground, a third bird attacked and Kass elbowed it, knocking it out cold. And then a fourth, fifth, sixth...on and on. It was a shitshow."

"You're like a little Ryan Garcia," Martin said.

"Who?" Olivia asked.

"He's a boxer. Never mind, I'm impressed, Kass."

"Hmm...you're shitting us, right?" Harlen said, still unconvinced.

"No, that's what happened," Kass said. "I can't explain it except the stone seems to give me unusual powers. It's totally weird and pretty scary, actually. In fact, I went to bed with bruises all over my body last night from the battle with the birds, and by this morning I was one-hundred percent good, better than good!"

"Wait, so you have some type of superhero strength and healing powers, too?" asked Harlen.

"No, well...maybe. I don't know," Kass replied.

"Prove it," Harlen persisted. "Show us how you were able to fight off those big-ass birds."

"Harlen, cut it out. Can't you see he's not in the best headspace right now?" Olivia reprimanded.

"Hey, Kass, mind giving the sofa a try?" Martin's suggestion came with a comforting tone, as if offering a gentle solution to the tension in the room.

Surveying the expectant faces around him, Kass rose from his spot on the floor and exchanged glances with Olivia and Martin, who remained seated on the sofa. With a shrug of his shoulders, Kass tentatively approached the challenge. His attempt to lift the sofa, though, was met with frustration. He strained, attempting to summon superhuman strength, but the furniture refused to budge.

"So, how do you even start explaining what went down last night?" Harlen inquired.

"I can't wrap my head around it," Kass confessed. "Honestly, battling those birds was like I tapped into a whole different side of myself. Fear, anger...it all kind of melded together."

The room seemed to hum with a charged atmosphere of uncertainty. Gab's voice broke through the tension.

"But what's next? Are we looking at more vultures dive-bombing you? Is this just the beginning of some weird cosmic rollercoaster?" she asked.

"Maybe we should just toss the darn stone," Olivia suggested. "It's as if those vultures are hell-bent on keeping you away from it or taking it from you."

Martin reached over and picked up the gem resting on the carpet.

"Ouch!" he exclaimed, hastily dropping the stone. In an instant, the energy in the room underwent a dramatic shift. Martin's involuntary response to the stone spread a ripple of fear among the others, their own expressions reflecting his startled reaction.

"Yeah, I dared to try and hold it, too. Hotter than hell! But Kass is on a different wavelength with that thing. There's something going on between them," Jack mused, both fascinated and uneasy.

When Martin heard this, his ears perked up. "Kass and the gem have a special relationship?" he remarked with a grin. Martin looked directly at Kass, raised his eyebrows and said, "Interesting."

"I think we should take it back," Olivia said. "This thing is going to haunt us. Think about it, it's sending vultures to come get it or to kill you, Kass, for taking it."

"Ah come on, you're exaggerating. We don't know for sure those birds were after him. I say we keep it and sell it for some serious cash," Harlen added.

"Okay, hold on. We're not selling anything or traveling back to Costa Rica. That's absurd," Jack said. "Let's sit on this for a while and figure things out."

"I agree," Gab said.

"Okay, I can agree with that," Olivia added.

"Ya, all right," Harlen said, chagrined.

"Sounds like a plan," Martin agreed.

"Kass, what do you think?" Jack asked.

"I'm thinking we should find a place to hide the gem so it's not in the house, but also where no one can find it."

"Good idea," Jack agreed. "So let's brainstorm about the best place to hide it."

"Gab, how about your dad's bakery?" Kass suggested.

"Wait, Kass, now that I think about it, we can't hide the gem at the bakery or anywhere away from you," Jack explained. "If more vultures or some other creatures show up, you'll need the gem."

"I don't know, Jack. I don't want the stone anymore. I want to get rid of it before someone gets seriously hurt."

"I know you're scared, but nothing can hurt you as long as you have the stone."

"Well then, we need to return it like Olivia said," Kass insisted.

"Kass, there's no way we can get on a plane and travel across the continent and return it by ourselves. We're going to have to wait until next year's camping trip. Then we can all go back and return it," Jack said.

"We don't know if next year's trip will even be to Costa Rica and I'm not keeping this damn thing for a year anyway!" Kass practically yelled.

"Okay, okay. Relax, bro. Let's just take it one day at a time. We'll figure something out. Come here, man," Jack said, giving Kass a hug. "It will be alright. We will figure it out."

Chapter 9

J essica 5:04 p.m.: Martin, where are you?

Jessica 5:04 p.m.: Are you with Jack and them again?
Jessica 5:05 p.m.: How come you're not replying?
Jessica 5:08 p.m.: Martin?

Martin's thumb glided across his phone screen, each message from Jessica adding to his mounting exasperation. The decision ahead weighed on him, a knot of tension forming as he realized the gravity of what he needed to do. Text messages wouldn't suffice—this was a conversation that demanded more.

Summoning his resolve, he dialed her number, his heart racing as he waited for her to answer. When she did, her voice filled the line with a flat, terse, "Hello."

"Hi," he ventured, his voice carrying both uncertainty and determination.

"Umm...hi?" Jessica's voice then crackled as demanding questions tumbled out in a rush. "Where have you been? Why haven't you replied to any of my messages? Were you with—"

"Jessica, stop! Just...relax," Martin interjected, his tone steady yet urgent enough to diffuse the mounting tension.

"Relax? What's gotten into you lately?" she blurted.

"Jessica, this isn't working for me anymore. I just need some time. I think we need some time apart," he admitted.

The silence that followed was charged with the unspoken complexities of their relationship.

"What, are you breaking up with me!?" Jessica shouted.

"Yes, I just don't think this is working out anymore," Martin replied, feeling guilty, but not even sure why he felt that way.

"I can't believe you're doing this! You're such an asshole!" Jessica screamed, ending the call.

Martin looked at his phone and sat on a stool at the kitchen counter.

Jessica 5:11 p.m.: I can't believe ur doing this!

Jessica 5:12 p.m.: Let's talk. I'm sorry I overreacted.

Jessica 5:14 p.m.: WTF!

Jessica 5:14 p.m.: OK! Fine. You're an asshole!!!

Jessica 5:15 p.m.: Don't call me. I'm fine with this. I hate you

so much!

Martin turned his phone over and set it down. With folded arms, he leaned onto the counter next to his phone, seeking a physical anchor for his emotional turmoil.

"Hey honey, I overheard your phone call," Martin's mom said as she entered the kitchen, her voice a soothing presence in the room. Her hand landed gently on his shoulder.

"Yeah, she's just so high maintenance and demanding. I couldn't take it anymore," Martin said.

"Well, you're young. You'll find someone else. Now you know a little more of what you want and what you don't want," she responded with comforting words of wisdom.

Her hand remained on his shoulder, a grounding touch that reminded Martin he wasn't alone in navigating the complexities of his emotions.

***

Jack and Gab made their way to Gab's house and down the hall to her bedroom after the intense meeting with Kass and the gang. The young couple had a lot to discuss.

"Hey, keep the door open," Jason's voice echoed down the hall. "You're seventeen, not twenty-five."

"Oh, Dad, no one is trying to make babies around here," Gab quipped. Her lighthearted banter was indicative of her close bond with her family. Nevertheless, she left the bedroom door open a crack then ran to the bed and sat on Jack's lap, moving in close.

"Stop, he's going to come in," Jack said, backing his face away.

"Well, if he wants to watch us kissing, he can be my guest," she said, kissing Jack.

The two of them were often affectionate with each other and had no problem with public displays. After two years in a kind and supportive relationship, they were comfortable hugging, even kissing, in front of their friends and families.

"How bad does it hurt?" Gab asked, lifting Jack's t-shirt and brushing her fingers across the bruises on his torso.

"It hurts, but not too bad. The second one really knocked me down hard and used its talons. I still can't believe the way Kass battled them. I seriously thought I was in a superhero movie."

"I can't imagine," Gab said.

"When I was on the ground, I saw the birds coming at him. Like so many of them coming full force. I thought for sure he was going to be killed. I was so scared."

"Well, maybe that stone did save him then. Maybe it saved both of you. Is it possible the connection he has with the gem gives him special powers at critical times like that?"

"I think you're onto something here," Jack concluded.

Gab leaned in with tenderness, pressing her lips softly against each of Jack's wounds, tracing the contours of his bruised body with a gentle touch. Her affectionate gestures aimed to comfort, each kiss a whisper of reassurance. Gradually, as their embrace deepened, their mouths came together in a moment of shared intimacy.

***

Martin's family held the keys to a charming winery nestled in the highlands surrounding Kelowna. While modest in size, their winery had achieved remarkable success. This haven for wine enthusiasts wasn't just about the delightful vintages they crafted, it was a symphony of experiences, where the ambience of the vineyard itself became the main attraction. Perched atop a steep hill, the winery commanded a breathtaking view of Lake Okanagan, stretching endlessly both north and south of the city. The outside seating area had been transformed into a canvas of relaxation, inviting guests to savor their glasses of wine while soaking up the richness of the fertile Okanagan Valley and the expansive lake beyond.

Martin was the second oldest of five siblings: four boys and a girl, with his younger brothers, Mike and Markus, identical twins looking forward to attending Cypress High as eighth graders in the coming year. The twins were both academically bright, with extending marks. Martin's sister, Lori, was a tenth-grader and the sibling with whom he shared an unbreakable bond. They frequently found themselves spending ample time together. Meanwhile, Ross, his elder brother, had graduated from Cypress High just a year earlier.

Ross had developed a drug problem during the latter part of his junior year, leading to his absence from school for a month to participate in a residential drug treatment program. This created a division between him and the rest of the family. In fact, Martin harbored strong resentment toward his brother stemming from Ross's stealing, lying, and manipulation. Building a relationship with Ross proved difficult for Martin, regardless of their close proximity in age. This circumstance also cast a shadow on Martin's presence at Cypress High due to the stigma linked to his older brother's behavior.

Fortunately, Lori excelled as an extending student, showcasing remarkable academic achievements. While Martin enjoyed positive relationships with Markus and Mike, the twins shared an inseparable connection that left little room for others.

"Mom told me that you and Jessica broke up. Are you okay?" Lori asked.

"Yeah, I'm good. I'm surprisingly better than I thought I would be," Martin replied.

"Well, that's good. How did she take it?"

"Not so good. You know she can be quite intense."

"I didn't like her for you. The whole 'I'm the most popular girl' was tiring and the mean girl act was ugly. But she is very pretty. I have to give her that," Lori said.

"Yeah, she is, but pretty isn't everything and it's not enough. At least not for me. School might be a little awkward for a while, but I'm fine," Martin said. "Come on, you want to go to the mall with me?"

"Definitely. Who knows, maybe you'll find a Girlfriend 2.0 upgrade there," Lori joked.

"Well, I hope they have a good return policy, just in case," they both chuckled.

As the days passed, the town of Kelowna tried to return to some semblance of normalcy, but the memory of the vultures' haunting presence lingered like a shadow over the community. Media outlets continued to buzz with reports of the bizarre bird behavior at the high school and the violent attack on Gab's dad, leaving residents shaken and bewildered.

However, one incident remained shrouded in secrecy—the harrowing battle Kass and Jack had faced on the high school field. Only their closest friends knew the truth of what had transpired that night.

When Jack and Kass had later returned to the scene to gather evidence, there was none to be found. No trace of the birds or their feathers. It was as if the terrifying encounter had never happened.

The media, eager to find an explanation for the other strange events, attributed the vultures' presence to an unusual migration pattern caused by climate change. But Kass and his friends knew better. They knew the creatures had come in search of the jewel or seeking vengeance for its theft.

Despite the town's attempts to move on, an eerie tension hung in the air. Kass couldn't shake the nagging intuition that dark and sinister forces were at play because of his possession of the gemstone.

The students of Cypress High and their parents were getting into the groove of their morning, and like clockwork, Jack showed up at Kass's place at 8:40 a.m. sharp. This gave them the usual sixteen minutes to hustle their way to their first class.

"Is it in there?" Jack asked, referring to the gemstone and pointing to Kass's backpack.

"Yes, I have it," Kass replied, somber and serious.

"Okay, have a good class and I'll see you in a couple of hours."

After morning classes had wrapped up, the lunch bell rang and the five friends gathered around a picnic table outside the school. Amid the laughter and bites, Gab's attention was drawn to Martin not far away.

Seated solo, his back against a tree, Martin was engrossed in a book while nibbling on his lunch. It was an uncommon sight. In the months prior, Martin would always hang with his jock friends and Jessica.

"Hey, where are you going, Gab?" Olivia asked when she saw Gab rise from the bench and walk away. Gab didn't respond and made a beeline for Martin.

"You do know this is every dog's favorite pee spot, don't you?" she said with a smile.

"What?" Martin replied, jumping up. "That's gross!" He took off his canvas jacket and smelled it.

"I heard about you and Jessica," Gab said more seriously.

"It's cool," Martin said. "I anticipated it happening, but just not this soon."

"We all thought you two would get married and have a bunch of babies. I mean, by surrogacy, of course. No way Jessica was going to allow a baby to come out of her. Not with that body," Gab said with a smile.

Martin laughed. "True that."

"Hey, come have lunch with us. I mean, why not, right?"

Martin agreed and felt relieved when everyone was receptive to his honorary membership. Well, everyone except Harlen, who continued to be leery of Martin's newfound kindness.

After lunch, they dispersed to their various classes, but that didn't stop texts, memes, and emojis from flying back and forth.

The students in the math class found it difficult to stay focused on anything Mr. Yung was saying. Instead, they kept glancing out the window with concern. Not that they wanted the vultures to reappear, but they did hope something would happen to add excitement to their otherwise dreary day.

Mr. Yung noticed the students were even more distracted than usual. He walked to the windows and closed the blinds.

"Isn't it better if we can see out there just in case we're under attack?" a girl asked.

"Attack? This is not a movie, Candice, this is a math class. You'll be fine," Mr. Yung said.

Moments later, Mr. Yung realized keeping the blinds closed resulted in so much anxiety the students were even less attentive.

"Okay, I'll reopen the blinds. I just need you all to focus. In fact, let's get into groups of four, starting with you four, and you four, and you four, and so on," he instructed.

The chairs shuffled into groups, refocusing the students so Mr. Yung could make some progress with his lesson. Soon the class period ended and students had one last class before their school day was over.

"Hey, Kass," Martin said, stopping Kass at his locker.

"Hey, Martin, what's up?"

"Well, I was wondering, would you take me shopping? I'm looking to change my wardrobe a bit and could use some help."

"Shopping?" Kass wondered. "Yeah, I guess. Hey, change of subject, mind if I ask why Jessica dumped you?"

"Actually, I broke up with her."

"Wait, you broke up with one of the prettiest girls in school? Clearly the most popular. What happened?"

"It just wasn't working out," Martin said, not wanting to talk about it. Instead, he repeated, "So, shopping?"

"Sure, Martin. How about Saturday?"

"I was hoping maybe tomorrow."

"I guess tomorrow could work. It would have to be right after school, though. I need to be home by seven to watch my sister while my mom and dad attend an event."

"That's great. Awesome!" Martin was all smiles.

After school that day, Jack, Gab, and Olivia helped out at Keith's bakery, an occasional and typical routine for the teens. In this case, they helped with the quarterly inventory, along with Jason.

"It's weird being around your dad today, Gab. I keep feeling like a creature is going to attack at any moment," Olivia said.

"I feel the same."

"Well, we can pretty much assume it's not over," Jack added as he counted the bags of flour on the shelf. "We just don't know what or when."

"That doesn't help, Jack," Olivia said.

"Probably not, but reality is reality, and we can't ignore it. We need to stay alert, watch each other's backs, and especially keep an eye out for Kass."

"He should have never gone back for that gemstone. And then to take it on the plane and back here. What was he thinking?" Olivia said, exasperated.

"Ah, come on. I would have done the same thing. A jewel falls off a gigantic creature that was attacking a creepy creature that was attacking us. I mean, what a souvenir of an unforgettable experience."

"Yeah, I see your point," Olivia admitted, "but that souvenir has come with a price."

"A big price," Jack agreed. "But Kass wouldn't have gone back if he'd known all of the ramifications of his actions."

"True," Gab added. "Kass would never have done anything to bring such violence here."

"Well, we know how much he likes his bling," Olivia added with a smile.

***

On that day after school, Martin pitched in at the family winery alongside his twin brothers, while his sister dedicated her time to homework in the winery's office.

"Hey, let me know if you need any help with your homework," Martin mentioned to Lori. "I'll be downstairs in the tasting room."

"Thanks, but this is easy stuff," Lori said.

"Yo, I heard you and Jessica broke up," Markus said, sitting with Mike in a section of the tasting room. Patrons were sparse, leaving room for their banter.

"Yeah, she finally dumped you," Mike joked.

"Haha...I broke up with her and it's all good," Martin replied.

"You're never going to find a prettier girl than Jessica. All downhill from here, pal," Markus laughed.

"Yeah, she's a ten and you're a solid three," Mike said, laughing along with Markus.

Their banter was all in good fun. Mike and Markus would be more empathic in a more serious situation, but they could see Martin was fine with the breakup.

***

After school, Harlen and Kass studied together at Harlen's house, taking occasional breaks to play Nintendo Switch.

"Are you doing okay, Kass?" Harlen said, pausing the game.

"Sure, I'm fantastic."

"Who do you think you're fooling? You must still be tripping."

"Okay, yeah, I'm freaked out," Kass admitted. "You weren't there. You watched those birds knock over Jason, but it was nothing like the way they hit Jack. They were looking to do some serious damage. And when they came at me, I turned into this different person."

"Jack said it was some superhero stuff."

"I actually don't remember it all. It happened so fast. I just remember having the overwhelming feeling I needed to save Jack and protect myself. Sure, I was angry and afraid at first, but I became protective more than anything else," Kass explained. "I've never physically helped anyone before, like from a bully or fight. The only person I've protected is Kallie, and that's more socially, not physically. I'm always on high alert to shield her from ignorant people who make hurtful comments. But I can use my words for that."

"Okay, so it wasn't a David Banner Incredible Hulk moment?" Harlen joked.

"Nah, it was more like one of those *Matrix* scenes, you know? In-the-flow fighting, almost effortless. As I mentioned earlier, it all unfolded in a blur. I'd estimated around ten birds, but when the dust settled, there were dozens of vultures scattered across the field. And here's the kicker, a few were like thirty yards away, all the way to the opposite side."

"Man, that's just insane."

"I was seriously thinking we should throw the jewel in the lake. But I'm afraid that's not going to solve the problem," Kass said. "There's more to what's happening than that."

"Throw it in the lake? That'd be a crazy move, man. That massive gemstone needs to be dismantled into individual jewels and sold to the highest bidder. I'm dead serious, you don't just flush dolla's down the drain," Harlen said, gesturing his hands as if it was raining money.

"Let's wait for things to cool off a bit and then we can brainstorm how to turn this into some serious cash," Kass replied. "And this gemstone stuff is not the only trippy thing happening these days," Kass said.

"Now what?" Harlen asked. "We don't need any more drama."

Kass laughed. "No drama. It's just that Martin asked me to take him shopping tomorrow."

"Actually, that's pretty cool, Kass. You're the perfect person to go shopping with. If it wasn't for you, I'd look homeless."

"That's true," Kass laughed again.

"Plus, I think he has a boy-crush on you," Harlen teased.

"*Whaaat*? No, I don't think so."

"No 'what'. He does. It's obvious," Harlen giggled. "And he just broke up with Jessica, so now he's ready to make his move. Plus, you're not dating anyone and he's a good-looking guy. So why not?"

"Because he likes girls. And he's always been an annoying jock like his idiot buddies."

"I know, but he's been making an effort. He's not that bad anymore. Plus, he's no longer with evil Jessica and those dufus girls. I'm just saying, try not to judge him and instead try to understand him," Harlen said.

"Whoa, look at you, all grown up and sounding smart," Kass replied, smiling and nudging Harlen with his elbow.

"Ouch! Be careful, Mister Superhero. I'm not a vulture."

Chapter 10

T he evening in Kelowna was calm and quiet. The sky was just starting to darken with the sunset casting a warm glow over everything. Hummingbirds darted from flower to flower, while the spotted towhees made their presence known with distinctive calls. Overall, it was a peaceful scene, the local birds contributing to the city's natural surroundings.

Despite the passing of several days, the gang still felt haunted by the vulture attacks and the mystery surrounding the gemstone. They couldn't help but wonder if the vultures would make a return appearance. Were those two dragon-like creatures somehow connected to the vultures? Were they after the gemstone? These questions plagued their thoughts.

Kass, in particular, was grappling with the responsibilities connected to possessing the gemstone. He knew that simply getting rid of it wouldn't guarantee anyone's safety. In fact, keeping the gem close for the special powers it gave Kass seemed like the wiser idea. Tossing it into the lake might not be enough to deter the creatures, and he might then find himself vulnerable if they came back for another confrontation.

Meanwhile, the vulture attacks continued to be the talk of the town, especially at *Butter!*, the busy bakery. The gossip mill was in full swing as curious townspeople flocked to *Butter!* to exchange rumors and stories about the recent incidents at the school and the bakery owner's house. Keith and Jason found themselves constantly bombarded with hushed conversations and questions. Everyone wanted to know what had happened and why the vultures had targeted their house.

"Why was Jason attacked?"

"Have you encountered these birds before?"

"Where are the vultures now?"

The two dads were at a loss for answers and had grown weary of the constant inquiries.

Their house was the neighborhood's most infamous. With contemporary elegance, the minimalist design featured clean lines and large windows. Its sleek and modern construction boldly contrasted with the quaint, Victorian-style homes that encircled it. A house ideal for entertaining, Keith and Jason were often chosen to host neighborhood gatherings and parties, particularly during the holiday season.

The history and connection the two dads had with their surrogate and egg donor, Halle, was truly special. Halle had played a pivotal role in their journey into parenthood, including dear memories that dated back to when she was Jason's high school sweetheart. The bond she shared with Jason, including her understanding and acceptance of his sexuality, had resulted in a unique and enduring friendship.

Despite the divergent paths their lives had taken, Jason and Halle's close relationship remained steadfast, resilient in the face of life's ups and downs. Halle had always occupied a central role in Jason's partnership with Keith—she had officiated their wedding and played a significant part in Gab's early days. Halle provided Gab with not only the crucial first days of colostrum but also continued to offer breast milk for the following six months. Her nurturing presence extended beyond nourishment, as she showered Gab with gifts and affection, becoming an influential figure in Gab's formative months.

The news of Halle's terminal pancreatic cancer diagnosis when Gab was nearly fourteen months old struck everyone deeply, especially since it meant she wouldn't be present to witness Gab's childhood unfolding. Halle valiantly fought for seven months against the disease, but eventually, she succumbed.

Amid the heart-wrenching challenges of illness and loss, Keith and Jason held onto their gratitude for Halle's selflessness and the incredible gift she had bestowed upon them—their precious daughter, Gab. Every single day, Gab brought immeasurable joy into their lives. Their little miracle. A living, breathing symbol of enduring hope and boundless love.

***

Like the town of Kelowna, Kass's house was calm and quiet. Wonderful smells were coming from the kitchen, drawing Kass out of his room and down the stairs.

"Mom, what's for dinner?" Kass asked eagerly.

"Mom, tell Kass about dinner. Share the delicious news," Kallie chimed in with a grin.

"It's lasagna. I made a huge batch, so I hope you've got your appetites ready."

"I'm practically famished," Kass admitted with a chuckle.

"Hey, Dad."

"Hello, Champ," Jay said as they crossed paths in the living room.

"Hey, Dad. Hey, Son. Dad's playing Son, and Son's playing Dad," Kallie echoed mischievously.

Gathered around the dinner table, they all savored their meal, swapping stories and connecting as they shared their favorite part of their day.

Then Kass's dad discussed his upcoming business escapade, a semiannual ritual that whisked him away to Central America and Asia to curate gems, fabrics, and crafts for their family boutique, *Heritage Crafts*. He was to leave in two days for Asia.

These journeys weren't just about commerce, they were about orchestrating a symphony of cultures and experiences with skillful finesse. Upon returning home, Jay would delve into his downstairs sanctum, engaging in meticulous artistry of restoration, preparing each item to gleam in pristine perfection for premium sales.

"Hey, Dad, when's the next trip after this one?" Intrigued by his father's tales, Kass seized the opportunity to probe further. "I mean, which month will you be traveling to Central America?"

"September seems to be the sweet spot, right before the holiday frenzy. Why do you ask?" his dad replied.

"Think you'd be up for some company? Yours truly?" A sly smile curved Kass's lips as he put forth his audacious proposal. A pause hung in the air, a moment of suspended possibility, as Jay considered his son's out-of-the-blue proposal.

"September, huh? School bells will be ringing, but I'll ponder on it."

"Missing a bit of school might not be the end of the world, especially if you can juggle your studies with the travel schedule," interjected Kass's mother, the steady voice of reason in the family. "Plus, your academic track record can handle a little detour. Quality time with your dad would be priceless."

"Absolutely, Mom. I've aced the art of balancing, and the prospect of bonding with Dad on an adventure like this is an education I wouldn't trade for anything." Kass said, laying it on thick and seizing his mother's support like a lifeline.

"Alright, that's still a few moons away," Jay said, shifting his gaze to his wife. "How about we circle back on this in a couple of months and lay down some serious plans. Perhaps Kass can have a chat with his teachers before the school year wraps up."

"Absolutely, we'll figure it out," Bailey affirmed with a determined nod.

After dinner, the living room buzzed with energy as Kass and Kallie nestled together on the sofa, locked into the vibrant world of *Rupaul's Drag Race*. Their fingers dipped into a giant bowl of popcorn and their laughter echoed in sync with the silly show. Snuggled under Kass's arm, Kallie giggled and playfully echoed Rupaul's iconic lines, "Can I get an amen? You better work!"

"Alright, Kallie, it's bedtime," her dad's voice interjected.

"Just one more go, Dad. One more go," she pleaded with sparkling eyes.

"You mean one more minute, not go," Kass instructed.

"Okay, one more minute, not go, Dad. One more minute, not go," Kallie repeated.

"Ready for some serious fun, Kallie? Hop on my back and let's kick off an epic, action-packed adventure."

"Yay, let's do this!" Kallie exclaimed, leaping onto Kass's back for a piggyback ride through the house and up the stairs in a whirlwind of youthful spirit.

***

Kass 8:36 p.m.: Hey Jack, I have the perfect plan!

Jack 8:36 p.m.: You're planning on kissing Martin?

Kass 8:36 p.m.: Hey, Harlen has a big mouth. LOL

Jack 8:37 p.m.: Okay, what plan?

Kass 8:37 p.m.: Dad goes to Costa Rica in September. Let's go with him and return the stone!!

Jack 8:38 p.m.: Brilliant. Wait...we? LOL

Kass 8:38 p.m.: Yes, goodnight. See you in the morning.

Kass set his phone on the nightstand and pulled the blanket snugly over his shoulders. Thoughts swirled in his mind: going to Costa Rica again, returning the stone, making sense of the vulture attacks and his superpowers. Kass was well aware how challenging it was going to be to navigate the times ahead. Yet he found solace in the unwavering support of his friends and drew strength from the powerful aura of the gemstone.

***

The school day unfolded without any feather-flying incidents and Kelowna continued to be a town of relaxed tranquility. Life at Cypress High adhered to its usual routines, unremarkable and calm, and as promised, Kass took Martin shopping. Together, they browsed a local clothing store, one of Kass's favorites.

"So, what's on our shopping agenda today?" Kass queried Martin in the men's section of the large boutique store.

"I'm not entirely sure. That's where your expertise comes into play. I'm your muse," Martin replied with a bashful grin.

"My muse, huh?"

"What? That's a word."

"Yeah, it's a word. Just didn't peg you for using it," Kass noted, sliding hangers left and right on the hunt for the perfect shirt for Martin.

"Do you think I'm unintelligent?" Martin inquired.

"Nah, I used to think you were a bit of an idiot. But now, you're alright," Kass reassured him with a smile. "Hey, check this out. This is so you," Kass raised a multi-colored floral shirt and held it against Martin's torso.

"Uh, really?" Martin yelped.

"Nah, I'm just kidding," he laughed, returning the shirt to the rack.

Kass gathered a collection of clothing before sending Martin to the changing room. Martin's facial expressions were hilarious: No way! You think so? Oh, hell no! Maybe?

"That shirt's perfect," Kass said. "You look really hot—I mean, it looks good on you." Each time Kass paid him a compliment, Martin smiled, and with each compliment, another garment went into the purchase pile.

"Hey, I don't know about these pants. My balls can't breathe," Martin said, hiding in the dressing room.

"Haha, come out, let me see," Kass requested.

"My balls?"

"No, not your balls, you in those pants," Kass laughed.

Martin slowly came out of the dressing room.

"Ah man, those look great on you," Kass said with a huge smile.

"I don't think so. I can't wear these," Martin squirmed, adjusting his legs and crotch area in the skinny jeans.

"Wait, I'll prove it. Turn around."

Martin turned around and showed his backside.

Kass snapped photos. "Okay, turn this way again." *Click. Click.* Kass then sent the photos out on the group chat.

"Don't share those with anyone!" Martin shouted.

"Too late. Wait for it...wait for it..." he grinned as the two of them watched the replying icon.

Gab 4:11 p.m.: Hot!

Harlen 4:11 p.m.: Dude, I can see your balls!

Olivia 4:11 p.m.: Shut up, Harlen. He looks great!

Jack 4:12 p.m.: Man, you're in good hands.

Gab 4:12 p.m.: I like the shirt too!!

Olivia 4:13 p.m.: Martin has some serious drip!

"See, it's unanimous," Kass grinned at Martin. Then addressing the sales clerk, "Three pairs of these in different colors, please."

Later, in the parking lot, Martin asked, "Want to grab a bite to eat?" He stowed the shopping bags in his dad's car.

"I still need to head home and hang out with my sister," Kass explained. When he noticed a hint of disappointment on Martin's face, he quickly added, "Hey, why don't you come over and have dinner at my place? I'm sure my mom has whipped up something or there might be leftover lasagna."

"Okay, cool, that works," Martin accepted with a smile.

Martin and Kass had enjoyed their after-school shopping spree as a one-on-one opportunity to get to know each other on a more personal level. The synthetic aura that had previously surrounded Martin no longer existed. Kass found him fun and kind, and appreciated witnessing his more vulnerable, gentle side.

***

"Martin, meet Kallie. Kallie, say hi to Martin," Kass said as they entered the house and found her eagerly waiting by the front door.

"Say hi to Martin. Martin, hi Martin. Hi Martin," Kallie greeted, her face lighting up with a smile and bouncing a bit in the excitement of meeting her brother's handsome new friend.

"Hi, Kallie," Martin replied, glancing at Kass and then back to Kallie with a puzzled look.

"Oh, Kallie has autism," Kass mentioned casually. "Come on, I'll introduce you to my mom. My dad's upstairs packing for his business trip—he leaves tomorrow," Kass added, guiding Martin through the house with Kallie trailing close behind.

"You must be Martin," his mom said with a welcoming tone.

"Hi, Mrs. Kane."

"Oh, please call me Bailey," she laughed.

"Yes, call me Bailey. You can call me Bailey," Kallie added.

"We will call you Kallie," her mom added, pulling Kallie in for a hug.

"Nice to meet you, Bailey."

"So, you're staying for dinner and Kallie gets two babysitters. Sounds good."

"I'm not a baby!" Kallie yelled.

"Kallie, remember, you have to use your kind voice. Try again," Kass reminded.

"I'm not a baby. I'm a young lady," Kallie said, changing her tone and using her calm voice, as she often practiced.

After dinner, Kass and Martin spent time playing games with Kallie, then took on the task of putting her to bed. Once Kallie was settled, they joined forces again to clean the kitchen and tidy up the board games they had enjoyed earlier. The camaraderie between Kass and Martin was taking root in a genuine and tenderhearted way.

For Martin, this connection was different from the friendships he had experienced before. His previous companions often displayed an abundance of ego and testosterone, rarely delving into personal matters or family discussions. Those relationships mainly revolved around sports or school gossip and lacked the intimate dimension he was experiencing with Kass.

Curiosity got the better of Martin and he ventured into a conversation about Kallie.

"What's it like having a sister with autism?"

"She's pretty cool actually. To be honest, I'm used to it. It's all I've ever known. Having a sibling any different from her is beyond my imagination. She's sweet, cute, and has this incredible sense of humor."

"Yeah, she really is sweet," Martin said as he placed a plate into the dishwasher.

"The challenging part is when people stare or give judgmental looks when she's having a tough moment. It's not that she's being unruly, it's just her being autistic."

"I think I'd end up punching someone."

"Oh, I've thought about it many times, trust me."

"Well, it's great she has you," Martin said. He recognized the nuances Kass was sharing about Kallie's world and the challenges she faced as a child with autism. Given this vulnerable exchange of feelings, their friendship deepened further.

"Do you have to get going or wanna hang out some more?" Kass asked when they had finished cleaning the kitchen.

"Well, I don't have to get going. We can chill a bit longer."

"How about PS5?" Kass suggested. "I have *Call of Duty: Vanguard*," he said, walking up the stairs to his room.

Martin looked around Kass's bedroom and noticed his immaculate decor. Everything was clean, tidy, and organized—unlike Martin's room.

Martin also noticed Kass's fashion posters and his collection of cool shoes when Kass opened his closet door. His bed looked like it was from a department store display: posh pillows and a pristine duvet cover.

"Who's this?" Martin asked, pointing to one of the posters.

"John Galliano. He's a designer," Kass replied.

"And who is this?" Martin asked, pointing to another poster.

"Um, this is Adut Akech," Kass said.

"Adut Akech?"

"You've never seen her anywhere? Like, on billboards, shopping bags?"

"Nope, not that I recall," Martin admitted.

"She's an iconic fashion model," Kass replied, chuckling.

"Okay, and who is this?"

"That's Alexander McQueen. He was a brilliant designer, too," Kass explained.

"Was?"

"Yeah, he passed away about a decade ago. He hanged himself. Despite having everything, he still battled severe depression."

"Oh, wow," Martin commented, settling onto Kass's bed. "Goodness, this bed is comfortable." He flung his arms overhead and sprawled onto his back.

"Here you go," Kass said, handing Martin a controller.

"Okay, I've got to confess, I've never played PS5. My little brothers play it at home, but I haven't had the chance."

"Alright, I'll show you how to play. It's easy."

Kass and Martin got lost in the video game for about an hour. "Oh, man, it's late," Martin said, looking at the time on his phone, then placing the controller on Kass's desk.

"Hi, boys. Martin, I'm not paying you overtime for babysitting," Kass's mom teased.

"Sorry, Mrs. Kane. I'm on my way home," he responded with excessive politeness.

"Bailey."

"Yes, Bailey. Thanks, Kass. I'll see you at school tomorrow," Martin said, taking his leave. Martin and Kass exchanged a handshake-hug, awkward yet friendly.

"He seems like a nice kid. Where did he come from?" his mom inquired after Kass had shown Martin out.

"He's an idiot-turned-nice-kid," Kass joked.

"And?" his mom pressed, with a smile.

"Nah, just friends. He just broke up with his girlfriend. I think he's looking for a new group of friends to hang out with."

"Oh, well, that's nice."

Kass sauntered back to his bedroom, a whirlwind of uncertainty swirling within him. He couldn't shake the feeling he might just be developing a crush on Martin. Determined to push those thoughts aside, he turned his attention to his phone.

Harlen 7:41 p.m.: Haven't heard from you all day. Date must be going good. How good? LOL

Gab 7:42 p.m.: Looks like shopping went well. Did you have fun?

Harlen 7:53 p.m.: Okay, what are you two doing that I don't want to be doing?

Jack 7:59 p.m.: Let's talk about this plan of yours.

Jack 8:16 p.m.: Oh right. You're on your date with Martin. HAHAHA

Jack 8:27 p.m.: Just kidding, bro.

Olivia 8:31 p.m.: Well, how did it go?

Harlen 8:45 p.m.: Who's the top or bottom?

Kass continued scrolling through his messages, a smirk playing on his lips. From his perspective, Martin's quest for new friends and the whole idea of him being on a date was quite amusing. Yet, in the midst of his amusement, a flicker of curiosity also emerged. He found himself briefly pondering if there might be a grain of truth to it. As the day's events drifted through his mind, Kass dwelt in those memories for a few minutes, then closed his eyes and allowed the day's experiences to dissipate.

Chapter 11

"Kass, come quick!" his mom screamed from the bottom of the stairs. "Kass!"

Kass jumped out of bed, but before running downstairs, he stopped and looked in Kallie's room to see her still sleeping.

"Kass!" his mom screamed again.

He closed Kallie's door and ran downstairs to find his mom at the closed back door, leaning against it in terror. When she saw Kass, she ran to the kitchen window.

"Look!" she screamed. "What are those things doing here?"

Kass gasped when he took a look for himself. In the backyard, at least eight large monkeys stood like angry, intense statues.

"Wow, what the heck! I don't know, Mom."

"Why are they in the backyard? And why are they just staring at us?"

"Completely freaky," Kass agreed, feeling ill-at-ease yet fascinated.

"Where are you going?" his mom shrieked in panic.

"To get my phone. I'll be right back," Kass replied, rushing to his room.

"Mom, is it breakfast time?" Kallie asked, approaching her mom, who quickly closed the window shades.

"Yes, go to the dining room. I'll be right there."

Kass returned with his phone in hand, ready to document the weird event with video. His mom hovered behind him as Kass prepared to open the back door.

"Wait, hold on," she said, her eyes scanning the room before rushing to the nearby utility closet. With determination, she grabbed a broom.

"Are you going to hit them or do some spring cleaning?"

Kass cautiously cracked open the door and took a hesitant peek outside. To his surprise, there were no monkeys in sight. Encouraged, he opened the door wider and stepped out onto the deck, surveying the entire area, finding it devoid of angry-looking monkeys.

"What in the hell is going on?" his mom asked.

"I don't know, Mom," Kass replied. The unexplained disappearance of the monkeys left them feeling relieved, yet puzzled and uneasy. The sudden turn of events added an additional layer of mystery to an already bizarre situation.

Bailey retrieved her phone from the living room and dialed the Animal Wildlife Hotline—an agency she often phoned when a hungry bear ransacked the neighborhood's garbage cans. After activating the speakerphone, she detailed the strange scene in her backyard, where the monkeys had inexplicably vanished into thin air.

"Disappearing monkeys, huh? Well, that's a new one," quipped the officer on the other end. "We'll assign our top-notch monkey detectives to crack this case. Expect to hear from us later today. And if those crafty monkeys decide to put on a repeat performance, don't hesitate to give us a shout."

"But—" was all Bailey had time to say before the call was terminated.

She scowled at the phone, not for a moment believing she'd receive a callback.

"You sounded like a delusional crackhead telling a tall tale," Kass laughed.

"Geez, how embarrassing. Well, I'll call your father. He's on his way to the airport. He'll believe us."

"Okay, I need to get ready for school."

"No, please feed your sister first. Just some cereal will be fine. I need to meditate for a minute or two. I'm completely discombobulated."

After preparing a bowl of cereal for Kallie and before dressing for school, Kass took a quiet moment in his bedroom to think about the events of the morning. An undeniable insight had already convinced him the monkeys' mission was intertwined with that of the birds. All these events seemed to circle around the gemstone and, by extension, the monstrous jeweled creature still lurking in the distant Costa Rican mountains.

Kass 8:14 a.m.: You won't believe what was just in my backyard!

Gab 8:14 a.m.: BIRDS!?

Olivia 8:14 a.m.: Oh no, are they back!?

Kass 8:15 a.m.: No, not birds. MONKEYS!

Kass 8:15 a.m.: Big ass monkeys!!

Harlen 8:16 a.m.: LMAO

Jack 8:16 a.m.: What do you mean, monkeys?

Kass 8:17 a.m.: There were about eight tall monkeys in our backyard. Mom saw them first. They were just standing in the yard staring at us.

Harlen 8:17 a.m.: He's fucking with us guys.

Harlen 8:17 a.m.: Good one Kass LMAO

Kass 8:17 a.m.: I'm serious!!

Jack 8:18 a.m.: I hope you got pics but right now I need to get ready. I'll see you in a few minutes.

Martin 8:20 a.m.: Wait, I just saw these texts. Are you serious???

Harlen 8:21 a.m.: Let's meet at our spot before school. Get there early?

Olivia 8:21 a.m.: Yes!

Gab 8:21 a.m.: Yes!

Martin 8:21 a.m.: For sure

Harlen 8:22 a.m.: See you there

***

The gang's meeting spot was on the side of the school, at one of the three picnic tables. This had been their meeting location since ninth grade. As planned, they gathered early to discuss what had just transpired at Kass's home. Kass described the monkeys while Olivia and Gab searched online in hopes of identifying the exact species.

"They were big and black. They stood as tall as fourth graders."

"Come on, we need more details than that," Gab probed.

"They had long limbs. And the tail. The tail was long, super long. It almost looked like they had five legs," Kass continued.

"Five legs?" Harlen shrieked.

"Oh! Their faces were white," Kass added.

"Hey everyone, what did I miss?" Martin said, out of breath from rushing to join them. "I had to wait for my brothers to get ready."

"The monkeys were black with white faces, stood like humans, and had a long tail that looked like an extra limb," Olivia summarized.

"Were these them?" Gab asked, showing Kass her phone.

"Yes, that's them! Sort of," Kass exclaimed.

"Black-headed spider monkey," Gab identified.

"Yep, that's definitely them. But the monkeys in my yard were much bigger with shiny red eyes. Or maybe orange. It was creepy," Kass added.

"Okay, we need to know as much about them as possible. We need to figure out how they got here from—" Jack started.

"From Central or South America," Gab interjected.

Everyone fell silent as Gab confirmed the monkeys' connection to their camping trip.

"Okay, let's meet after school somewhere. My house?" Jack suggested and everyone nodded in agreement.

The friends entered the school together as usual then scattered to their classrooms with monkeys, vultures, large creatures, and an electrified gemstone on their minds.

***

"Okay, what did we learn about these monkeys?" Jack asked the group when they met at his house after school.

"Well, they mainly eat fruit," Olivia mentioned.

"Great, mainly eat fruit and not humans," Harlen said with a sarcastic tone.

"They eat mainly fruit and sarcastic people," Olivia added, rolling her eyes.

"They grow to be about two feet tall," Gab added.

"Two feet? These monkeys were more like four feet tall," Kass said.

"Four feet? Are you sure these are the monkeys you saw?" Jack asked, showing Kass several pictures of black-headed spider monkeys.

"Yes, that's them…but taller," Kass confirmed.

"Black-headed spider monkeys are active diurnally and are arboreal. They form fission-fusion groups upwards of one-hundred individuals," Martin read.

"English, please," remarked Harlen.

"It means they're active during the day rather than at night and live primarily in trees," translated Olivia.

"And they break off into small groups for some activities, but then gather into large groups for other purposes," explained Gab.

"A group of up to one-hundred?" Kass exclaimed, his voice filled with panic. "Great. What have we gotten ourselves into?"

"We? You're the one that brought the bling back here," Harlen snarked.

"Come on, guys, we're all in this together. We need to listen and learn so we know what to do if they attack us," Jack advised.

"I'm scared," Olivia exclaimed, taking Gab by the arm and pulling her close.

"We're all scared," Jack acknowledged. "Martin, keep reading."

"The large groups are composed of multiple males and females."

"But how did they get here? They called an Uber?" Harlen quipped.

"Dude, are you always cracking jokes? Can't you be serious for even a moment?" Martin shot back.

"Why don't you shut up and go back to your idiot friends. Not sure who invited you anyway." Harlen's tone seemed to reveal a hint of jealousy toward Martin for some reason.

"Come on, we are all in this together. How many times do I have to say this?" Jack admonished.

"So, how did they get here, and how did they quickly disappear from your backyard? Did they have wings?" Gab asked.

"I didn't see any wings. They had a good thirty seconds between my mother turning around and us looking back outside," Kass recounted.

"Sleeping is an example of a fusion-type behavior, where monkeys congregate in trees to protect themselves from predators like snakes and jaguars," Olivia explained.

"This tells us we need to find them when they're not sleeping," Jack proposed.

"Find them?" Kass sighed. "We should stay put and wait to see if they appear again."

"I'm with Kass," Gab added.

"Me too," Olivia and Harlen chimed in simultaneously.

"But I have to agree with Jack," Martin asserted. "We need to find them, confront them, and do whatever we can to keep them away from our homes and families. It's Kass's family that's in the most danger."

"If we find them, I'm giving the stone back," Kass said with resolve.

"Okay, Martin's in. Who else is up for it?" Jack inquired.

One after another, each friend confirmed their willingness to join the quest for the black-headed spider monkeys, recognizing it could be another thrilling and potentially dangerous adventure.

"Myra Provincial is the nearest and most populated tree location. It makes sense to start there," Kass suggested.

"Not much fruit for them, however. We should bring fruit with us to lure them out," Olivia said.

"Good idea. And the backpack with the gem needs to be securely strapped onto Super Kass," Jack added.

"I'll drive. I can pick a few up around say 7 p.m.?" Martin offered.

"I'll pick up the others," Olivia said.

"Great. That should give us enough time before sundown," said Jack.

"Their bite can prove deadly," Gab read more. "Because it can cause anaphylactic shock in humans, killing them."

"How do we protect ourselves from being bitten?" Olivia asked.

"We all hide behind Kass," Harlen said, joking but also serious.

"Okay, you guys...we can do this," Jack concluded.

Chapter 12

"Kass, we need to unravel what you're made of—your strengths and limitations," Jack said, casually pressing a drinking glass against the water dispenser lever on the refrigerator door and filling it with cold water.

"What's the plan, then? Am I suddenly going to sprout wings? Become bulletproof? Survive a monkey bite? Or maybe I'll surprise everyone by spitting fire like those mythical dragons," Kass said, his familiar mischievous glint in his eyes.

"Exactly," Jack nodded with a grin.

They headed out to the backyard, ready to dive into their mission of uncovering Kass's hidden powers. After a string of experiments, they reached the conclusion that Kass didn't currently wield any exceptional strengths or superpowers to fend off aggressive creatures.

"Maybe Gab was right and the powers only kick in when you're threatened or protecting others," Jack suggested.

"I think that's true, but I'm getting the jitters, Jack. This ain't my thing; I'm not built for this. You should be the one leading. You've got that whole Thor vibe going on," Kass admitted.

"I know, Kass. I know you're nervous. But we can't go to the cops and we can't tell our parents. We just need to figure things out until we can get the stone back to where it belongs."

"Why not tell our parents, though?" Kass asked.

"Because, they will involve the police. And if the law gets a hold of this, the media will, too."

"Alright, you're right. I'm serious Jack, why don't we just drop the gem in the woods with the monkeys? Just be like, here, here's your damn stone, now leave us alone, and run!" Kass said.

"We could, but what if it's not theirs and then something else comes for it later? We won't have it or know where it is," Jack explained. "I'm also scared that if we give up the stone we'll be without protection. Clearly, your connection with the gem is what gives you extra strength and that was the only thing that saved us from the vultures. Hopefully, that same power will kick in should the monkeys attack."

"Okay, I get it, just please don't leave my side. No matter what, Jack. Don't leave me alone," Kass said with tears in his eyes.

"Ah man, I am so sorry you have to go through this. You're not alone. I'll be right next to you," Jack reassured Kass, giving him a hug.

***

The two vehicles carrying the six friends made their way to Myra Provincial Park, a seventeen-minute drive. Packed in their trunks were an assortment of items that might come in handy: two baseball bats, thirty pounds of bananas, passion fruit, rope, tape, flashlights, lanterns, and a small axe.

Upon arrival at the park, they set off on the paved trails, gradually disappearing into the embrace of towering trees.

With a mixture of excitement and uncertainty, the friends ventured forth. They had a problem to solve, but the solution remained elusive. They weren't entirely sure how to find the monkeys, let alone comprehend the potential risks involved. In their pursuit of a solution, these curious teenagers were about to encounter challenges beyond what they could have anticipated.

"Okay, so who's going to do the talking if their leader wants to negotiate?" Harlen asked.

"Wait, you think they talk? Haha...now we're in *The Planet of The Apes*?" Martin joked.

"Hey, at this point, they might speak Spanish and play the drums. I'm not underestimating these monkeys," Harlen added with a smirk.

"Let's just find the damned things before it gets dark and they go to sleep," Jack said.

"We're already running out of bananas and passion fruit," Olivia mentioned, dropping her last banana on the ground, after creating a long trail behind them.

"I'm almost out, too," Kass added.

Dusk gave way to night, and soon they were forced to rely on the beams of their flashlights to navigate. The gentle sway of the treetops in the breeze was illuminated in flashes as they moved their lights.

"Wait, I heard something over that way," Gab whispered. She swung her flashlight around, scanning the trees and the ground.

"I heard it too," Jack confirmed.

"I love you," Gab whispered to Jack, drawing his face close and planting a quick kiss. "If something happens to me, take care of my dads for me," she added with a half smile.

"Stop it, you're making me nervous," Harlen muttered.

"Shhh...did you hear that?" Olivia exclaimed. The group's senses sharpened as more unidentifiable sounds emerged from the trees and underbrush.

"I did," Harlen said.

"I heard it, too," Martin agreed.

"Okay, let's form the circle we practiced," Jack directed.

Olivia, Martin, Kass, Gab, and Harlen formed a tight circle with their backs to each other and their flashlights on. Jack pulled out two battery operated lanterns and placed them on the ground. He then completed the circle.

"Okay, on the count of three, we scream," Jack instructed. "One, two, three..."

"Ahhh!"

All six voices united in a collective shout while their flashlights sliced through the darkness and into the surrounding treetops, anticipating the monkeys' arrival. Martin clutched a flashlight in one hand and gripped a baseball bat in the other, a poised stance signaling his readiness. Positioned next to Jack, Kass exuded a determined demeanor, prepared for whatever might unfold.

"Kass, remember, keep that backpack secure."

"Jack, don't worry. I've got this."

Harlen wielded his nunchucks along with a flashlight, his hand movements weaving an entrancing dance above his head.

"Don't hit me with those things," Olivia said, once again annoyed by Harlen's antics. "Where did you even get them from? They teach you how to use 'em in Taekwondo?"

"They sure do and I'm going to karate-kid their asses," he said.

"It's been forty minutes and still no sign of them," Gab announced.

"Hey, shh…I can feel them coming from over there," Kass said, pointing to his left. "No, they're right in front of us."

"Um, they're right in front of us?" Martin gasped.

Within moments, the group was encircled by over-sized black-headed spider monkeys. Their sleek black fur served as natural nighttime camouflage, allowing them to blend seamlessly into the shadows except for their white faces, which stood out in stark contrast to the obsidian back-drop. But it was their round, fiery-orange eyes that truly captured attention, radiating an intensity that both pierced through the darkness and intensified their intimidating presence.

"Hey, we come in peace," Jack's voice echoed. "Why have you come?"

"If these monkeys start chatting, I'm going to shit myself," Harlen said.

"They're just staring," Olivia remarked, her shaky voice laced with intrigue.

Amid the charged atmosphere, one of the monkeys dared to approach Kass, causing Jack to subtly shift closer, ready to intervene if needed. The monkey's intent gaze locked onto Kass, its gestures beckoning him forward.

"Sorry, but he's not going anywhere with you," Jack said.

Suddenly, and with great speed, two other monkeys charged. One shoved Olivia to the ground, then joined his buddy to seize Jack's arms in a vice-like grip. The swift maneuver left Jack defenseless, the monkeys' strength insurmountable.

Meanwhile, the first monkey repeated its persistent invitation to Kass, urging him to follow.

Jack's response was resolute. "Absolutely not!"

Emerging from the shadows, several more pairs of monkeys sprang into action, capturing Harlen, Gab, and Martin.

But then, a glimmer of hope appeared.

"Oh, it's actually working!" Gab exclaimed, as she observed one of the monkeys staggering, then collapsing to the ground.

Harlen's excitement matched Gab's. "Check that one out! It's going down."

The monkeys released their grips on the teens' arms. Olivia couldn't contain her excitement. "I can't believe this is happening! They're all going down!"

As the scene unfolded, more, then finally all of the monkeys in their proximity succumbed to the effects of the drug and toppled over in an unconscious stupor. The teens had ingeniously crushed two bottles of Jack's dad's sleeping pills, then injected the drug into the fruit.

"Yep, my dad's Temazepam did the trick!" exclaimed Jack.

"Who knew these apes were party animals?" Harlen said.

"Now what do we do?" Kass asked, realizing they hadn't thought this through far enough.

"Tie them up," said Jack. "We can call the police and let them deal with these animals."

"They'll know we're involved if we call," Olivia reminded Jack.

"Just tie 'em and leave 'em!" Harlen pleaded. "Let's get out of here."

"We can't just leave them tied up for someone else to find," Jack said.

"Oh, no! Look guys!" Olivia's voice quivered as she pointed at six monkeys just arriving, furious, their hostility directed straight at her.

"Oh yeah, we totally thought this brilliant idea through, didn't we?" Harlen snarked, his poorly timed sarcasm not at all appreciated by the others.

A monkey lunged at Olivia, but before it could strike, Kass intervened and moved her out of harm's way, then deposited her into Harlen's arms. The same enraged monkey then redirected its fury toward Kass who reacted faster than the monkey, seizing its hairy hand and flinging it into the surrounding trees. Several more pernicious primates charged at Kass. Propelled by his restored extraordinary strength, Kass met his attackers head on, employing a flurry of kicks, punches, and throws, often launching them up to fifty feet away and rendering them unconscious.

During the chaos, one of the monkeys struck Gab in the head, causing her to stumble. Jack, fueled by fury, leaped to his girlfriend's defense, caught her before she hit the ground, and held her close. The scene was a whirlwind of violence and danger. Kass continued to protect his friends, battling the ferocious onslaught with a vengeance.

The troop of monkeys then directed their anger at Kass, launching themselves at him with unprecedented ferocity.

Despite their formidable strength, Kass effortlessly subdued them, ending their frenzied assault.

Just when it seemed the attacks had relented, a horde of even more menacing black-headed spider monkeys emerged from the darkness and descended upon the teens. The shrieks and growls of the attackers filled the night, drowning out any hope of escape.

In that very moment of hopelessness, a surge of wild electrical vibrations coursed through Kass's entire being. With a brutal clapping of his hands and a warrior-like primal roar, Kass unleashed a wave of explosive energy. The shockwave propelled every monkey backward, their bodies colliding with trees and creating a momentary pause in the ruthless onslaught.

Silence settled over the scene, broken only by the heavy breathing of the exhausted and injured teens. Kass fell to his knees, his body trembling under the strain of the intense battle. Jack rushed to his side. "Is he alright?" Olivia asked, her voice trembling.

"He's...he'll be okay," Jack replied, his own voice filled with disbelief and awe. "But right now, we need to get out of here. Get to the cars. Now!"

Jack and Martin pulled Kass's arms up and around their shoulders and the six friends high-tailed it to the cars.

Jack placed Kass's limp body into Martin's car. He remained quiet, clearly exhausted.

"I'll take Kass back to my house and stay with him until he's recovered," Martin offered.

"Are you sure?" Jack said.

"Yeah, it's cool."

Olivia dropped off the others at their homes, everyone still in shock over what had just transpired at Myra Park. Besides Kass, Olivia was probably the one most affected by the monkey melee, since she had spent the past five years advocating for animal rights. How bizarre she had engaged in drugging animals with sleeping pills and battling them.

The others hadn't quite resonated with Kass and Jack's earlier description of their battle with the vultures on the school's field when they first heard the story. However, after this experience with the monkeys, everything clicked, and they developed nothing but respect for their two heroic friends. None of them had ever been in a physical altercation before this battle with the vicious four-foot monkeys.

The gravity of what they had just encountered left the entire group stunned and shaken. But with the indomitable spirit and special powers Kass had displayed, they now hoped they could overcome any threat that may come their way. Though battered and bruised, they were a bonded team, ready to face the challenges ahead.

***

"Hey, we can chill in here," Martin said, closing the front door of the little house behind him. "Do you want something to drink?"

"Whose place is this?" Kass asked, looking around the humble yet comfortable dwelling.

"It's the winemaker's cottage, but he's in Italy for the next couple of months. All the wine has been made for the year and not much for him to do, so he goes back home during this time."

"How about some water?" Kass requested.

"I also have plenty of wine," Martin offered.

"How about water for now?"

"You got it."

"Hi," Kass said, answering his phone. "Yeah, I'm good. Just sitting at Martin's. Yep. I know. Yeah, I'll see you tomorrow morning."

"Jack?"

"Yeah, he's just checking up on me," Kass said.

"You two have a pretty cool friendship. You're like brothers."

"He's definitely like a brother. Whatever that feels like," Kass said.

"I like your friends," Martin said.

"Well, they're your friends now, too, it seems to me."

They both smiled. Martin handed Kass a glass of water and then went to the main house for some food. While Martin was gone, Kass sent his mom a text letting her know he was over Martin's house and would be home before curfew, which only left him ninety minutes. When Martin returned, he found Kass asleep on the sofa. Martin sat next to him and pulled the throw blanket over the two of them. Soon, Martin was asleep, too.

Later, when Kass opened his eyes, he discovered himself cuddled up to Martin under a fluffy blanket with his head resting on Martin's chest.

"Oh, no!" Kass blurted, waking Martin. "I need to get home. I'm an hour late for curfew."

"Okay, okay, I'll get you home," Martin said, jumping up and grabbing his wallet and keys.

The cuddling wasn't mentioned during the boys' drive to Kass's home. They both felt awkward but also intrigued by how comfortable they felt being together.

"Hey, thanks for everything tonight," Martin said, parking in front of Kass's home. "Really, you protected us from those crazy monkeys...and...well, it was really nice chilling with you at my place."

Kass smiled and locked eyes with Martin.

"You're welcome. That's what friends are for."

Martin leaned in for a kiss. Kass felt his heart racing with desire and anticipation, freely surrendering to the sweetness of the moment. When their lips finally met, an invigorating surge of electricity ran through them—from the hair on their heads to the tips of their toes. It was a much more subtle and pleasant surge than the one Kass had experienced at Myra Park. Their embrace grew tighter, pulling each other closer as if trying to meld into one. All the awkwardness and uncertainty melted away, leaving only an uninhibited passion between them. Their kisses deepened, fueled by a newfound connection that clearly transcended the boundaries of friendship.

Time seemed to stand still as they explored each other's lips, savoring the taste and the touch. It was a symphony of sensations that left them both breathless and craving more. In Martin's car, parked in front of Kass's home, they got lost in each other, caught up in emotions they had never before experienced.

When they finally pulled apart, their eyes remained locked, speaking volumes without the need for words. "Incredible," Martin whispered, the timbre of his voice soft and tender.

"Absolutely," Kass responded.

On his drive home, Martin couldn't shake the taste of Kass on his lips—nor did he want to. The heat of their contact burned in his memory. Meanwhile, Kass stood at his doorstep, his heart pounding with a newfound sense of excitement and contentment, certain that he had stumbled upon something undeniably precious with Martin.

Chapter 13

"Should I ground you or was it worth breaking curfew for?" Kass's mom asked as Kass entered the kitchen the next morning.

"Sorry, Mom. I fell asleep watching a movie," Kass said, trying to hide his smile.

"Then I'll assume it was worth it considering that smile on your face," she said, smiling back at him. "So, *Martin?*"

"Yeah, I think so," he answered, feeling pleased with what had happened in Martin's car.

"That's nice, Kass. I'm happy for you. But let's not make a habit of being late and just make sure you keep your grades up. And for goodness sake, wear a condom."

"Mom!"

"Wear a condom. Wear a condom. And wear a for goodness condom," Kallie chanted as she entered the kitchen, making Bailey's comment even more cringeworthy for Kass.

"Now look what you started," Kass said, looking over at his mom while picking up Kallie and swinging her around.

"What's this about condoms?" Jay said, entering the kitchen.

"Dad, I didn't know you were here. What happened to your trip?"

"Well, your mum called me frantically talking about some monkeys in the backyard."

"Alright. Alright. I wasn't frantic, just concerned."

"So I postponed my trip for a few days," Jay said. "And now I'd appreciate the backstory on the condom comment."

***

The morning was calm, yet the minds of the six teens were far from it—filled with unsettling echoes and uneasy thoughts. The lingering sights and sounds from the previous night's events played on a loop in their heads, casting a cloud of disbelief and apprehension.

They reached for their phones out of habit, scrolling through the digital realm in search of any news, chat, or comments about the inexplicable vulture attacks. They also were curious if anyone else had encounters with giant monkeys.

Fingers swiped and screens lit up, each notification adding tension to an already tense situation. The more they sought answers, the clearer it became they were grappling with a puzzle that defied all reason. The unknown lingered like a ghost, and the teens wrestled with a whirlwind of questions. When would the next incident occur? Where would danger strike? Who or what was orchestrating these events? How could they possibly prepare for what lay ahead?

The first bell rang, a five-minute warning until classes would begin. Gab grabbed Jack's hand and led him and the rest of the group through the front doors of the school.

"Don't even think about it," Kass whispered, looking at Martin, then over to Jack and Gab's hand holding, and then back to Martin. They smiled and took their walk together, side by side, hands to themselves.

"Have a good class," Martin said.

"You, too, Martin."

Everyone split up to attend their individual classes, except Harlen and Olivia, who had their first class together. Olivia was the most academically advanced member of their group and often attended classes without her friends, but Olivia and Harlen were lucky enough to have Socials together.

Olivia 9:14 a.m.: Umm...why is Jessica glaring at me?

Harlen 9:14 a.m.: Better you than me. She's looking a bit crazy.

Olivia 9:16 a.m.: Did I do something I don't know I did?

Harlen 917 a.m.: She's probably upset that Martin has been spending a lot of time with us since they broke up.

Harlen 9:17 a.m.: Wait, maybe she thinks he broke up with her to be with you!

Olivia 9:17 a.m.: No, it can't be. Ew!

Olivia 9:18 a.m.: How do I tell her it isn't true and that would never happen?

Harlen 9:18 a.m.: Just ignore her. That's what we've always done.

Harlen 9:18 a.m.: Poof, be gone girl!

Harlen 9:18 a.m.: LOL

"Class, please put all distractions in your pocket or in your bag, not on your desk or in your hands," the teacher said, glancing over at Harlen, Olivia, and several other students she noticed using their devices.

The students sheepishly put away their phones and presented themselves as more attentive.

***

Half the school day had passed with no reports of wild monkey sightings at the park or in the city, but the teens continued to check their social media, just for peace of mind.

"Okay, let's put our phones away. We're becoming obsessed," Gab suggested when the group gathered for lunch in the cafeteria.

"I agree. This isn't helping us get through our day," Jack said.

"See, perfect guy for me: someone who agrees with me," Gab said, kissing Jack.

"Anything for you, Baby," Jack said, kissing her back.

"Ah, get a room, you two," Harlen said, causing most of the group to laugh.

Kass and Martin sat across from one another at the lunch table and didn't laugh at Harlen's comment, too wrapped up in sneaking little glances and smiles, and sending texts.

Martin 11:45 a.m.: Hey, want to hangout after school?

Kass 11:45 a.m.: Sure!!

Martin took a peek at his phone, read Kass's response, and smiled when he saw all the yellow emojis that followed.

"Okay, what is going on with you two?" Olivia asked.

As usual, Olivia was the one who didn't hold anything back. Her motto: ask or you'll never know.

"What?" Kass snapped.

"What?" Harlen mimicked, laughing.

"Hey, what did you two get up to after we left the park?" Jack asked.

"Nothing!" Martin said, looking at Kass, unsure what to say or even what to feel.

"Okay, Martin kissed me," Kass blurted.

Simultaneously, their four friends started singing and dancing around the table, as the other students in the cafeteria watched and wondered.

"I kissed a boy and I liked it. I kissed a boy and I liked it. The taste of his watermelon chapstick..."

"Ugh, this is why I didn't want to say anything," Kass admitted, showing annoyance, but also laughing at their mini performance.

"Well, I sure did like it!" Martin smiled.

"I bet you did. I'm not even gay and I'd like to kiss those puckery lips, too!" Harlen said, grabbing Kass's face and pretending to kiss his lips.

"Okay, wait...so, you and Martin..." Olivia said, wrapping her head around this unexpected connection, especially considering Martin had acted like an arrogant heterosexual jock for so many years, and had been dating Jessica.

"I know, I know. But please, please don't tell anyone," Martin pleaded. "If my brothers found out they would tell my mom and dad, and I'm not ready for all that potential drama."

"Man, I don't think that's a thing anymore. We don't announce if we're gay, straight, bi, or whatever. We just do our thing, and what comes up in conversations or actions, happens. Let things unfold naturally," Jack said. "Right, Kass?"

"Yeah, easy for you to say. You're straight and don't have brothers or parents that might disown you," Martin said.

"Whoa, really? You think your family would be upset, or worse, disown you?" Kass questioned.

"Blah, I don't know. What do I know? One minute I'm with Jessica and the next minute I can't stop thinking about kissing you," Martin said, causing everyone to smile at his sweet comment.

"I agree with Jack. Just be you. If people don't like it, well, you know, fuck 'em. I don't think most people really care anymore," Harlen added.

"Maybe, but I just read there were over one hundred hate crime incidents last year in Canada alone, and those numbers have only increased since then," Martin shared.

"Wow! That's wild," Jack said.

"Hey, I'm gay. Does anyone care?" Harlen shouted, standing on a chair in the cafeteria. His announcement was followed by cheers, claps, and laughing. "See, no one cares. You'd have to live under a rock or in a closed-minded suburb for people to have a problem with our gay people," Harlen added.

"It's your journey. You two do you. We won't say anything to anyone," Gab confirmed.

Crash.

"Ah, damn! They're back!" Kass shouted.

The cafeteria windows shattered. Chaos exploded. A frenzied horde of vultures stormed in, their screeches mingling with the sickening thud of wounded birds hitting the beige tile floor, splattering blood and creating a grisly mess. Panic gripped the students, driving them to scramble for safety wherever they could find it. More windows exploded, each opening unleashing yet another wave of swooping vultures, escalating the nightmare.

"This doesn't look good!" Harlen's shouted understatement rose above the chaos as he dove under a table. Around him, other terrorized students sought cover, too. With every new breach, more students scrambled in desperation, the once-orderly cafeteria now a vortex of mayhem and fear.

Several teens lay on the cafeteria floor, wounded, some unconscious from the impact of the vultures' large bodies ramming into them. Kass knew he and his friends had to act fast, or risk being torn apart by the scavengers' merciless assault.

"Move! Now!" Kass's voice rang out like a battle cry, as he took charge. He led the group in a daring escape, running as fast as they could out the cafeteria doors and into the halls of Cypress High.

But the vultures were not their only foes. Turning a corner, they confronted a terrifying line of the overgrown spider monkeys, their orange eyes locked onto the trembling teens like predators marking their prey.

"We're trapped!" Harlen gasped, his voice hoarse with desperation.

"We have to find a way out," Kass said. He tightened his grip on the backpack that was slung over his shoulder, his fingers digging into the strap and his knuckles whitening as if to channel determination through that touch. The heft of the gem, a symbol of hope and survival, pressed against his side as he subtly adjusted the bag, ensuring it remained secure during their urgent search for an escape route.

Martin scanned the surroundings, his mind racing. "There must be a way. We can't let them get to us."

As if the wild kingdom itself had turned against them, the school had become a battleground of wild beasts and terrified teens. Fear and adrenaline coursed through their veins.

"Mr. Carter!" Kass screamed, catching sight of the principal stationed in the hall adjacent to the school office. He stood between the agitated monkeys and the cluster of six friends.

Mr. Carter stepped forward, a beacon of courage within the chaos. "Kids, stay there!" His commanding voice cut through the tension and asserted control.

In the school office, Mrs. Mather, the vigilant school secretary, observed the scene through the hall window. Swift and determined, she dialed for help, fully aware of the urgency.

The monkeys, their unyielding gazes fixed on the teens, seemed almost attuned to the apprehension in the air. The suspense of the moment was underscored by the distant echoes of screams from the lunchroom—a stark auditory reminder of the urgency.

"Steady, everyone," Mr. Carter said. "Kids, get back!"

Mr. Carter placed his body in the center of the hallway but when the monkeys took several steps closer, Mr. Carter slowly stepped back.

"Stay right there!" he demanded, with his palm up in the HALT position. He hoped the monkeys either understood the English language or body language.

With adrenaline surging through his veins, Kass couldn't stand by and watch the monkeys attack Mr. Carter. So, ignoring the principal's command, he sprung into action, becoming a fierce protector. With lightning speed, he ran toward the charging monkeys. Then in a blur of motion, Kass ran up the side of the wall, defying gravity with a display of superhuman agility and landed behind the bewildered monkeys, catching them off guard.

"Whoa, did you see that?" Gab exclaimed, her eyes wide with amazement as she exchanged incredulous glances with her peers. Murmurs of amazement rippled through the hall, along with whispers of disbelief at witnessing such an extraordinary demonstration of physical skill.

The monkeys turned around, clearly astonished, only to see Kass making his escape through the double doors of the school's main entrance. Like a streak of lightning, he dashed away with the intention of luring the troop from the school. It worked. Without delay, the monkeys were in hot pursuit.

The chaos in the cafeteria subsided as soon as the monkeys left the building. It felt like the vultures and the monkeys shared some kind of telepathic connection. A tense silence descended upon the room, only interrupted by the sound of heavy breathing and the occasional whimper of fear.

The vultures, their presence looming large just moments ago, flapped their wings and soared out through the broken windows they had created. Students cautiously emerged from their hiding spots under tables and behind the cafeteria counter, their eyes wide with apprehension as they scanned the room for any lingering threats. Among the remnants of the vultures' presence were feathers, blood, and fresh carcasses.

***

"Kass is a real life superhero!" Martin exclaimed, dumbfounded.

"I've seen him do impressive things before, but this is on a whole new level," Jack replied, still trying to process what he had just witnessed.

After Kass led the monkeys away, Harlen sprinted toward the same exit, following Kass's lead.

"Come on, we need to follow him!" Harlen shouted, urging the others forward.

Olivia clung tightly to Gab's hand as they ran, fear and determination intertwined in their young hearts. They couldn't let their friend face the danger alone, even if he seemed to possess extraordinary abilities.

Kass slowed his pace to allow the monkeys to follow, but not actually catch up to him. The monkeys jumped onto cars, smashing the roofs and hoods. They scattered and scurried over the rooftops of houses, offices, and shops. Kass stayed just far enough ahead to keep them engaged in the pursuit.

Kass's friends jumped into Martin's car and followed Kass's ever-changing location through a tracker app they had downloaded when the vultures first appeared. This safety measure had been integrated into their plans should danger arrive. And danger had definitely arrived.

"They're headed to Myra Park!" Gab yelled.

"Take a left!" Gab said, looking at her phone and navigating.

"Slow down, Martin!" Jack demanded.

"Sorry, just trying to get there."

The monkeys continued to chase Kass through the residential neighborhoods of Kelowna.

"Kass is still running at such a fast speed! He must be exhausted by now," Gab reported, staring at her phone and watching the red dot navigate through the city. "He's getting on the 97."

"Unbelievable," Olivia said.

"Okay, just stay steady on the 97 'til we get there," Gab informed Martin.

"Hey, Martin," Harlen began with a sly grin. "Now that we've got you cornered, spill the beans—what's the deal with you and Kass?"

A burst of incredulous laughter erupted from Jack. "Seriously, Harlen? Right now?"

Harlen shrugged, undeterred. "Why not? It's now or never! Come on, spill it, Martin. Are you head over heels?"

"Can't say for sure. All I know is this feels pretty amazing. But watching him in danger? That's a whole different story."

"He's got that gemstone, remember? He'll be alright. And by the way, just so you know, I'm all for it. You two make a seriously cute couple," Gab said.

"Yep, you got my vote. You break his heart and I'll break your face," Olivia snapped.

"She's not lying. She's tougher than she looks," Jack added.

"I have no plans to hurt Kass. In fact, I have a feeling I might be the one to get my heart broken," Martin confessed.

Chapter 14

Martin stayed on the 97 while Gab continued to track Kass. Even with his newfound strength and speed, Kass remained in grave danger, and his friends were eminently concerned.

"He's there. He's at the park," Gab announced. "We're seven minutes away."

"Call his phone again," Olivia suggested.

Kass had accelerated his speed over the last mile to arrive at the park well ahead of the monkeys. He was exhausted but with enough reserved energy and just the right amount of time to locate a large tree with a substantial hollow to hide in. Within seconds of getting himself nestled inside, the monkeys arrived. The leader of the troop walked in the middle of six other monkeys, who served as sentries and protectors. The dozens of remaining monkeys scattered about in search of Kass.

Minutes later, Jack, Olivia, Martin, Harlen, and Gab arrived at the park. Their eyes widened at the sight: people pointing frantically into the trees and discussing massive monkeys darting about. Eager for answers, the teens grabbed their backpacks and retrieved the equipment from Martin's trunk—supplies from their initial Myra Park trip.

"Hey, where are you?" Jack asked when Olivia had Kass on speaker.

"I'm in a tree trunk," he whispered.

"A tree trunk?" Jack repeated.

"A tree trunk?" Gab echoed.

"We have you on the tracker. Stay where you are and we'll find you. Don't move," Jack said.

"I don't hear them, so I think I'm cool for now. But hurry, Jack, I can't do this without you."

"I'll be there in a minute, buddy. Stay on the phone so I can give you updates."

While the group journeyed through the forest in search of Kass, they perceived rustling sounds among the trees and witnessed loosened leaves descending sporadically.

"Hey, I think the monkeys are above us," Jack reported to Kass. "Now I see a large tree with a hollow, so I think we're right across from you."

"Okay, don't move. I am coming out."

"Form the circle again," Jack directed, and the group huddled in their defensive position with their backs toward each other, shoulders almost touching.

Kass came out with caution, walking toward his friends. The rustling noises stopped and a last few leaves fell. An ominous silence inhaled their fears.

Then a half dozen monkeys dropped from the trees and formed a well-coordinated security detail directly in front of Kass. They parted, creating a path for their formidable leader to step forward. Kass instinctively backed up and Jack moved in closer to protect his friend. In the next instant, the rest of the monkey troop surrounded the group of teens in a tense and foreboding standoff.

Kass's eyes narrowed in focused concentration. When it became clear two of the giant monkeys were preparing to lunge, he sprang into action. With lightning reflexes, he raised his arms in a dramatic defensive posture. To everyone's astonishment, a shimmering, transparent shield materialized before him. When the primates charged, they were halted in their tracks by the impervious and invisible barrier. The surge of crackling electricity was generated when the two monkeys contacted the shield, leaving them zapped and disoriented. They tumbled to the ground in a daze.

The shield vanished as quickly as it had appeared, leaving Kass and his friends in awe of what had just happened.

"Did you guys see that?" Martin gasped, barely able to believe his eyes.

Olivia's excitement bubbled over. "Kass, that was incredible! You just pulled off another superhero move!"

Kass grinned, feeling a rush of adrenaline and newfound confidence.

"How did you do it?" Jack asked.

"I don't know. I closed my eyes and thought only of protecting us and defeating them."

"Do it again! Wait, everyone hold hands," Jack commanded.

"Quick, everyone behind me," Kass said.

The monkeys' rage had reached a boiling point. Their eyes blazed with fury, their bodies trembled with anger. The leader's club swung down with deadly force, aimed directly at Kass. In a split-second decision, Kass again braced himself for impact, fully prepared to shield his friends from harm. He clenched his fists and shut his eyes in what appeared to be another deep and focused state of concentration. An enigmatic energy surged through him—a surge of power far greater than his previous experiences, including the mysterious powers that led him to victory over the vultures, and later these monkeys. And in the very next moment, something inexplicable happened. Defying all proven laws of physics, the six teens vanished into thin air.

The monkeys, taken aback and frustrated by the sudden disappearance of their would-be prey, screeched in confusion and anger. They searched frantically, but there was no sign of the teenagers anywhere in the park.

***

News of the unprecedented wild animal invasion at Cypress High, and the teenagers' determined pursuit of the violent monkeys, spread like wildfire across the city, stirring a sense of alarm and urgency. Soon after, concerns about the disappearance of the teens prompted citizens to alert authorities, setting off a frenzy of activity among law enforcement and emergency responders.

Sirens soon filled the park and the monkeys scurried into the trees of the surrounding forest and out of sight. Helicopters circled the area in search of the teens and the wild monkeys. Police officers and firefighters, including Gab's dad Jason, swarmed into the park.

An abandoned car was spotted near the trailhead, and firefighters immediately used a long reach tool known as a "slim jim" to unlock the front door. All eyes were fixed on the vehicle, wondering if its contents might yield clues to the whereabouts of the teens.

The police officers examined the car's contents and located the registration identifying Clark Landis, Martin's dad, as the owner. The police contacted the Landis family without delay, and then the families of the other teens who had also chased after the monkeys. Witnesses, still shaken by the unusual events, came forward one-by-one to provide their accounts to the police. They shared every detail they could recall, from the monkeys' erratic behavior to the group of teens rushing into the forest shortly after.

The atmosphere around Myra Park became increasingly tense and anxious. Concerned bystanders exchanged worried glances and speculated about what might have happened to the group of friends who had ventured into the forest.

As the scene attracted more attention, news reporters arrived to cover the unfolding mystery. They went from person to person, capturing eyewitness accounts and interviewing anyone who might have additional information.

With the police, firefighters, and citizens all working together, the search for the missing teens began in earnest. Time ticked away and the level of anxiety grew, but the determined efforts to find them remained steadfast.

Keith wasted no time leaving their bakery and rushing to Myra Park. He located his husband Jason, then joined the other equally anxious parents of the missing teens, who had arrived soon after receiving the distressing calls from the school and police. A dedicated team of volunteers, led by an experienced rescue coordinator, sprang into action, organizing a methodical search of the vast park. They stationed groups of people at each entrance road, ready to spot any sign of the missing teens. The signal to begin the search was given and the dozens of volunteers moved toward the park's center, carefully covering every square inch of the vast area. The police mobilized their trained dogs, trying to cover as much ground as possible.

Hour after hour, the search persisted, with everyone hoping to find a helpful clue or sign. As dusk approached, the search was called off for the night. With heavy hearts, the volunteers had to accept they hadn't found any trace of the teens. Nor had they found any clues regarding the elusive monkeys.

Despite their growing fear, Kass's mom never gave up hope, repeatedly calling his phone. But just like the other parents, her calls went unanswered.

"Bailey, there's nothing more we can do here," Jay said to his wife. "It will be dark soon. Let's get home to Kallie and wait for Kass to call or walk in the door."

"Yes, let's agree to call each other as soon as we hear from any of them," Keith said.

"I can't just go and sit at home. Something has happened, I can feel it," Bailey bemoaned in her desperation.

"I'll drive around the city looking for them and call you every fifteen minutes," Jay reassured her. "Let's go home."

"They'll search the area again tomorrow morning. Nothing more can be done here tonight," Jack's dad Carlton said, with the confidence and authority of a successful attorney. His meticulous grooming and tailored suits were professional requirements for a man who represented prestigious clientele in the entertainment industry.

Jack's parents had parted ways when Jack was just nine years old. Following the divorce, he primarily resided with his father while his mother resided in England, her attention primarily consumed by her new family and their life across the Atlantic, rather than Jack's well-being. Jack's interactions with his mother were limited to a couple of occasions each year—typically a few weeks during the summer and the occasional Christmas or Thanksgiving.

"Alright, let's get home," Bailey agreed with watery eyes.

"Everything will be fine. We'll figure it out," Jay said to comfort his wife as he opened the passenger door then closed it after Bailey was seated.

The parents of the missing children returned to their vehicles and drove home.

The whole province was holding its breath, waiting for any news that would lead to the discovery of the six friends and explain the mystery surrounding their sudden disappearance.

Upon arriving home, the parents of the teens were bombarded by more photographers who waited on the adjacent sidewalks and even in their driveways. Walking from their cars to their houses, they heard the constant clicking of cameras and the intrusive questions of reporters.

"Mr. Kane, do you know where your son is?"

"Mr. Evans, have you heard from your son?"

"Have you heard from your daughter? Where could Olivia be? Did she run away?"

"Mr. and Mrs. Landis, do you think Martin is in danger?"

Front doors were shut and window shades pulled tight, but the aggressive news reporters could still be heard, further upsetting the already distressed parents.

✳✳✳

"Still no answer," Olivia's mom Nia said, setting the phone on the counter.

"What in the hell is going on? Where are they?" her dad Larenz quavered.

"What's wrong? What is going on? Where is Olivia?" her sister Adriana asked.

"The news said she's been kidnapped by apes!" her brother Faris announced.

"We aren't sure, kids."

"Where is she?" Adriana cried.

"The authorities are still searching and we will hear something soon. For now, we have to keep our spirits up," their mom said.

"Why are the reporters on our sidewalk like that?" Faris asked, looking out the window.

"They'll go away soon. Let's just stay away from the windows, go to the family room, and watch something on TV. We won't be able to hear them then," their dad suggested, directing his family to the opposite end of the house.

That conversation, with almost identical dialogue, was happening at the other families' homes. So many questions for which the parents had no answers.

Chapter 15

Morning arrived and the city was restless. The teens' parents were panicked, even though it reassured them, somewhat, to know the city's resources were being fully utilized to find their children.

"What are we going to do?" Bailey asked her husband.

"I don't know, honey. I just don't know. I called the police department before you woke and still no word."

Bailey, frail and exhausted from lack of sleep, was still in tears. She had spent most of the night roaming around the house and rummaging through Kass's room in hopes of finding information that might help locate him. She had found nothing.

"Bailey, please go get some sleep. I'll wake you up if I hear anything. We are no good for Kallie if we're zombies. I'll make her something to eat and make some more calls," Jay said.

"Alright, but promise me you'll wake me if you hear anything at all."

"I promise," he said, kissing her forehead and then her cheek. He watched her climb the stairs, using the handrail to lift herself up each step.

Bailey went into the bedroom, sat on the edge of the king-sized bed, then plopped her body back onto the mattress as if in defeat. She stared at the ceiling as more tears trickled down her face. After a few minutes of reflection and worry, she wiped the tears away and rose to disrobe. She walked into the ensuite bathroom to stand in the shower and let the warm water from the large showerhead give her an opportunity to release her pent-up emotions. She sobbed, slowly lowering herself to sit on the tile floor of the shower. Her crying was intense, gut-wrenching. She covered her mouth so Kallie and Jay wouldn't hear her. But he did. He looked up at the ceiling, then lowered his head in despair before climbing the stairs to comfort her.

"Bailey, everything will be fine. Kass will be home. I know it," he said, as he turned off the water, wrapped a towel around his weeping wife, and lifted her up out of the shower.

He carried her to their bed, placed her under the blanket, and kissed her forehead again before walking out of the room. With the door gently shut behind him, Jay leaned his back against it and listened. He heard some gentle sniffs but soon all was silent.

Before lifting himself away from the door, he stood in the hallway for several minutes of solitude, then headed downstairs to the kitchen, where Kallie sat patiently waiting for her breakfast.

***

"Mr. Roads?"

"Yes, this is Jason and Keith. You're on speakerphone," Jason said.

"Hi, this is Detective Camber. I have been assigned to your case and will be the person leading the investigation regarding the disappearance of your daughter."

"Have you heard anything yet?" Keith asked.

"No, we are still canvassing the area and creating an extensive log of where Gabrielle and her friends had been seen before their disappearance. Can I come by today and talk with you more?"

"Yes, we're home."

"How does 11 a.m. sound?" Detective Camber proposed.

"Yes, that will be fine."

Jason placed his phone on the coffee table and Gab's dads shared a comforting embrace before settling onto the living room sofa. The house, usually vibrant with Gab's energy, was oddly quiet—too quiet. Not hearing her usual banter and infectious laughter created an unmistakable void. It was like the house paused, as if it were poised, eagerly waiting for her to burst through the door and infuse it with life once again.

"We'll find her," Jason said.

"This is just too bizarre. How do six kids just vanish from a park? Vanish from a city? Where in the hell are they?" Keith said, his voice trembling. The two dads held each other again and, this time, dissolved into tears.

***

"Hey Mike, you okay?" Martin's older brother Ross asked, sitting on the edge of his younger brother's bed. "Mike, talk to me."

"He hasn't said a word all morning," Markus said, standing nearby and staring down at his twin brother.

"Dude, our brother is going to be just fine. They probably just got lost in the woods and there are hundreds of people looking for him."

"You think so?" Mike turned over, faced his brothers, and leaned up. "You really think he's just lost? The news is saying he's been abducted."

"Man, don't listen to those idiots. We are going to find our brother. Come on, you have to eat something," Ross said, guiding Mike out of his bedroom and into the kitchen.

The doorbell rang. Detective Camber embarked on his rounds, beginning with the Landis family. The detective, clad in jeans, a polo shirt, and a casual suit jacket, possessed a lanky six-foot frame. He had a head of short, fiery red hair, and his face was clean-shaven. As he entered the house, he unceremoniously slipped off his shoes, adding them to the collection of footwear already gathered by the door.

"Hi, nice to meet you," he said, shaking hands with Martin's parents.

"I'm Rose and this is Clark."

"And these are our boys: Ross, Mike, and Markus," Clark said, introducing his sons as they entered the living room.

"Nice to meet you boys."

"And this is our daughter, Lori."

"Nice to meet you."

"Here, come in and have a seat. Can we get you tea, coffee, or espresso?" Clark offered.

"An espresso sounds great. Thank you."

"Can you boys go upstairs or something?" their dad said.

"Dad, we want to hear too. We're not little kids anymore," Markus said.

"You're right," his dad acknowledged after a pause.

"It's fine with me if they stay," Detective Camber said. "They might prove helpful with locating the whereabouts of your son."

"Martin," Clark said firmly.

"Yes, Martin. So, I'll be asking a bunch of questions in order to put things together. They might seem silly but the more information I gather, the better our odds in finding Martin."

"Okay."

"Do you know why Martin was at the park yesterday?"

"Same story that you heard," Clark said. "Their school was being attacked by vultures and monkeys, and Martin and his friends chased after the monkeys."

Then directing his next question at the boys, the detective asked, "Why would Martin and his friends chase the monkeys? Why were they the only kids to do so?"

"I don't know. He's never mentioned anything about monkeys before," Ross offered.

"No, I've never heard him mention them either," Mike said.

"Same," Markus added.

"How long has he been friends with the other kids?"

"Just about a month, I think," Rose answered. "Since they got back from their camping trip in Costa Rica."

"Costa Rica? Nice. And he didn't mention anything about his new friends?"

"No, not a word," she said.

"I have five names: Jack, Gabrielle, Kass, Harlen, and Olivia. Which one is he closest to?"

"I'm not sure..." his mom began before being interrupted by Lori.

"Kass. He's closest to Kass."

"Why Kass out of the five?" the detective inquired.

"I think they just have more in common than the other four," Lori replied.

"Were there any family fights recently? Can you think of any reason at all why he would not come home?"

"Nothing. We all have positive relationships with him. He's a good kid and never causes any problems," Martin's dad said, glancing over at Ross.

"Great, you don't have to look at me when you say that," Ross snapped.

"I didn't."

"Right, Dad. Whatever..." Ross said before grudgingly leaving the room.

"Sorry about that. We have some unresolved issues with that one. But like I was saying, I've asked the kids and my wife and we all agree—Martin was acting normal when he left for school yesterday morning."

"Can I take a look in Martin's room?"

"Certainly. It's right up the stairs," his mom said, leading the detective who, upon entering Martin's bedroom, looked through his belongings: inside his closet, in the pockets of his pants, in all of his drawers, in the trash can, between his mattress and box spring, and he even shuffled through multiple notebooks on Martin's desk and bookshelf.

The detective then asked a slew of more questions, which the Landis family answered in full. Detective Camber stayed for nearly an hour and then left for his next appointments with the other teens' families, saving Kass's house for last.

***

"I'm going to ask you some questions, and just answer them the best you can," Detective Camber said to Olivia's parents, Nia and Larenz. Olivia's aunt, uncle, and their two children, were also present—a supportive gathering that often occurred whenever someone in their family was in crisis.

Nia and Larenz were the pillars of their tight-knit community, their real estate genius shaping the very landscape of their surroundings. Nia, with features mirroring Olivia's, radiated elegance with her dark brown skin and long lustrous hair, while Larenz, standing tall at 6'3", had a tackle guard physique. The attractive couple had two additional children: Olivia's siblings, Adriana and Faris.

Detective Camber had a calm demeanor and approached the interaction delicately, reassuring the family as he inquired about Olivia's last known whereabouts, recent activities, known associates, and any potential leads that might assist in locating her.

"Has Olivia exhibited any unusual or concerning behaviors in the days or weeks leading up to her disappearance?"

"No, she's been acting normal in the past weeks," Nia answered.

Larenz nodded in agreement. "Olivia's a responsible girl; she wouldn't just disappear like this. Something's not right."

Detective Camber listened attentively, jotting down notes before asking further questions about Olivia's friends. And like he did in all six interviews that day, he asked to search the missing person's bedroom for any helpful information. In Olivia's case, he found only science awards and evidence of an organized and responsible young woman.

After his thorough interview and inspection, Detective Camber concluded, "We're going to do our best to locate Olivia. If you think of anything else or if you hear from her, please contact me immediately. Here's my card."

With that, he offered a warm smile and took his leave, proceeding to Jack's house to continue his diligent efforts to locate the missing children.

***

"Your son has quite the collection of accolades," the detective said as he viewed Jack's trophies, ribbons, certificates, and plaques all prominently displayed in his bedroom, as well as a pile of medallions stored in a box.

"Yes, he's been athletic since he was five," Carlton replied.

"And he's been with his girlfriend, Gabrielle, for how long?"

"Gab, about two years now, I guess."

"Any drug use, excessive drinking, or concerning behaviors?"

"Seriously, Jack is just a great kid. He's kind and compassionate, and he has a nice group of like-minded friends. He's never been in trouble with anyone."

"How did he get himself involved in a situation like this?" the detective probed. "I mean, a high-speed chase pursuing wild monkeys with his friends?"

"Detective, I just don't understand it. He has to be protecting one of his friends or something," Carlton insinuated.

"The question is, which friend?"

"They are all good kids and one isn't more likely than the others to get into trouble," his dad firmly stated, agitated by the detective's questions.

"I'm just trying to find the root of the problem, which will hopefully lead me to finding your son and the rest of the kids," Detective Camber said.

"I get it, but I'm telling you, these are all good kids. Jack and I are quite open with each other and I'd be very surprised if something has happened that he didn't feel comfortable telling me about. We talk about everything."

"Well, I have a feeling there's at least one thing he hasn't mentioned to you. And I think whatever it is has pulled him into an unfortunate situation," the detective concluded. But then he thought of a follow-up question. "I hope this isn't too personal, but is there a Mrs. Evans?"

"She's Mrs. Dillard now. She remarried and lives in England. She's been there since Jack was nine," Carlton answered.

"Amicable divorce? Is Jack in contact with her?"

"Not so amicable at first, but we're friendly and have moved on with co-parenting Jack. Well, sort of co-parenting."

"So, she knows he's missing?"

"Yes, she'll be arriving tomorrow."

"Can I have her contact information?"

"For sure. I'll write it down for you."

Carlton picked up Jack's notebook and pen, wrote down the requested information, and tore the piece of paper from the notebook. Before closing the notebook, however, he noticed a to-do list written on the next page. It had a list of supplies, such as flashlights, rope, bananas, and most alarmingly, Temazepam. He quickly closed the notebook and placed it back on the desk, without calling the detective's attention to it.

"I need to call Jack's mom back and make a few other calls. Can I answer any more questions for you?" Carlton asked the detective.

"I'm good for now. I'll call you if I have any additional questions or updates."

"Okay, great."

Carlton escorted Detective Camber to the door, then watched him walk to his car before running upstairs to Jack's room to read more of Jack's to-do list. *Temazepam, syringes, knife...* Without delay, he went to his bathroom and looked in the medicine cabinet, where he discovered a full container of Temazepam missing and a second container with many tablets gone, as well. With a pensive demeanor, he walked back to Jack's bedroom to search it more thoroughly in hopes of finding more clues or helpful information. Instead, he only found several books: *Jewels and Gems*, *Gems*, and *Diamond Appraisal*.

***

"Hey Jason, it's Carlton."

"Hi Carlton. I have you on speaker. Have you heard something?"

"No, nothing. But the detective just left and while we were in Jack's room, I found Jack's notebook with a to-do list."

"What's on the list?" Jason asked.

"Rope, flashlights, bananas, knife, syringes, and Temazepam," Carlton shared.

"Temazepam? Sleeping pills?"

"Yes, and over forty pills are missing from the prescription bottles in my medicine cabinet."

"Oh, no, what are these kids up to?" Jason said.

"Did the detective see the list?" Keith asked.

"No, I was shocked when I saw it and hid it from him. I called you two instead. Should I have shared it?"

"Yes, for sure. It might help the police find out where they are or what these kids have been up to. I understand your hesitation, but the list is concerning," Keith added.

"We'll check Gab's room again and have a more thorough look," added Jason. "We'll call you back if we find anything."

"Okay, thanks guys. And I'll call you if I hear anything else."

***

"Hi Cynthia."

"Hello, Frank. I haven't heard anything yet," Harlen's mother said to his dad, her ex-husband.

It had been many years since Frank and Cynthia had seen each other in person. Once in a while, she would catch a glimpse of Frank, his wife Gloria, and Harlen's half-brother Hanson, when Harlen was on a video call. Over time, Harlen's divorced parents became kind and civilized toward each other, even though their split was far from amicable.

"Nothing?" Frank asked.

"No, although a detective called an hour ago and will stop by around noon today."

"Okay, Hanson and I will be there tomorrow night."

"And how is Hanson?"

"He's fine. Just turned five. He's a fun kid."

"And Gloria?"

"We're getting a divorce," Frank announced.

"Oh, I'm sorry to hear that."

"Yeah, me too. Harlen doesn't know yet. Hell, Hanson doesn't know yet either."

"Why?" she probed.

"Why don't they know?"

"No, why the divorce?"

"Well," Frank paused. "I see you are still direct with your questioning. Let's just say Gloria has a pretty severe drinking problem."

"Oh, no."

"Yes, we've tried rehab, marriage counseling, and nothing has worked. She comes from a family of alcoholism. Divorce became inevitable when the drinking started affecting her parenting as well as our relationship. I just can't do it anymore."

"Frank, I am really sorry to hear this."

"Thanks, Cynthia. She'll live with her family in London and Hanson and I will move back to Canada in the summer. I've been offered a job in Vancouver, and this way I'll be closer to Harlen—and Hanson will have a brother to grow up with."

Frank's news had given Cynthia an opportunity to momentarily forget about their missing son.

"I know I've said this before, Cynthia, but I am truly sorry for how I handled everything. I did something horrible years ago and I will always carry the guilt and pain for my actions. I'm sorry," Frank said. "I know, karma, right?"

"Frank, karma doesn't work like that. You did some things back then that changed everyone's life, but I no longer have hard feelings for you. Harlen is happier having you in his life, and he's always talking about his little brother. He's going to be delighted to know you will be moving back to Canada. I appreciate your apology but let's figure out how to get our son back home so you can tell him the news."

***

Detective Camber sat down with Kass's parents in their living room. They had been through a restless night and the concern on their faces was palpable. The detective, with a reassuring yet focused demeanor, began to ask a series of questions.

"First, I want to assure you that we are doing everything we can to find Kass and his friends," Detective Camber began. "I know this is a challenging time, but your cooperation in answering these questions could greatly assist our efforts."

"Of course, Detective. Ask us anything," Bailey nodded, her eyes filled with hope and worry.

"We just want our son and his friends to come home safe," Jay added.

"How long has your son been able to run along a wall? I'm sure you've seen the video by now."

"Honestly, I have no idea. I'm guessing he's been practicing and perhaps the added adrenaline from the encounter with the monkeys contributed to what looked like a pretty extraordinary feat," Jay said.

"And running at high speeds?"

"He's always been a fast runner." Bailey said, a bit on the defense. "He was running for dear life and wasn't going any faster than..."

"Than?" the detective interrupted Bailey.

"Detective, we just don't know what is happening," Bailey finally admitted.

Bailey and Jay dove into their recollections, weaving a tapestry of information for the detective. They divulged every tidbit they could recall, including Kass's recent energy level and his bruises from a doubtful game of football. They did their best to offer Camber an expansive view of their son's activities and social circle.

"Mind if I have a look at his computer?" Camber inquired, leaning in with a furrowed brow.

Bailey hesitated, uncertain. "I'm not sure, Detective. I'm wary of invading his privacy."

"Your son's missing, Mrs. Kane," Camber pressed gently. "This is the moment when invading his privacy might just help us find him."

Bailey sighed, flipping through her phone gallery to retrieve Kass's password. "Alright," she sighed, handing it over with reluctance trumped by worry.

As Detective Camber commenced with his sleuthing via Kass's computer, he entered a digital portal into the teenage mind.

He combed through Kass's browsing history, stumbling upon a surprising fascination: jewel appraisal. It was a subject that seemed incongruous with the typical interests of a teenager. This sparked his curiosity. The screen became filled with searches, articles, and discussions, suggesting that Kass had been diving deep into the world of precious gemstones. Detective Camber couldn't help but wonder what had ignited this newfound passion.

But the digital trail didn't end there. With each keystroke, the detective ventured further into Kass's virtual realm and discovered a captivating interest in Costa Rican creatures. Monkeys and vultures had taken center stage in Kass's online explorations, with detailed articles and images painting a vivid picture of these exotic animals. It was a peculiar fascination for a teenager and Detective Camber was intrigued by the connections among the online articles, the monkeys and vultures that had invaded Kelowna, and the missing teens.

After concluding his interview with Kass's parents, Detective Camber shook their hands and offered a reassuring nod. The investigation was well underway, with the gathered information serving as valuable pieces to the puzzle of the missing teenagers. The detective left Kass's home, determined to piece together the clues and complete the puzzle to safely reunite the teens with their families.

Chapter 16

"**G**ab?" Jack's voice pierced the murky space, a stifling scent of sulfur and damp cool oppression hanging in the air. His words echoed in the darkness with urgency. Jack's former reality seemed to have morphed into an alternate realm draped in an impenetrable blackness.

"I'm here!" Gab responded, her fragile voice quivering with trepidation.

Jack activated the flashlight on his phone and urged Gab to do the same.

"Where are you?" Gab yelled. "I can't see your light."

"Over here! Stay where you are. I'll head in your direction and look for your light."

Moments later, Jack's light and then his touch materialized out of the darkness, pulling Gab close as if to confirm the reality of their togetherness. Their embrace transcended words, an unspoken reassurance in the midst of the inexplicable. In the dim light, Jack's face drew nearer, and their lips met, a fleeting but intense connection that spoke of shared vulnerability in the face of the unknown.

"Where are we?" Gab's voice trembled.

"I don't know. Seems like a cave," Jack replied as he swept his flashlight across the unfamiliar cavernous space.

"Kass! Olivia! Harlen! Martin!" Jack's and Gab's calls rang out, but only a faint echo replied, a haunting reminder of their solitude.

Threading through the darkness, Jack and Gab navigated the cavern's twists and turns and finally, distant responses broke the silence.

"Hey, I'm here!" Olivia's voice pierced the stillness.

"Over here!" Martin's shout followed from a distance.

"Where are we?" Harlen's voice wavered.

Jack anticipated hearing Kass's voice next, but that did not happen.

"Kass? Where's Kass?" Jack cried. "Everyone, use the flashlight on your phone," he instructed.

Driven by fear yet determined to reunite, they all maneuvered the rocky terrain, their movements accompanied by the splash of puddles and the scrape of stones. In those moments, the cave seemed to reflect their apprehension, its darkness mirroring the challenges that engulfed them.

Within a matter of heartbeats, the friends drew together in the cave, their embraces a symbol of solidarity. Flashlights then danced across the cave's expanse in their search for Kass, whose absence remained a puzzle to be solved.

"Here, let's go this way," Jack suggested. The group followed behind, continuing to flash their lights. Jack navigated the way but without a clue as to which direction led to the mouth of the cave. As they sloshed through the puddles, careful to avoid tripping on the rocky surface, they heard what they assumed to be troglobites crawling along the walls and the plip-plop of water dripping from the high ceiling or down the sides of the cave.

The cave's expanse stretched out before them. A heavy silence enveloped the space, broken by the faint sound of their breathing. It was as if they had entered a place tainted by an uncanny presence, a tension that crept into their senses and made their skin prickle with unease.

Questions surged through their minds like a storm. How did they find themselves there? Where, precisely, had they landed? Yet two questions rang loudest: where was Kass and was he safe? The mist of uncertainty clawed at them, leaving them to wonder whether Kass still lingered within Myra Park or had become prey to the ferocity of the monkeys. Could he have endured such a relentless assault? It was the unknown that gripped them most tightly.

Suddenly, as Jack made his way around a large boulder at a sharp and narrow turn, he felt an odd warmth on the side of his face and inhaled a strong stench that burned his nostrils. He shined his light in that direction and came face-to-face with an enormous bear-like beast. It growled.

"Back up!" Jack instructed while keeping his voice soft and calm.

Standing upright with its paws outstretched, the powerful seven-foot creature displayed its unique features and projected an imposing presence. The bear-like beast possessed the sturdy and formidable build characteristic of its common species along with otherworldly traits. Its fur shimmered with an ethereal luminescence, each strand pulsing with the muted light of distant galaxies. Instead of conventional claws, crystalline appendages adorned its massive paws.

The teens quickened their retreat, putting a distance of around twenty steps between them and the beast. However, their relief was short-lived as the bear, with deliberate, plodding strides, closed in. Its ominous approach caused the ground to quiver with each lumbering step.

"Okay, guys..." Jack whispered. "Slowly retreat and pick up fist-sized stones to throw if the bear attacks. Gab, unzip my backpack and see if there's anything in it I can use."

Gab did as directed and shined her light inside. "What's this?" Gab asked, pulling out a knife with a thick wooden handle.

"Oh, wow! Kass must have put it in my bag. I've seen it in his dad's shop but Kass has done something to it." Jack took the knife from Gab—one eye on her and the other on the creature.

"It's warm in my hands," Jack said.

"Jack, you can't use that on the bear. Don't hurt the bear, Jack," Olivia pleaded.

"Olivia, if I don't hurt this bear, or whatever it is, it's probably going to hurt us...maybe even kill us."

"Kill the damned bear, Jack!" Harlen hissed.

The tension in the cave reached a breaking point as the beast closed in further, its massive form filling the space with raw power and menace. Jack's heart pounded as he brandished the dagger, every muscle in his body on edge. The bear's growls and grunts echoed in the darkness, signaling its dogged pursuit.

In a flash of movement, the creature lunged at Jack, its enormous claws slashing through the air. Jack managed to dodge the full force of the attack, but one paw swiped his shoulder, tearing his shirt. Jack grimaced in pain as he hit the cave floor. The creature loomed over him, its fangs dripping saliva onto Jack's face like grotesque rain. The other teens threw the rocks they had picked up, but the bear paid no attention. In that instant, Jack understood the urgency—his actions had to be swift and merciless. With a flood of adrenaline, he plunged the dagger into the side of the bear's neck, the blade finding its mark with eerie precision. The impact unleashed a potent surge of electricity coursing through the beast's body. Its fur illuminated in a dazzling and unearthly display of radiance. Jack pulled the knife free but maintained his grip. With lightning speed, he took the dagger in both hands and stabbed the bear's throat with a series of rapid, calculated thrusts. Each motion produced a burst of sparks, an almost mystical dance between weapon and flesh.

The creature began to falter. Its roars became gasps for air, all vitality draining from its hulking form as it struggled to remain upright. Desperate and disoriented, the bear's gasps grew more halting until, with a final, defeated exhale, it lost its balance and crumpled to the ground.

The gang stood in awe, staring, as their once fearsome adversary lay motionless before them. The cave fell silent. Relief and disbelief swept through the teens.

"Umm...what the heck just happened?" Olivia mumbled.

"Did you just kill a goddamn bear, Jack?" Harlen gasped.

"See if it's dead," requested Gab.

"How am I supposed to do that, Gab? Take its pulse?" Jack asked, still in shock and out of breath from the fight.

"Put your hand up to its mouth and nose to see if any air is coming out?" Martin suggested.

"After you," Jack countered.

"How about we just assume it's dead and get the hell out of here," Harlen proposed.

"I second that," Olivia added.

"That was no ordinary bear and this is no ordinary dagger," Jack said, holding it in his hand.

"You said it felt warm. Like when you picked up Kass's gem?" Gab asked.

"Yes, but not as hot. I can also feel an unusual force pulsating throughout my body. Definitely not a regular ole knife."

"Excuse me! Can we cut the chit-chat and get the hell out of here?" Harlen said again.

"Excellent idea," Olivia said. "Hey, I think I can feel a breeze coming from that way. Let's go."

Jack remained quiet as they walked along. His battle with the bear had seemed like an out-of-body experience and he was feeling traumatized by it. He found himself attempting to wrap his head around the rage that had engulfed him—a level of rage he had never before been forced to explore.

"Eureka! I see a speck of light ahead!" Gab shouted.

"Ahh, this is great," Martin added.

"Yes, it's getting bigger and brighter," Olivia announced.

"Harlen, please stop humming!" Olivia snapped.

"Hey, I'm celebrating. Don't snap at me. Can't you hear how nice I sound?" Harlen's humming turned into singing and the acoustics of the cave echoed the lyrics and melody of *Watermelon Sugar*.

"Okay, you do sound pretty good, but now I'm craving watermelon," Olivia chuckled.

Harlen's voice ebbed but he continued to hum his way through the cave and toward the light while Jack, still holding the knife and enjoying the power of its special energy, sliced troglobites as he walked. The damp, dark, dreary cave had been terrifying, but after a few more minutes of walking toward the light, the five teens were ecstatic to finally be out. It took a moment for their eyes to adjust to the piercing sunlight and for their bodies to adjust to the oppressive heat and humidity of the foreign climate. The vibrant green trees and lush vegetation of a tropical forest surrounded them while an abundance of birds chittered, unseen but noisily present.

"Hey, look. Look at those gems," Olivia said, pointing to the dagger Jack was holding and the bright specks of jewels that sparkled in the sunlight.

"They look like pieces from the big gemstone Kass had," Martin said.

"He must have chipped these off of it and glued them on. Smart, Kass, real smart," Jack said, making better sense of the special energy within the weapon.

Jack, how's your shoulder?" Gab asked, opening the tear in his shirt to take a look.

"It barely got me."

"Yes, it looks like a scratch and there's only a little blood," Gab confirmed. "Still you need to wash it as soon as possible so it doesn't become infected."

"Jack, look at your hands. They're all red," Martin noticed.

"Must be from the dagger," he said, placing the dagger on the ground.

"Look in the bag. What else is in there?" Harlen asked.

Jack put the backpack on the ground and opened it. He pulled out another dagger. Similar, yet smaller. It, too, had small specks of gems glued onto the handle. He then pulled out several granola bars, a half of a ham-and-cheese sandwich, two bags of Sour Patch Kids, a filled water bottle, a lighter, and a magazine.

"Of course, *Fashion Forward*," Jack said, smiling. "He's impeccable."

"What's in your bag, Olivia?"

"My math book, a notebook, pencil and pens, lip gloss, gum, and a granola bar."

"So what if Kass is still in the cave?" Martin asked.

"Good question. We can sit around for a bit and see if he comes out or we can leave him a note and go exploring so we know where the heck we are," Jack replied.

"I'm hungry."

"Harlen, you're always hungry," Olivia said.

"Here, let's split this bar," Gab suggested, unwrapping the granola bar. "Take a small bite and pass it around."

"There's no reception," Martin said, holding up his phone. "I got nothing."

"Neither do I."

"Same here."

"This means we don't have any idea how far we are from home or even civilization," Jack said. "Wait, my phone just shut off."

"Mine too!"

"So did mine."

"Great. No reception. No flashlights. Nothing," Gab said.

"We're clearly not in Canada," Olivia concluded.

"How do you know?" Harlen asked.

"Look at the trees. We don't have trees like these in Canada. And the air here is much more humid. You know, guys," Olivia continued, "this tropical environment, the beast in the cave, and those gems in the dagger have me hypothesizing we are somehow back in Costa Rica."

"So many weird things have been happening," Martin added, "I wouldn't be surprised. And this sure does feel like the rainforest we were in."

"So how did we get here?" Harlen asked.

"It was some kind of teleportation," said Martin.

"Get the hell out of here. There's no way that is a real thing," Harlen said.

"Okay, well, how do you explain the fact we were in the park one minute, then here the next?" Martin said.

"Okay, so maybe teleportation is a real thing, but where is my boy Kass and how do we get back home?" Jack asked in desperation.

"How about I hang my baseball cap on this branch as a marker?" Martin suggested, lifting the cap and letting his long blonde bangs fall over his eyes. With a quick swipe, he cleared them away and tucked the strands behind his ears.

"Hand me a pen, Olivia," Gab said. "I'll leave a note as well."

Kass, we're all safe and heading west, hopefully toward water. We'll circle back to check if you're here or if you've left a message.

With the cap hung on the branch and the note left behind, the friends, sans Kass, embarked on their journey in the direction Olivia had suggested.

The rainforest teemed with trees and dense vegetation, along with the constant buzz of insects and the calls of birds. The unfamiliar, jungle-like terrain didn't deter the resilient teens; they pushed forward, determined and undaunted.

"Olivia, does this mean we don't have to take the test tomorrow?" Harlen joked. "Wait, is it still today? What year is it? Ah man, maybe we teleported back to the 1500s."

"Harlen, can't you just keep quiet for a minute?" Martin said, annoyed. Gab, Jack, and Olivia all laughed at Martin squabbling at Harlen.

"How about I jab you with that dagger and see how quiet you get," Harlen said.

"Now, now, boys. We're a team through all this and have to stick together," Jack said.

"Sorry, Harlen," Martin said.

"No worries, I know you're just scared about your boyfriend," Harlen said, continuing the sarcasm.

"Okay, boys, if you're done kissing and making up, let's pick up the pace," Jack said, leading the group.

It was mid-morning and the trees provided only partial shade from the oppressive heat as they made their way through the forest in search of civilization, water, and Kass. They took breaks, drank a sparing amount of water, shared small portions of food, and wiped away the sweat that dribbled from their brows.

"Do you smell that?" Olivia asked.

"Uh...Martin's B.O.?" Harlen said.

"Dude!" Martin snarled.

"No, I'm not talking about Martin's emanating odor," Olivia said, winking at Martin. "I can smell fish and water. We are close!"

"Oh my gosh, what would we do without you?" Gab said, as she gave Olivia a tight hug.

"Wait, I can hear the water now, too," Harlen said.

The teens ran fast, following Olivia, and arrived at a glistening river about a dozen yards wide.

The riverbank was lined with tall swaying grasses and small trees that provided occasional patches of shade. Wildflowers in various colors added a touch of vibrancy to the scene. The area had an untouched, serene quality, with no signs of human development in sight.

Jack dropped his backpack and shed his clothing down to his boxer briefs. The others followed suit, and together they enjoyed a frolicking good time in the cool invigorating river.

Jack left the water and stood on a large boulder that overlooked the river. When he spotted a fish jumping, he realized their meal was soon to come. He searched for a straight, narrow, yet strong stick he could whittle down smooth. Martin did the same and eventually they had two solid sticks, each about four feet long. They then gathered vines which they used to tightly wrap their daggers onto the ends of the sticks. Thus, they created spears, sturdy hunting tools that also could serve as strong weapons with remarkable powers due to the miniature gems already embedded in the daggers.

"This should also prevent the daggers from heating up our hands," Jack said.

The teens were knee-deep in the water, taking turns trying to jab fish that were hardly larger than a pen. They had no luck because the fish were so small and too quick. But when the sun started to set behind the trees, an abundance of larger fish started to jump out of the water to catch mosquitoes and other flying insects. The scene became a playful fishing frenzy with the gang trying their best to catch dinner, grabbing and stabbing at the jumping fish. They failed.

"Okay, stop, everyone!" Gab shouted. "It's not going to work if we are all in the water splashing around. The fish are in different pockets of the river. We have to be strategic."

"You're right, but I think you're the problem, Gab," Jack teased.

"I'm the problem? How am I the problem, Jack?"

"You're distracting the fish with your sexy body," he said with a wink and a smile.

"Haha...very funny," she smiled back.

"Get a room," Harlen interjected.

Jack laughed, then said to Harlen, Gab, and Olivia, "Okay, you three get out of the water. Martin, you go over there. It looks like a fishing hole. I'll stay here."

"Stay quiet, Jack. Don't move, and jab fast," Martin advised.

And that's exactly what they did. One by one, Jack and Martin were able to stab several fish, each about a foot long. Harlen and Gab then took turns with the spears and also had success. Olivia kept her distance. As a vegan and advocate for animal rights, she was never keen on witnessing the death of sentient beings. She had spent the past five years avoiding the consumption of animal-sourced food, but was in a current situation where she would have to decide: starve to death or eat fish and live.

After Gab skillfully speared a couple of fish, she passed the weapon back to Jack, and in that exchange, playful glances were shared between them. With a hint of charm in his tone, he murmured, "You know, I could get plenty of fish for the both of us."

Gab blushed and replied, "Oh, really? And what do I have to do in return?"

"Maybe a kiss?" he suggested with a cheeky grin.

Gab playfully rolled her eyes, but her smile gave away her interest. "Deal," she said, leaning in for a quick kiss on the lips before Jack returned to spearing fish with renewed energy and a playful spark between them.

With the lighter retrieved from the backpack, Gab skillfully ignited a small campfire using dry kindling, sticks, and sheer determination. The crackling fire roared to life, providing ample heat to cook the fish. After just ten minutes, the glowing embers infused the fish with a tantalizing smoky essence.

"I feel bad for Olivia, she hasn't had meat in five years," Gab said to Jack.

"I know. It was hard not to cringe each time she took a bite. But you know what, at least it's healthy."

"True."

"She'll be fine. We don't know how long we'll be out here and she has to eat something."

They lost track of time and the sun suddenly disappeared beyond the mountain just west of them. Dusk was quickly turning to nighttime, making the teens feel vulnerable and concerned for their safety in the open forest with scant knowledge of where they were. They realized they didn't have enough time to get back to the cave before dark, so they spent the next hour quickly constructing a temporary eight-by-eight-foot lean-to. With Olivia's assistance, their shelter was quite sturdy after tying a rafter between two trees, then leaning branches onto both sides with brush piled on top. The result was a shelter large enough for the five to get some much-needed sleep.

"Think we're going to be okay?"

"Yes, Olivia, we have smart-you, these dagger spears, and my muscles," Harlen said, flexing his skinny biceps. "Hey, you know we will have to be together eventually, don't you?"

"What? What are you talking about, crazy?"

"Well, think about it. If we're trapped in this place forever, we will be the only two single people. Jack and Gab have each other, Martin will have Kass when we find him, and well, we can't sit around forever watching them be happy while we're alone and miserable," Harlen explained.

"Harlen, I love you, but I would rather eat a raw, bloody deer than even kiss you," Olivia stated.

"Whoa, savage," he replied.

"But...I have to say, you did look pretty good in your undies," she chuckled.

"See, you didn't know this bod was right here waiting for you."

"Alright Romeo, let's get settled inside the shelter before it gets too dark."

Olivia, Martin, and Harlen laid down on the grass-covered ground inside the shelter while Jack and Gab stood watch just outside the entrance. Sitting side by side, Jack wrapped his arm around his girlfriend and held a spear in his free hand.

"Gab, please go get some rest," Jack pleaded after a half-hour of watching her yawn.

"Okay, I will. Wake up Martin when you're ready to switch."

"Yes, deal," he said, kissing her goodnight.

"Okay, okay...I can hear the exchange of saliva," Harlen said from inside the shelter. "Like I told you before, get a room!"

They giggled while Gab made her way to bed.

Jack remained awake for several more hours, holding the spear and leaning his body against a large rock the group had rolled into place earlier to help guard the entrance to the shelter. The pitch black night was mostly quiet with only the sporadic sounds of small crawling creatures to help keep Jack awake. But during the next hour of guard duty, his eyes began to slowly close.

Chapter 17

The morning sun broke through the dense canopy of the tropical forest, illuminating Jack, who had fallen asleep during his watch. As Martin emerged from the shelter, his expression turned to one of alarm.

"Jack, don't move!" Martin whispered.

Jack flinched, opened his eyes, then immediately stood up, trembling. An enormous snake-like creature was slithering out of the river and inching its way toward him. With a smooth, shiny head the size of a semi-truck tire and dinner-plate-sized eyes, the creature glared at Jack, baring its razor-sharp teeth with tusk-like canines.

The other friends, now awake and huddled at the entrance of the lean-to, watched the creature grow in length—six feet, eight, then ten feet long! Its head moved closer and closer to Jack, water dripping from its slithering body. The closer it got, the more vicious it appeared.

Jack slowly lifted his spear. With quivering hands, he took on the role of protector. Although he realized his friends were perhaps smarter, he had always considered himself the leader and guardian of the group.

When the massive snake-like creature lifted its head, its elongated body displayed rows of sleek silver scales that bristled along its spine, resembling the raised hackles of a fierce wolf. Jack clutched his spear, poised to strike the creature's face should it advance any nearer.

"What are you doing, Martin?" Jack hissed when, out of the corner of his eye, he saw Martin moving to the side of the creature, the other spear in hand.

"Both of us in the same spot probably isn't a good strategy," Martin said.

"Slow...move very slowly," Jack said, barely moving his mouth and whispering his command.

"Don't you worry, I'm...nice...and...slow."

The creature's eyes moved side-to-side, from Martin to Jack and back again.

"Harlen, get back!" Jack said, as Harlen slowly crawled out of the shelter. "You don't even have a weapon!"

"I'll stay back but also try to distract it. Besides, three are better than two," replied Harlen as he positioned himself at what he hoped would be a safe distance away.

"Okay, no sudden moves. Nice and slow," Jack reiterated.

"Five are better than three," Gab said, as she and Olivia followed Harlen's plan to stay back but serve as distractions.

The five teens had a lengthy western stare-down with the creature. It had discontinued its advance and took a striking position with the front part of its body arched up like a cobra. It then began to salivate, large globs of drool dripping from its fangs.

Suddenly, it lunged at Jack and extended its incredibly long tongue. Jack and Martin attacked back. Jack sliced part of its tongue and Martin stabbed the side of its head. The creature squealed and attacked again, just missing Jack. It then fully emerged from the water and swiped its tail at

Martin, knocking him to the ground. When Gab ran over to help Martin up, the creature took a swipe at her, too. She stumbled, hitting the ground hard, her body reeling from the impact.

The creature's momentary interest in Gab gave Jack another opportunity to stab it on the side of its body. It let out another loud squeal. Although injured, it continued to keep an erect body, even as yellow liquid oozed from it, which then flowed into the river. Again, it lunged, unfurled its long tongue, and wrapped it around Harlen's leg. The muscled tongue pulled the terrified boy toward its wide-open mouth, ready to engulf Harlen's body. There was no doubt as to the creature's intentions. It was going to sever Harlen with its razor-sharp teeth and devour him.

"No!" Jack shouted, throwing his spear as hard and fast as he could.

Martin howled and thrust his own spear into the creature's side, deeply imbedding it.

Jack's aim had proved impeccable with the spear finding its mark directly in the creature's beady eye. Martin's strike had penetrated so deeply that the weapon stayed firmly lodged in the creature's body, causing Martin to lose his grip.

The creature, attempting to retreat, was once again partially submerged in the water, dragging the spear down with it. Undeterred, Martin maintained focus and determination. He dove into the water and seized the shaft of the spear. The impaled creature screeched and flopped around like a fish out of water, swinging Martin from side-to-side while he fought to hold on to the spear. Harlen, his leg still wrapped with slobbery tongue, was tousled and dragged about. Liquid squirted and leaked from the creature's eye and body, causing it to lose strength, and perhaps appetite. Harlen managed to loosen himself from the beast's tongue and fell to the ground, shaken and banged-up, but otherwise unharmed. Jack rushed to extract his spear from the creature's eye.

Within the next few seconds, the creature surrendered, defeated and dying. Its body collapsed and slid back into the river surrounded by thick yellow fluid.

"Well, there goes my morning bath," Harlen said, still lying on the ground and out of breath.

"Dude, you almost got eaten by a monstrous eel and you're still cracking jokes?" Martin said, running over to help Harlen. "Get up!"

"Ah, you were scared for me. Ahhh...you love me, you love me."

"Yeah, yeah...come on," Martin said, helping Harlen regain his balance.

As the adrenaline slowly dissipated, and the full impact of their victory settled upon them, the group gathered their spears, homemade utensils, and backpacks. Each piece of equipment felt like a tangible trophy, a reminder of their courage and resilience in the face of untamed adversity. They exchanged glances of triumph and relief, and a shared understanding that they had just come face-to-face with nature's raw power.

✳✳✳

The sun climbed in the sky, and the group trekked away from the river, back to the cave. The journey consumed nearly three hours, a stretch during which their faces turned a shade redder—though Gab's sunburnt nose outshone them all.

Arriving at the cave, their eyes were drawn to the baseball cap that stubbornly clung to the tree, a silent testament to Kass's absence. This somber moment, where they collectively mourned their missing friend, marked the poignant beginning to a day poised to unfold with a profound sense of loss.

"This doesn't mean he's not okay," Jack said.

"Exactly. Let's stay positive. Remember, he has extra strength on his side," Martin added.

"Well, what do we do now? What *should* we do?" Gab asked.

"Yeah, what's the plan, Jack?" Harlen inquired.

"We need to continue our search for Kass and also seek out civilization so we can get home."

"Okay, then let's leave another note for Kass, but Martin can I borrow your cap to shade my lobster face?" Gab asked, then grabbed it when she got a nod from Martin. "Thanks. And now I suggest we keep heading west and parallel to the water. After all, the Pacific Ocean is somewhere out west and we know the coast is populated."

"Yeah, good idea, Gab. But let's leave time to catch some fish. Your face is so red we can cook them on it," Harlen added.

The group laughed, except for Gab, who scrunched her face and glared at them. Olivia replaced Martin's cap with a piece of paper from her notebook. *We were here. Heading west to find civilization,* she wrote. She set the note on the ground and placed several small rocks on top to keep it in place. Then the group set out on their journey west.

The sun reached its peak and sweat ran down the muscles of Jack's broad shirtless back. The water they had boiled the day before was running low and their food supply was almost gone. Moments of silence and sadness came over them as they continued to think about Kass's whereabouts—how he was alone and probably frightened, perhaps hurt, or even worse, dead. They would shake their worrisome thoughts, only to have them soon return. The dire reality of their situation was taking its toll.

Fortunately, the forest had remained quiet after their battle with the river-eel and their walk became uneventful, almost enjoyable. They could finally take a moment to breathe and relax, appreciating the lush trees that gave them comfort from the piercing sun.

"We need to make three more spears." Jack stated. "It's important that we are all protected."

They scoured the surrounding area, collecting stout branches, and with deliberate focus, crafted makeshift spears, meticulously sharpening each one using a dagger's keen edge.

"Not as flashy as the jeweled ones, but they'll do the trick," Jack remarked, a glint of resolve in his eyes.

"Oh my gosh!"

"What, Olivia? What?" Gab shouted back.

"I hope we get back before Kane Brown's concert."

"Olivia, what is wrong with you? I thought another creature was about to attack," Jack said.

"Sorry. I got a little excited. I've been waiting for this concert for like forever. We gotta get back before Friday," she said.

"Okay everyone, let's make sure Olivia is back in two days so she can get to the concert in time," Harlen said.

"Hey, I'm just thinking of something positive during this chaos we're in."

"We're all under a lot of stress and over-sensitive," Jack interjected. "Let's remember that and try to be more patient with each other."

"What's your favorite Kane song?" Harlen said, approaching the conversation with a different angle.

"*What's Mine is Yours.*"

"That's a good song. I hope we get back so you can go to the concert."

"Thanks, Harlen."

"See, nothing but love," he added, giving Olivia his best smile.

They continued walking while searching for some form of civilization or *any* sign that Kass was alive. The temperature reached an oppressive high and walking through the forest became much more challenging.

"We need to find water."

"We will, Olivia. I have a feeling we're getting close," Gab said, as they walked side by side. "Until then, let's chat about other stuff to keep our minds occupied."

"Good idea."

"So, are you still interested in that new guy in your English class?"

"No, he's too immature," Olivia said.

"Well, give him time to mature. Then you'll have someone hot and datable."

"I don't have the energy for that. Plus, there are too many other interesting people out there," she said.

"That's true. What do you think about Kass and Martin?" Gab asked.

"I think they could be good together. I actually think it's pretty awesome the way Martin made a decision to follow his true feelings. Whoa! What was that?" Olivia asked, as she suddenly stopped and looked behind her. A rustling noise followed.

"I heard something, too," Gab said.

"No, I can't face another creature; one almost ate me!" Harlen squealed.

"Keep walking," Olivia said, pushing Harlen to move ahead.

The sounds of cracking undergrowth became louder and more frequent. It was evident something was crawling in the bushes. Soon, Olivia and Harlen saw the leaves moving only a few yards from them.

"What is it?" Martin asked.

"I don't know, but there's more than one," Olivia exclaimed.

The group picked up their pace, but that didn't stop the unseen creatures from getting closer.

"Run!" shouted Martin.

The gang's heartbeats raced in tandem with their pounding footsteps as they sprinted through the open terrain. When they dared to look back, terror gripped them. Insect-like organisms were pursuing them, each one the size and shape of a cantaloupe. These creatures had a dozen spindly legs that moved with remarkable agility, two large, piercing, yellow eyes emitting a haunting glow, and long twitching antennae.

Amid their fear, the absurdity of the situation struck them. It was like a nightmare straight out of a sci-fi movie, but there was no director yelling "cut" to save them.

"Go! Go!" shouted Jack.

"This way," Martin navigated.

Harlen tripped but hopped back up and resumed running. The cantaloupe creatures gained speed and quickly approached the anguished teens.

"What is that smell?" Olivia said.

"Ew! It's repulsive," Gab exclaimed. "And why is the ground getting soft?"

"Oh my gosh, is this shi—" Harlen called out.

"Sure is!" Gab screamed.

The group soon realized they had traveled into a dung field and their shoes were depressed in feces. Each sticky step was met with the squelchy sound of feces splattering, adding a disgusting layer of difficulty to their desperate escape. The combination of terror and the nauseating environment intensified their determination to outrun the nightmarish cantaloupe-creatures and find clean ground as quickly as possible.

"Keep running!" Jack shouted, fighting to take each mucky step.

"This is just horrific!" Martin yelled.

"I think I'm going to throw up," Jack said.

They finally reached the edge of the dung field, which would have been good news if it wasn't also at the edge of a tall cliff.

"What do we do now?" Olivia cried in panic.

"Look! We're over a big river. We're going to have to jump," Jack proclaimed.

"What?" screamed Harlen.

"Yes, we are going to have to jump off of the edge of this damn cliff and into the water below! We have no choice."

"No way, man, that's impossible," Harlen said. "Wait! They've stopped. They're not coming across their own crap."

"You're right, they've stopped," Gab confirmed. "But they're still surrounding us and we have nowhere to go but here in this crap...or down."

"Exactly. So let me say it again: we have to jump. Yes, it's quite the jump, but we don't have much of a choice, do we?" Jack reiterated.

Suddenly, the insect-like organisms underwent a mechanical transformation. Their spindly legs, composed of intricately interlocking components, extended. The teens could hear a metallic hum as the leg extension process unfolded with precision. The cantaloupe-critters increased their height by two feet, giving them an even more imposing presence.

"They're starting to move again!" Olivia shouted.

"Okay, okay! I'll jump first," Jack offered.

"It has to be at least a hundred feet down," Gab gasped.

The creatures made their way across the poop field accompanied by the sound of sloshing as hundreds of long mechanical legs flung feces in all directions. Their bulbous, segmented feet were equipped with twisting tendrils sprouting out like deformed toes and ending in sharp, claw-like tips. With each step, these tendrils firmly gripped the ground, propelling the creatures forward.

"I'm too scared. I can't do it!" Gab said, looking over the cliff.

"Gab, we don't have a choice," Jack said again.

With his heart pounding like a drum, Jack took a bold leap off the precipice and plunged into the shimmering abyss below. The world above disappeared and he was swallowed by the stinging shock of entering the cool river water. His friends perched themselves at the edge of the cliff, eagerly anticipating Jack's triumphant return to the surface of the water.

Seconds seemed to stretch into forever, but then, with an infectious grin, Jack emerged from the water, his excitement radiating to those far above him.

Martin, driven by anticipation and a fierce competitive spirit, couldn't wait any longer. He stepped to the edge, ready to embrace the thrilling challenge. With a spirited whoop, he launched himself into the air, aiming for the perfect entry into the river.

Olivia, her eyes sparkling with excitement and a dash of playful defiance, eagerly followed Martin's lead. She soared through the air with grace, her laughter merging with the rush of the wind as she descended toward the sparkling depths.

Harlen and Gab, both grappling with fear and reluctance, agreed to jump together. In their exchange of glances, a clear undercurrent of apprehension persisted, casting a shadow over their choice—which was not really a choice. After a hesitant pause, they took a collective breath and leaped.

Their bodies hurtled through the air in a breathless descent. As they plummeted toward the water below, the wind roared in their ears, drowning out all sounds except their screams.

Chapter 18

"**W**here's Gab!?" Jack shouted to his friends who had surfaced after their risky jump. Jack panicked and swam around the area where he believed she had entered the water. He then dove deep in search of his girlfriend.

"Over there!" Harlen pointed to a swatch of red liquid surfacing nearby.

"Oh, my gosh!" Olivia exclaimed.

Jack swam toward the blood as Gab's body floated to the surface, face down. He turned her over, wrapped his arms around her, and pulled her to shore where he laid her on her back.

"I know CPR!" Harlen shouted. "Move over, she's not breathing."

The group looked at each other with disbelief, but then with intrigue as they watched Harlen tilt her head back, creating an airway.

Her wound was noticeable—blood soaked the soil underneath her head. Olivia tore a piece of her shirt and used the fabric to apply pressure and stop the bleeding. Harlen began his CPR treatment with thirty compressions to her chest, then breathed twice into her mouth after squeezing her nostrils closed and sealing his lips to hers. Jack paced around frantically with his hands gripping his head and hair. Tears fell as he mumbled worrisome words.

"Harlen, maybe you're doing it wrong," Jack blurted in panic. "Do you even know what the hell you're doing?"

"Will someone please shut him up? I'm losing my count!" Harlen shouted.

Harlen repeated the resuscitation sequence, but Gab's body did not move.

"Come on, Gab, you can do it!" Jack pleaded. "You're strong, you got this."

Olivia and Martin watched anxiously, their hearts weighed down by concern. Suddenly, Gab coughed and sputtered, struggling to catch her breath. She opened her eyes to find her four friends hovering above her.

"You're okay! You're alive!" Jack exclaimed.

"I am?" Gab questioned, still coughing, feeling groggy and disoriented.

Jack dropped to his knees, profoundly relieved by the turn of events. He gently wrapped his arms around Gab's weakened body and held her softly without disturbing her head. With care, he brushed the hair from her face, his touch tender. Tears streamed down his face, mixing with the mucus on his upper lip. But he didn't mind—in that moment, the only thing that mattered was Gab.

As their emotions swirled in the intense moment, Jack leaned in and kissed Gab, a soft silent expression of relief and joy that spoke volumes.

He looked over to Harlen, who was still out of breath, and whispered, "Thank you."

Harlen nodded, his own eyes filled with tears. "I couldn't let anything happen to her," he said, his voice trembling.

"You're one tough cookie, Gab," Harlen grinned.

"Wow, Harlen, I can't believe you just saved my life," Gab said, looking at him with gratitude.

"I knew CPR would come in handy someday," he joked, trying to lighten the mood.

"You're amazing, Harlen," Olivia said, with tears in her eyes.

"The gash on your head doesn't look too deep," Jack said, gently pressing the cloth against her wound.

"I must have grazed a rock under the surface of the water," Gab said.

With Gab safely breathing and conscious, the group gathered around her. Their adventure had taken an unexpected turn, but they were thankful that quick thinking and teamwork had saved Gab's life. The bond between the friends was unbreakable, and now, more than ever, they realized the depth of their love for each other.

After Gab regained her composure, the five teens cautiously made their way down the riverbank. Here, they found a remarkable transformation in the surroundings. The trees and shrubs displayed a brilliant, almost fluorescent shade of green, in stark contrast to the disquieting landscape they had encountered earlier.

They ventured deeper into this mysterious realm. The towering trees remained strong and resolute, yet they also seemed to exude an unusual warmth. It was as if the branches reached out like welcoming arms, inviting the teens to embrace the serenity of this place. The soil underfoot shimmered, casting a unique and enchanting charm.

Here, an intriguing blend of tranquility and joyfulness coexisted, casting a spell that embraced the teens and filled them with an inexplicable sense of happiness.

"Hey, wow! That's *amaaazing*!" Martin exclaimed, waving his hand in front of his face like he was trying to conjure up ancient spirits.

"What do you see?" Gab asked, trying to decipher the code of Martin's bizarre hand dance. The others stared at him with concern and bewilderment.

"All these butterflies. They're magnificent," he said, holding his hand out like the chosen butterfly whisperer.

"Um, this dude is so high, he's orbiting the moon," Harlen joked, secretly wondering if they had accidentally stumbled into a parallel universe.

"It certainly looks that way," Gab added, suppressing a giggle that threatened to burst like a shaken can of soda.

"Ahhh...this rain is pure ecstasy right now," Harlen proclaimed, caressing his face like he was trying to charm the raindrops to dance with him.

"Wait, what rain? Are they messing with us?" Olivia asked, shooting a doubtful look at Gab. "These two have officially booked a one-way ticket to the *Black Mirror*," she muttered, watching Harlen's theatrical rain ritual and Martin's butterfly-catching extravaganza.

"Ah, damn! You too?" Olivia gasped, gazing at Gab, who was on a quest to be crowned the Forest Hide-and-Seek Champion.

Moments later, Olivia couldn't resist the siren-call of the trippy forest, and she joined in the hallucinogenic carnival, running around like a warrior princess seeking enlightenment.

"Look! It's Kass!" Martin yelled, pointing at the water as if he'd found the legendary Fountain of Youth.

"Kass! Where have you been?" Jack chimed in, giggling like a mischievous sprite.

"Kass! Kass! It's Kass!" Gab echoed, her laughter harmonizing with her imagined universe.

Jack glanced over at the river, and his eyes sparkled with excitement. There was Kass, sailing down the river on a makeshift raft like a wild river deity, his bare-chested magnificence causing even the trees to swoon.

Martin stripped down to his underwear, dived into the water, and swam like a possessed Olympian. But as soon as he reached Kass, *poof*! Martin's beautiful boyfriend-mirage disappeared into thin air.

"Where's Kass? He vanished. What kind of mythical riddle is this?" Gab exclaimed, staring at Martin's wet escapade. "We've crossed the threshold into the realm of epic mind-bending, and I'm not sure I want to return."

"I've never been high, but this feels like being on a roller coaster through the cosmos," Harlen admitted, half enjoying the wild ride and half wondering if they'd ever return to their familiar reality.

"It's starting to wear off," Jack said.

"Do you think this water has somehow become imbued with hallucinogenic properties?" Olivia pondered.

"Indeed," Harlen said, his eyes locked on the mysterious river.

"Let's get Martin back over here," Jack said.

Jack, Harlen, Gab, and Olivia waved their hands, trying to get Martin's attention.

But Martin, still under the influence of the hallucinogen, had become engaged in an eccentric dance, twirling a large branch like a lover. His movements were hypnotic as he continued to revel in his altered state of consciousness.

Soon Martin's psychedelic journey subsided and he regained some semblance of coherence. He looked around, only to discover he was on the opposite side of the river—alone, nearly naked, and dancing with a stick, which he had deliriously mistaken for Kass. A bewildered expression crossed his face as he pondered the comical predicament he had unwittingly stumbled into.

"Martin! Swim back across but don't swallow any of the water," Harlen shouted.

"What? Swim on my back across the water?"

"No, don't drink the water!" Gab and Olivia shouted together.

"Don't drink the water?"

"Right, don't drink the water. Hurry, swim across," Jack yelled, signaling with a swinging arm.

It was inevitable Martin would consume at least a small quantity of water on his journey across the river. He arrived high, delusional, and filled with joy. Olivia and Harlen sat near him on the bank while he sobered.

Jack and Gab sat together, overlooking their friends keeping a vigilant watch on Martin. When Gab turned her head toward Jack, she was surprised to see tears welling up.

"Jack, what's wrong?" she asked.

"I thought we saw Kass. This whole thing is messing with my head. I'm now genuinely worried about him." Jack wiped away a tear.

Gab wrapped her arm around his shoulders. "I'm scared too," she admitted. "I'm worried for all of us, but especially for Kass."

"Where do you think he might be?" Jack's voice quivered.

Gab took a deep breath, trying to keep her own emotions in check. "I don't know, but I'm hoping he's at home organizing his shoes alphabetically."

Jack forced a smile, which quickly faded. "I don't think so. I think he ended up somewhere around here and didn't survive. I know it's a terrible thought, but come on, we know Kass. He wouldn't last an hour in this violent forest alone."

Hearing Jack's words, a single tear fell from Gab's eye. She fought to remain strong for both of them, but the fear was overpowering. "Well, let's hope for the best. Let's keep our spirits up and stay optimistic," she said.

"You're right, my boy is strong. There's a whole 'nother badass about him now," Jack said, proudly.

"Exactly, we will find him and he will be fine."

Jack and Gab soon joined the group to walk downriver together in search of food and shelter, and possibly Kass.

They trudged on in silence, each lost in their own thoughts, searching for a glimmer of light within the darkness.

Chapter 19

The dawn of the next day found the group of five friends still entranced by the lush greenery, the exotic birds, and the hidden secrets within the dense foliage. But on this particular day, dark clouds amassed overhead, unleashing a torrential downpour that seemed to foreshadow an imminent and harrowing disaster. Lightning illuminated the sky and the roar of thunder echoed through the forest, shaking the ground beneath their feet.

The faces of the teens showed concern even after seeking refuge and finding temporary sanctuary from the downpour under the thick foliage of a massive ancient tree with gnarled roots.

Jack surveyed their surroundings, his brows furrowed with worry. "We can't stay here. The wind speed is accelerating; this tree won't protect us for long. Things are getting out of control."

Olivia, clothes already soaked and clinging to a tree branch for stability, nodded vigorously. "I can't believe how fast this weather turned on us. It's like the jungle knows something we don't."

"We'll get through this. Let's keep moving and find shelter," Gab said.

The group set out but not more than ten minutes later, they realized they had lost sight of Jack. He had been with them moments ago, but was nowhere to be seen.

"He was right behind us," Harlen shouted through the downpour.

"Go back the way we came and keep shouting his name," Martin said, his body swaying in the savage wind.

The group began their frantic search for their missing friend, but their shouts were drowned out by the thunderous storm. They pushed back through the thick undergrowth. Visibility was poor and anxiety gnawed at them. Then, somewhere in the distance, they heard a weak and trembling voice. They followed the sound and there was Jack, huddled beneath a large fern with a heavy branch laying next to him. Jack's face contorted in pain as he clutched his chest.

"Jack! Are you okay?" Gab rushed to him.

Jack struggled to speak through gasps of pain. "This bra nch...broke...flew into my chest..."

Harlen knelt beside him and assessed the damage. "Maybe he broke a rib. Maybe just bruised. We need to find shelter and get him out of this rain."

Desperation fueled their efforts as they assisted Jack under the nearest large tree to somewhat shield him from the rain and wind. The storm showed no sign of letting up, making their isolation more apparent than ever.

They struggled to make Jack as comfortable as possible but their surroundings suddenly transformed into something straight out of a nightmare. Comfort was no longer an option.

A creature emerged, unlike anything the group had ever seen: a colossal frog, easily a hundred times the size of a regular one, with the bulk of a prize-winning hog. Its huge, webbed feet left a sticky residue on the wet jungle floor, while its skin shimmered with an array of iridescent blues, vivid greens, and fiery reds, creating a mesmerizing and surreal display against the backdrop of the forest. These colors stood out starkly against the dark and stormy atmosphere surrounding the area.

Olivia's jaw dropped as she stared in awe at the creature. "What is that thing? It's enormous."

Martin whispered, his voice barely audible, "Is it even a frog? Look at those teeth!"

Harlen's gaze locked on the magnificent but ghastly creature. "We can't stay here. It's coming closer!"

They watched in astonishment as the colossal frog moved with deliberate purpose, its vibrant colors captivating their attention. The amphibian's enormous predatory eyes stared at the teens like it had never seen anything as tasty. With elongated limbs ending in razor-sharp, hook-like claws, its deadly intent was obvious.

"It's not docile at all. We need to do something," Jack said, always the protector of the group and scanning the area for any possible escape route.

The frog came within striking distance. Jack, still in pain and struggling for breath, stood bravely in front of his friends. He held his spear with both hands in front of him and pointed it in the frog's direction.

"Jack, sit back down and rest," Harlen said.

"No, I'm fine. I'm okay now."

In a flash, the frog unfurled its tongue, a fierce appendage that shot out with incredible force, and wrapped it around Jack's arms still holding the spear.

"Jack! No!" Gab screamed, as the gigantic frog attempted to pull Jack into its gaping maw.

In a rush of adrenaline, Jack yanked himself free from the tongue's powerful grip, which then retracted into the creature's mouth. The frog continued to stand its ground before them.

"We can't stay here. We need to find a safer place to take shelter. Jack, are you okay? Can you walk?" Martin asked.

Jack, still catching his breath, nodded weakly. "I think I can. We have to get out of here."

"Watch out for that tongue! Spears ready!" Martin said.

They slowly and cautiously began to edge their way around the massive amphibian. The heavy rain continued, masking their movements. Each step was filled with tension knowing the creepy creature was watching their every move.

Except for its big bug-eyes, it remained perfectly still, limbs flexed, poised for action. The iridescent colors of its skin intensified, creating a hypnotic spectacle in the midst of the pouring rain.

Finally, the teens managed to circle around the obese beast and move further away. The adrenaline coursing through their veins made the driving rain a minor discomfort.

They forged ahead, their soaked clothes clinging to their bodies. The group's determination to find safety and escape the colossal frog's presence pushed them forward.

After an arduous journey through more jungle, they came upon a small indentation into the side of a hill. It wasn't much, but it offered some protection from the weather and a chance to regroup. They ushered Jack inside, where they hoped he could rest, regulate his breathing, and ease the pain.

The others gathered around him, understandably worried. But Harlen was beside himself. He paced back and forth, his mind racing with thoughts of their encounter with the colossal frog. "We can't stay here," he said. "We're not safe enough."

"Harlen, take a breath," Gab said. "Calm yourself. Jack needs to rest and the storm will pass. Then we'll move on. Until then, we need to stay right where we are. We've faced challenges before, and we'll face this one, too."

"And we should gather some supplies from the jungle as soon as we have the chance," Olivia added. "We don't know how long we'll be stuck here."

When the rain let up, the others left Harlen with Jack, and risked venturing out to search for anything that might be useful. They gathered branches and brush for a makeshift shelter, found some fruit to eat, and even managed to collect enough fresh water from an ephemeral stream that had formed from the rain runoff.

They then sheltered in place, huddled together to keep warm while simultaneously remaining vigilant should more danger be lurking.

"I've read about strange adaptations in Amazonian wildlife, but nothing like that frog," Olivia said. "Its colors were bizarre, almost hypnotizing and obviously designed to lure prey. But what could it possibly eat to explain its size?"

"Well, with that tongue and those weapons disguised as feet, I'd say it could eat a lanky boy with no problem!" Harlen said, not even trying to be funny.

"Relax, Harlen. You're safe with us," Gab said with a smile. "Maybe it's a guardian spirit of the jungle. Indigenous tribes have stories about creatures that protect their lands. Maybe we just wandered into its territory and it's no longer threatened by us."

"Ya, I'm going with Gab's theory," Jack said. "I mean, I love Gab's tongue but not a slimy frog tongue wrapped around me!"

Everyone laughed.

Despite their theories, they were all in agreement about one thing: they needed to get further away from the overgrown amphibian.

When Jack's pain began to subside, they decided to make their move and prepared to leave. With caution, they ventured back into the jungle, each step deliberate, sensing big bulbous eyes on them.

They slowly ventured away from the frog's territory, but the rainforest was unforgiving. Their path was fraught with obstacles. The relentless downpour had turned the jungle floor into a muddy quagmire, making each step a struggle. Vines and roots snaked through the underbrush, impeding their progress.

Their arduous trek eventually led them to a fast flowing river, swollen from the rainstorm. The river was too dangerous to cross at their current location, which left the group with a difficult decision: how to continue their journey without putting their lives at further risk.

Olivia scoured the area for options. "We need to follow the river in search of a safe place to cross. That should ensure we're out of the frog's territory."

They continued to traverse the muddy terrain, clambering over roots and wading through shallow tributaries created by the storm. After less than an hour of hiking, they stumbled upon a fallen tree, its roots exposed on their side of the river and its rather slim trunk lying the full width of the river. Crossing over was a daunting thought but the trunk appeared sturdy enough to serve as a bridge—albeit a skinny and slippery one. The turbulent river six-feet below posed a significant threat.

"This is our way across, but it won't be easy. We need to cross one-by-one and be extremely careful. If we slip, the current will carry us away," Martin said.

The muddy water of the swollen river rushed with an unstoppable force, another reminder of the jungle's staggering power.

"Okay, let's do it," Harlen agreed.

"We can do it," Jack said, even though he was still in considerable pain.

"I want to go first," Olivia surprised everyone by saying. Her steps were deliberate and she used a sturdy branch as a makeshift walking stick for balance. The others watched with bated breath as she made her way to the other side where she waved with a smile and a "thumbs up."

As Harlen made his way across, he glanced down at the fast-flowing river and immediately felt the effects of vertigo. He staggered but regained his balance and kept his eyes on the tree trunk in front of him for the remainder of the way. Martin was the last to cross. His steps were cautious and his heart pounded but he reached the other side successfully and the group let out the breath they didn't realize they had been holding.

Then, because the more tapered end of the tree trunk was near them, they worked together to swivel the tree away from the shore until the river's current pulled it to point downstream. They hoped this would deter the frog or any other dangerous creatures from attempting to cross the violent river.

Their journey continued with the group pushing through the underbrush. The heavy rain returned and the soil suddenly began to appear deformed with lumps rising as if sprouting seedlings. However, it wasn't vegetation emerging. Instead, hundreds of grotesque cucumber-sized caterpillars, moving with a synchronized, unsettling rhythm, began to inch upward. Slimy and semi-flaccid, their presence once again transformed the rainforest into something eerie, odd, and potentially threatening.

"What the hell are those!" Jack yelled.

"Caterpillars, no doubt!" Olivia echoed Jack's yell.

"Pick up the pace!" Jack demanded.

The teens struggled through the rain-soaked terrain, each step hindered by the slithering horde of caterpillars that were mysteriously emerging from the ground.

Even more mysterious, when those carrying the jewel-embedded spears turned to observe the caterpillar-creatures, the jewels on the spears emitted an unusual light.

And just as quickly as the caterpillars had transformed into chrysalises, their metamorphosis became complete when, within minutes, they emerged as bioluminescent butterflies. Their wings unfurled with intricate patterns, each delicate line and curve glistening.

The radiant energy that emanated from the gems in the spears had somehow triggered this metamorphosis process, turning the creepy caterpillars into mesmerizing beings of light.

In a surreal display of beauty, the butterflies encircled the group and a blissful sense of serenity washed over them. The air, once thick with tension, now reverberated with a harmonious hum.

Embraced by the soothing energy of the butterflies, the teens continued their journey through the rain-soaked terrain feeling renewed.

After hours of laborious trekking, they stumbled upon a clearing in the jungle. "We should rest here for a while and gather our strength," Jack suggested.

The rain had finally eased into a gentle drizzle and rays of sunlight began to filter through the canopy above. Jack's condition had mysteriously improved after their calming encounter with the butterflies and within twenty minutes the group felt ready to continue in earnest in their search for Kass and civilization.

They trekked along the river where humans would most likely be settled and came upon a waterfall, its cascading waters shimmering amid the rain-soaked surroundings. It provided a brief respite—a chance to bath and refresh themselves while taking in the glorious beauty surrounding them.

"This place is incredible." Olivia marveled. "Forgetting about the beasts and creatures for a moment, we've seen more beauty in a week than most people see in a lifetime."

"Yep. We'll have quite the story to tell when we make it out of here," Martin said.

"That's right. Soon this will all be like water under the bridge," Gab said.

"More like water over the falls," Harlen quipped.

Finally, the drizzle ceased and the sun cast its golden warmth upon the rainforest. The group of friends, though weary and battle-tested, enjoyed a moment of serenity and hope.

Chapter 20

"What are you collecting?" Harlen asked.

"This is a Manchineel tree, and I'm extracting parts of it," Olivia said, showing him the sap. "It is poisonous to humans and I'm hoping I can make a concoction to ward off any future creatures," she continued, slicing the bark with a knife and exposing the sap. "The toxins can produce an unpleasant smell. The milky white sap of the tree, in particular, has a strong, acrid odor."

"Oh, wow, that does stink," Harlen said, after taking a whiff of the sap on the tip of Gab's knife.

"It can cause severe skin irritation, blistering, and burning sensations."

"Ah, I'm so glad you're here with us. Wait, I mean, I'd rather you be home with your family, but I'm glad you're here with us. I mean, if I was going to wish someone—"

"Harlen, I get it," Olivia laughed.

The teens created another small, protective lean-to for shelter. Olivia then spread her concoction of plant poison along the outer wall and surrounding area. She knew she was putting innocent insects and animals at risk, but had decided it was a necessary sacrifice in keeping her and her friends safe.

The sun slowly disappeared and the moon illuminated, piercing through the trees like calm laser lights brightening the eerie forest. The serene night draped them in peace, granting the teens a deep and restful slumber.

Harlen leaned against the weathered wall of the lean-to during his watch duty. His thoughts swirled with both gratitude and dread. The survival skills he and his friends had honed during their harrowing journey seemed like substantial threads holding them together. He also understood that if it weren't for the support and courage of Jack and Olivia, the outcome for the five of them might have been a far more gruesome tale.

After enduring three long hours on watch duty, the teens rotated shifts, passing the torch to ensure vigilance.

In the light of the new day, they relished the comfort of the sun's rays and smiled at the chorus of birds that welcomed the dawn. Their melodious chirps filled the air as they flitted about with carefree exuberance.

The teens' ability to see their surroundings more clearly provided a glimmer of security in their battle for survival. They appreciated the reassuring ability to, at the very least, discern what might be hiding amongst the trees, concealed in the crevices of the rocks, or swimming beneath the surface of the river.

But with the new day also came their most pressing mission—the hunt for food. Having ventured far from the contaminated and hallucinogenic waters, they had endured a grueling twenty-four hours without a proper meal.

"If you say 'famished' one more time!" Martin snapped at Olivia, his patience worn thin as they followed the riverbank in search of a proper fishing hole.

"Famished, famished, famished. Find me food and I'll shut up," Olivia retorted.

"Here, give me this," Martin said, seizing the spear from Jack before wading into the river.

Martin moved with painstaking precision, careful not to disturb the water. He thrust the spear repeatedly, each jab aimed at an elusive fish darting beneath the surface. The group watched with anticipation, some masking their hunger with chuckles, while others stared with desperate longing.

Martin jabbed again and again...and again until, finally, he held up what looked like a nice-sized snapper with a spear piercing through its body.

Laughter and cheers of excitement resounded from the shore as his friends celebrated the accomplishment. Martin roared like a fierce hunter who had finally captured his prey.

He pulled the fish from the stick and flung it over to Harlen, then returned to the hunt. Within the next hour, Martin succeeded at catching four additional fish, then left the water feeling victorious.

His mates were proud of him and excited for their upcoming feast. Jack started a fire and Olivia concocted a birch bark sauce with berries and water.

In many ways, Olivia remained the backbone of the group. She kept them organized and her survival skills helped them immensely. She knew which berries, mushrooms, and other bits of nature were safe to eat and which were poisonous. She knew about rocks, insects, and animals. Olivia also knew about astronomy as well as minor medical remedies. She was by far the most knowledgeable person in the group. As much as she loved having this rank, she also sensed it taking a toll, being the informative one, the responsible one. Consequently, she often felt alone, even in the company of her friends.

Harlen and Martin sat away from the others while everyone was enjoying their grilled fish. "Hey, can I ask you a question?" Harlen asked.

"Yeah, sure, what's up?" Martin replied.

"Did you always know you were gay? Wait, you're gay, right?"

"Ha, yeah, I'm gay. I knew it even before dating Jessica. I think I knew when I was about eight or nine."

"So, why date Jessica? I haven't met your parents, but your siblings seem cool. Do you really think your parents would have a problem with it?"

"No, probably not. It was mostly my peers and my soccer teammates," he admitted with a touch of resignation. "I really wanted to play and I couldn't risk everyone knowing I was gay. I was sure I wouldn't make varsity or become a team leader—or so I thought. I believed I could hide it, blend in, perhaps even end up marrying a girl and having a family. You know, the typical dream every soccer player seems to have."

"Why eight or nine? What happened then?"

"Hmm...well, it wasn't like something happened. For instance, when did you know you liked girls?"

"I think I just always knew," Harlen said. "I mean, I don't know. I grew up thinking that boys and girls are supposed to be together. Cartoons, movies, TV shows, and even music on the radio. I don't think I knew being gay was an option. Wait, am I saying that right? An option?" Harlen's innocent ignorance challenged his approach to the conversation.

"Exactly. This goes back since I was five. My dad and I would watch soccer and all of the soccer players were either single, had a model girlfriend, or a wife and kids. I never heard of a gay soccer player. And by the time I was in the locker rooms with the dudes, there were so many gay jokes, and 'that's so gay' comments, there was no way I could even think about being true to myself. I spent my time hiding, being scared, and worse, lying for so many years," Martin shared, tears filling his eyes.

"Man, I never thought about it like that. Never thought about how rough it might be for some. But how did you *know*, know?"

"Well, I'm sure you had a moment when you saw a girl and was like, 'wow...I like that.'"

"Yeah, you're right. I did have that moment when I saw...well, I get it. I was about seven and I remember feeling all weird inside when I saw this girl for the first time."

"That's exactly what I felt when I was nine. And I have only felt that way toward boys, not Jessica or any girl. Jessica was the pretty, popular girl, and growing up, watching the athletes and all the shows...well, I thought I was supposed to do it the same way in order to be accepted and successful. And then Kass walked by me one day in the hallway, and I was like, 'whoa...there's that feeling again.' It was even stronger than when I was young. I started crushing on Kass big time."

"Hey man, it'll be alright. I'm sure Kass is okay and you two will be together again," Harlen reassured him with a few pats on his back.

"Yeah, I think he's okay. He has the special powers from the gemstone protecting him. It's us that I'm worried about. These jeweled dagger spears don't exactly scream 'confidence boost' for me right now."

"Well, we have Olivia. In fact, without you, Gab, and Jack, I'd be dead duck by now," Harlen said.

Jack, Gab, and Olivia looked over at Martin and Harlen laughing together and exchanged glances—a drastic difference from their usual banter and conflicting views. A deepening bond had clearly taken a leap forward.

"Well, nothing like connecting over fresh fish and a teleported adventure," Jack said to the amusement of Gab and Olivia.

After their meal, Jack extinguished the fire, making sure there was no chance of anything reigniting. Then he and Martin returned to the water to spear more fish for the day. Gab, Olivia, and Harlen gathered more berries and bark. With hours of daylight left, their appetites satisfied, and their bodies well-rested, they packed their bags, gathered their utensils, and began the next leg of their journey into the unknown. They were in great spirits, laughing and enjoying their quiet hike.

"Here, let's climb to the top of this hill and get away from the water for a while. We'll have a better view of the surrounding areas," Gab suggested, directing the group uphill.

"Let's do it," Harlen said, with a little more pep in his step.

They trekked through the shrubs and trees until the forest opened to an expanse of exotic flowers, birds, and small unusual trees. The teens were enchanted.

Then when they reached the top of the hill and looked further to the west, they noticed a bright green square of land and a pristine configuration of trees. The trees stood in a majestic formation, their graceful branches reaching skyward like outstretched arms embracing the sky. Each tree bore a crown of vibrant foliage.

Gab, Jack, Martin, Olivia, and Harlen all rested in a patch of shade as the sun rose higher in the afternoon sky and heated the land.

"This is just beautiful," Olivia said, sitting with her arms around her knees.

"Yeah, it sure is," Harlen added, lying on the grass with his hands comfortably cradling the back of his head. He was relaxed and enjoying the serenity with his friends.

"Okay, what do we do now?" Jack asked Gab.

"There has to be something out there besides creatures," she stated. "We need to find a road, a path, or signs of human presence."

"I think we're alone out here and we need to just start thinking about building something more sustainable," Jack said.

"Wait, we're going to get the hell out of here and I need you to stop talking crazy and get on board with that," Gab snapped with a tone quite out of her character.

"Whoa, Babe, hold up. I'm with you, completely. We're getting out of here, no question," he amended. "I'm on board with whatever plan you've got."

"Okay, I'm sorry."

"No apology necessary. I had a slight moment of defeat."

The five teens sat for another thirty minutes before descending the hill and continuing their journey. It wasn't much longer until they found themselves surrounded by the forest once again. They could no longer see the top of the hill where they had just sat marveling at the incredible beauty of their new mysterious world.

"Did you hear that?" Jack panicked in response to a worrisome noise in the forest.

"I think we all heard that one," Olivia added.

"We could feel it, too," Harlen said, as a dark shadow cast over them, even though nothing threatening could yet be seen.

"Stay close together," Gab said. "Martin, you keep an eye behind us. Olivia, look up. Harlen and I will look on the sides, and Jack, you keep focused on what's ahead."

They moved forward with haste yet caution, having already experienced the unthinkable and knowing worse could be out there.

Fortunately, whatever had made that sound, soon seemed to no longer be present or approaching.

Less than an hour later, the teens arrived at an open field of grass about a hundred square yards. It was the bright green square they had observed from the top of the hill. The grass was as green as grass could be. It was every gardener's dream. At the conclusion of the open field and on both sides, was a forest of perfectly aligned rows of huge trees. It had the appearance of a giant's tidy fruit orchard, except the trees were the old-growth deciduous trees of the rainforest.

"How odd!" Gab exclaimed. "How to even explain this?" The teens gawked in silence until Olivia continued. "Okay, which way, Captain?" she asked Gab.

"Hmm...this is where your guess is as good as mine. Although, I don't think we should walk straight through the middle of the field."

"I agree. Let's keep closer to one side where we can still see what's around us and above us, while not being too far from the protection of the forest," Martin added.

"I third that," Jack agreed.

"Okay, let's go closer to the right side," Olivia directed.

They continued their hike, finding the open air refreshing as they walked at a calm pace. The gentle breeze swept through the trees, bringing a sense of tranquility to their journey.

Chapter 21

"Wow, look at this!" Martin said with glee.

"Just spectacular," Gab said.

Little shiny stones, jewels the size of jelly beans, began to appear in the grass. Soon the jewels were plentiful at every step. The teens felt compelled to pick up a handful of the gems, then watch how they shimmered as they fell between their fingers and back onto the grass.

"These are rubies, sapphires, emeralds, and some other precious stones I don't recognize," Gab explained.

Harlen unzipped the backpack Martin carried and scooped several handfuls into it. Jack did the same with his backpack. They continued their walk while picking up more stones and admiring the beauty and possible wealth of them.

"This trip isn't turning out to be so bad after all," Harlen announced.

"Umm...this is no trip. Any minute now, the wicked witch of the east will be by with her flying monkeys to kill us," Olivia said. In an instant, time seemed to slow down as they found themselves shaded from the sun. Then, almost as if on cue, the teens simultaneously looked up to witness a flying creature.

"See, trip over!" Olivia exclaimed.

Even at a distance, the creature was enormous. It looked like a pterodactyl, but larger. As it flew closer, they could see bright, colorful feathers covering its body and bird-like wings. The flying creature sparkled, embroidered with what appeared to be the same jewels as on the grass—the same precious stones that had just filtered through the fingers of the teens with handfuls of them finding a home in their backpacks.

They stood as still as one could, watching the creature ascend. But when it started to swoop down toward them, they ran toward the safety of the forest. Jack and Martin gripped their spears with both hands. Harlen and Olivia grabbed hands without even looking at each other. The creature let out a loud shriek. Curiously, however, it suddenly veered away and disappeared. The teens were left relieved yet on high alert.

Mere seconds later, a dozen much smaller bird-like creatures emerged from the other side of the forest and converged in an in-flight circle around the teens. These diminutive creatures were roughly the size of a hawk.

They boasted long, slender featherless bodies—their only feathers adorned their wings. Their beaks were narrow with a subtle downward curve, and their disproportionately large eyes glistened like precious jewels.

"This does not look good," Harlen said.

"We're in trouble this time," Gab said.

"Not for long. On the count of three, stay as a group and run back into the forest. Keep your eyes open with weapons up," Jack directed.

"Okay, on the count of three," Martin confirmed.

"One, two, *three!*"

In a frantic rush, all five teenagers sprinted desperately toward the forest seeking refuge. Martin stumbled and fell hard.

"RUN!" he screamed to the others. They did.

It was a chaotic heart-pounding moment in their desperate dash for safety.

The winged creatures swooped across the grassy expanse, closing in on the fallen teen. In a heroic move, Harlen left the fleeing group to assist Martin rise to his feet, while the others continued to bolt for cover in the symmetrical rows of the oddly designed forest. Only a few strides from reaching the trees, Gab screamed as one of the birds grabbed her hair and lifted her a few inches off the ground. After carrying her a short distance, it lost its hold, causing her to fall hard onto the grassy field, a tuft of her hair still hanging from the bird's beak.

Jack ran over to Gab and helped her up. Together they ran and hid behind a large tree.

Just as Martin and Harlen neared the forest's edge, another bird swooped down, wielding a branch. It struck Martin with enough force to send him tumbling to the ground...again. His spear slipped from his grasp and landed within reach of Harlen, who without hesitation, retrieved it and stood guard over Martin until he could rise. But the combative bird dive-bombed the boys anyway. Martin braced himself for the impending strike but Harlen came to the rescue again. He leaped forward, positioning himself between Martin and the oncoming threat and thrust the spear into the creature with precision. The forest echoed with a shrill screech, followed by a thunderous roar of defeat as the bird fell lifeless to the ground.

Having yanked the fatal spear from the bird, Harlen handed it back to Martin, and the two boys ran into the forest. The birds landed and encircled the body of the slain bird. One comrade picked up the embattled creature's corpse and flew away with it.

"Over here!" Jack yelled to the others. "Run!" he repeated as he led them deeper into the forest.

Jack directed Gab, Olivia, and Harlen to hide inside a large tree hollow, big enough to fit only three people. Jack and Martin stood guard outside with the jeweled spears. They could hear the birds in the woods, but couldn't see them and didn't know if they had taken to the ground or were flying from tree to tree. Olivia pushed Jack away from the entrance to the hollow and commanded him to move so she, too, could stand guard. Harlen and Gab followed close on her heels.

"I don't need you protecting me!" Gab snapped at Jack.

"Yeah, exactly. Look what I did to that flying feathered fucker!" Harlen shouted.

"Here," Martin said, handing the spear back to Harlen with a grin and a nod of 'thanks.'

The teens heard the birds getting near and within the next minute they were surrounded by dozens of bird-like creatures, screeching at ear-piercing levels.

From somewhere in the distance, an angry roar materialized.

The screeching creatures began to approach the teens, whose backs were against the tree trunk. Their weapons erect. Their fears present.

"Aaah-aaah!" a Tarzan-like sound echoed through the forest.

"Shut the front door," Harlen said, as all the teens looked up to see where and from whom the call was coming.

They started hearing more and more loud screeching, but they couldn't see what was happening. The birds around them, now only a few feet away, turned toward the sounds, then flew off. The teens looked at each other, baffled but relieved.

The piercing screams continued along with the rumbling sounds of a violent conflict.

Then silence. Death was somewhere beyond their vision. They could feel it.

"Don't move. Keep looking up, side-to-side, and behind us," Jack advised.

"I'm going to go see what's happening," Harlen announced.

"Dude, this is not *Jumanji*; keep your butt right here," Olivia demanded.

"It's cool. I got this. Stay here," Harlen insisted.

Before Harlen could take a step, however, they heard movement coming toward them. They returned to their guarded position.

"Looking for me?"

"Kass!" Olivia shouted.

"Kass?" gasped Jack.

"Kass!" Harlen cried out.

"KASS!" screamed Gab.

"Oh my gosh, Kass!" Martin yelped.

The five friends lunged toward Kass and gave him an immeasurable amount of hugs and kisses.

Kass looked at Jack and noticed him crying, then scanned the faces of all his friends and noticed them all in tears, too.

Kass pulled Jack into a bear-hug and held him close. Jack sobbed profusely, soaking Kass's face, neck, and shoulder.

"I was so scared you were dead. I love you, Bro," Jack murmured.

"I love you, too," Kass said, still holding onto Jack's huge but diminished body.

The other four friends stood nearby, waiting for their opportunity to hold Kass. And one-by-one, each friend created their own special reconnection.

"This is the second best day of my life," Martin said, whispering into Kass's ear. Their prolonged hug was filled with passion.

"What was the first?" he chuckled.

"The night we kissed."

"Ah yeah, that was pretty awesome. I've thought about kissing you for days," Kass added.

"So, kiss me."

The boys shared their second kiss with Martin pulling Kass close. After the kiss, they took a moment to brush over each other's face with caring eyes, then kissed again.

"Get a room," Harlen said.

The six reunited teens all smiled and laughed. They were finally back together.

Kass had spent many days on his own, fighting to survive without anyone's support. He felt the epitome of loneliness—in a new world without friends, without family, without an understanding of where he was. Kass slept alone, ate alone, and thought alone. The solitude was terrifying.

"Well, let's get out of here. I have a hut set up not too far from here."

"A hut? Great," Harlen said, wrapping his arm over Kass's shoulder.

The group left the area and luckily, there weren't any more flying creatures in the vicinity.

"Wow! You destroyed all these birds," Jack said, looking at the dead feathered creatures sprawled about.

"You still got your superhero powers, I see," Martin added.

"I've been battling for days and my strength has tripled. In the middle of all the fights, I started figuring out some cool moves. With tons of time alone, I've been able to practice and just figure out new things. I assume you've been in battle, too?" Kass asked.

"Yes, every day there's something crazy going on. We thought this could be it for us until you came along," Olivia said.

Kass's friends followed him along the linear forest to his hut. They were happy, and for a moment, they didn't think about all the awful predators that continued to skulk in the forest.

"Kass, this is amazing," Gab said, admiring Kass's hut, which was more like a miniature compound than a simple shelter. It looked sturdy and had spikes on each exterior wall for added safety.

"What did you expect from this boy?" Jack said. "I mean, I agree, I get the designing part of it, but who built it?"

Each three-yard wall had two peepholes, so Kass could survey the outside areas as needed. The shelter was bare inside, but had a single bed frame elevated from the ground. His hut was surrounded by trees, which kept it cool enough to bear the oppressive midday heat.

"How did you do this?" Olivia asked with amazement.

"I had a lot of time on my hands."

"Yes, but how? You are the least skilled handyman on the planet," Harlen said.

"I just thought about all those home renovation programs and Instagram videos I've watched, and here it is. Look at this wall," he said, pointing to a wall with rather amateur construction. "It was my first. Obviously, I've improved my skills with practice."

"And how did you think of the spikes?" Gab asked.

"After being attacked multiple times, I just thought about spikes to prevent creatures from landing on the roof and attempting to enter the hut. I thought of all our buildings with pigeon poop prevention back home. The spike project was a good way to use the enormous amount of energy and stamina I have now."

"Stamina?" Harlen asked.

Kass had taken his passion for fashion and created a wall mural of carved sketches of dresses, suits, and floral patterns on each interior wall. He had transformed his rustic hut into a comfortable place to sleep and feel safe.

"This is much more impressive than anything I've seen in your sketchbook," Jack said.

"Just spectacular. I'm impressed," Gab added.

"Well, we might need to knock down a wall or two and build it bigger in order to accommodate all of us," Kass said, looking around at his creative structure. "Hey, how did you all make out? Did the daggers come in handy?" Kass asked as an afterthought.

"Oh my gosh, yes!" Olivia said.

"So glad you even thought of it," Gab said.

"I learned a lot from observing my dad restore antique pieces, and that inspired me. Despite the inherent hardness of the gemstone, I was able to utilize my dad's specialized tools. The drilling device required hours to chip away at the gem. It was not budging."

"Again, I'm impressed," Jack said.

"Yeah, thank you. These daggers saved our lives, a few times," Martin said.

Kass showcased his skill by leading his friends down an eight-foot path he had cleared from his home to a peaceful courtyard lined with neatly trimmed trees. And in front of his modest hut, he had built a fire pit enclosed by forty tall spear posts. Originally, he had only a single large tree trunk as a simple bench. However, Kass's friends had the opportunity to watch him in action as he brought in another log, smoothed its sides with a rock, and transformed it into a comfortable bench. His deft hand movements were enhanced by his jeweled power, adding an extra touch of craftsmanship to the scene.

Chapter 22

"**S**orry guys, I only got enough fish for one person this morning," Kass said. "We're going to have to venture further down to the river to get more. It will be a few hours before we can return here. Who would like to come?"

"I'm going," Martin said, eagerly.

"I'm not leaving your side again," Jack said.

"I'm in," said Gab.

"I'm tired. I'd like to take a nap or chill," Harlen said.

"I'll keep Harlen company," Olivia added.

Jack, Kass, Gab, and Martin embarked on their one-hour trek to the river. Armed with spears and laden backpacks, they ventured through the forest, acutely aware creatures could be lurking. Luckily, the forest remained relatively quiet as they pressed onward. Jack, Gab, and Martin found comfort in knowing that Kass, resolute and capable, would shield them if danger emerged.

Guided by Kass's knowledge of a prime fishing spot, Martin and Kass efficiently speared over a dozen fish, while Gab and Jack scoured the surroundings for edible berries, flowers, and bark, gathering provisions for their impending feast.

The sun dipped toward the horizon and a gentle breeze embraced the friends. In this tranquil moment, with the evening cooling and nature's embrace around them, they found themselves at ease, grateful for this shared respite.

"So, what's out there?" Harlen asked later, as he chewed a piece of hot, delicious fish.

"Besides animals, I'm not sure. I only know we're back in Costa Rica's rainforests, but I just don't know which way to go to get out of here.

"We'll figure it out. We have six resourceful brains now," Gab said.

"True," said Harlen.

"Wait, umm...Olivia, you're eating fish?" Kass noticed.

"Yes, I was left with minimal options around here. I'm fine though," she said, taking another bite.

"Shh, let her do her thing," Jack said with a grin.

"Olivia, I'm surprised you haven't figured all this out yet. Where are we?" Kass asked.

"Since we were teleported here, I have no clue," she replied.

"I want to know how we were separated from you," Martin chimed in. "How did you end up solo while the five of us landed somewhere else and all together? And since we've been traveling west for several days, we were obviously quite far from you."

"I have no clue. I haven't roamed too far from this spot. I've been to the river and walked a few hours in each direction, but didn't find anything, except havoc. Creatures of all sorts are out there, so I retreated back here each time."

"What's your worst experience?" Harlen asked.

Kass froze and looked down as if in a trance. His eyes became glassy, consumed with tears waiting to fall.

"Kass?" Jack called out from the other side of the fire pit when Kass continued to sit without moving.

"Yo, Kass," Harlen said, nudging him. "You alright?"

"Ah, yeah, I'm good."

"Where'd you go? What happened?" Martin asked.

"This happened," he said, lifting his pant leg to expose an ugly pencil-length scar on his calf.

"Oh no, what happened, Kass?" Olivia asked.

Kass's voice carried a heavy burden as he recounted his horrifying first day alone in Costa Rica. His eyes were haunted by the memories, and the gravity of the situation weighed on them all.

"My first day here was a living nightmare," he began, his voice trembling with the trauma that still haunted his mind. "I woke up, disoriented and face down on the ground, not too far from where we are now. My cheek was caked with gravel, as though I'd either taken a hard fall or had been lying there for an eternity. The world around me was silent, except for small, innocent-looking birds. Nothing vicious like the creatures we've encountered since. I was in shock, calling out to you guys repeatedly, but all I could hear was my own voice. I was terrified. I walked around for hours, oblivious to the setting sun, my panic growing with each passing minute. The realization dawned on me that I had no shelter, and darkness was approaching fast. Fortunately, I discovered that many of these massive tree trunks have hollows spacious enough to provide refuge. I cleared one out and nestled inside."

Kass's eyes welled with fear and sadness as he recalled the moment. "The next morning I awoke to a wolf-like creature, larger than a donkey, with dark black fur and ears grotesquely oversized. It wasn't like any wolf I'd ever seen. The creature stood, breathing heavily, saliva dripping onto my pant legs.

"My body froze while the wolf growled at me for what felt like hours. But then, something incredible happened. I had this burst of strength from fear and adrenaline and kicked the creature, sending it hurtling through the air at least a hundred feet away."

Kass shuddered as he concluded his harrowing tale. "I left the hollow and stood before the tree knowing the wolf would return. And it did—more angry and fierce than anything we encountered back home."

"Then what happened?" Harlen asked.

"The wolf whipped out its super long tongue with a sharp blade on the tip. It sliced a part of the tree trunk next to me and then, in a flash, the tongue returned like a fruit rollup back into its mouth. I'm not sure how it did that without slicing its own tongue, but it did."

"So, then what?" asked Gab.

"I held my dagger tightly and was ready to slice that tongue off if I got the chance. I ran through the forest at break-neck speed but the wolf was super fast, too. I managed to repeatedly dodge its brutal razor-tongue until it finally got me. It struck my leg and dug-in deep. I fell face first onto the ground, but immediately turned over, still holding my knife. The beast creeped up. I prepared myself and when it unleashed its tongue again, I timed it perfectly to slice it off."

"Yes!" exclaimed Harlen, jumping up with a fist in the air.

"It howled and ran off, disappearing into the forest. I haven't seen it or anything like it since."

"Why hasn't your leg healed like your wounds before? Those healed overnight," Jack wondered.

"That, I don't know. It only hurt for a short while and the healing process has been quick, but for some reason the scar is still here."

"Man, I feel so bad you had to go through that alone. Look at you, you're a warrior," Olivia said.

Tears returned to Kass's eyes. No one could fully understand what he had gone through. Around the fire pit, the friends joined hands and felt the familiar togetherness they had cherished over their years. Tears rolled down their faces. It was a solemn yet beautiful moment.

"Why don't we just teleport the hell out of here? What are we waiting for?" Olivia asked.

"Because we don't know how this whole teleportation thing works. I don't want to take the chance of being separated from you all again," Kass replied.

"Fair enough," she said, sitting back against the new seat Kass had just made.

The bright moon shot its rays in between the trees and branches. And given the brisk wind, the trees swayed to and fro, creating a laser-like show one might experience at a rave.

"We're going to turn in," Jack said, standing and guiding Gab with his hand.

"And we are going to sit right here for about thirty more minutes. Right, gang?" Olivia more than suggested, knowing Jack and Gab needed some quality time alone.

"Ah, that sounds great. Thanks," said Jack.

For the first time in many days, Gab and Jack enjoyed being alone and inhaled the privacy of a moment. It was dark, but they were able to capture the silhouette of each other. They undressed down to their underwear and laid their bodies on the ground. They kissed and caressed then, with Jack's body pressed against Gab's back, he gently kissed her neck, then kissed down to her lower back, and with both hands, undressed her completely. His tongue disappeared between her legs, giving her a pleasure she hadn't experienced for a long time.

Gab held her breath and silently released her moans.

"Wait, we can't," Gab whispered, pressing Jack's pelvis away from entering her.

"I know. I know. I just want you so badly," Jack said, returning the whisper.

Jack and Gab fought against their desires, their lips meeting in a passionate kiss before they settled into the perfect spooning position. Then finding a sweet closeness in each other's embrace, they drifted off to sleep.

Just shy of thirty minutes, Harlen pressed his ear against the door listening for any sounds that would have indicated, *Do not disturb.*

"Hey, leave those two alone," Kass said.

"Um...Jack is snoring," Harlen said with a big smile. He slowly opened the door. "They're asleep."

The four retreated into the hut. Martin and Kass also assumed the spooning position, while Harlen and Olivia slept solo, although close to each other. Soon, all six were asleep in a peace they hadn't felt in a long time.

$$***$$

The morning breeze was calm and subtle. The most beautiful birds circled the forest, bringing a sense of harmony to complement the restful balance the teens were feeling as they awoke. For too many mornings they had been waking to a nagging fear of facing another day.

"Where's Kass?" Martin leaped from the ground.

"I'm right out here," he said, outside the walls of the hut. "Who's hungry?"

"Wait, you went down to the river and back already?" Jack asked.

"Yes, remember, I can travel faster on my own and have a quick eye for nabbing the fish."

The other four trailed behind Jack, wiping their eyes.

"Wow, this is great. Thanks, Kass," Martin said.

"You're welcome. My pleasure."

"So, what are we going to do today?" Olivia asked, biting into her fish.

"We need to figure out how to get out of here," Kass said. "I've been focused on building the hut and discovering what is out there, rather than an exit plan. I was afraid if I found a way out, I wouldn't find you five, and I couldn't take the chance of leaving you behind."

"Please get us home, Kass! I don't know how many more nights I can take Jack's snoring and Olivia's farting in the middle of the night," Harlen said.

"Hey!" Olivia snapped, but then smiled.

"How long have you two known each other?" Martin asked.

"Since we were seven years old," replied Olivia.

"Seven? Ahh...that's a long time," Martin said, smiling over at Harlen, who had conveyed his love for someone he had met when he was seven.

Harlen looked at Martin with a caress of blush over his face. Martin put his index finger on his lips to gesture, *Shh. Your secret is safe with me.*

The teens spent their morning revamping their weapons and sharpening their spears, which would help strengthen their ability to conquer the unthinkable.

Carrying their leftover fish, berries, water, six spears, several handmade daggers, and other useful tools, they ventured west, zig-zagging forty-five degrees each day in hopes of discovering civilization or encountering any sign of human life. They were careful to never stray too far away from the river, their dependable water source.

The softball-sized gemstone Kass had retrieved when it rolled off the spine of the huge bejeweled creature remained nestled securely in his backpack and had been his faithful companion since the school camping trip. Upon his transported return to Costa Rica, his intuitive powers had grown proportionately with his physical powers. And his inner sense reinforced his belief that a personal connection with the stone was behind all the attacks from the bizarre creatures. He still didn't know who or what was orchestrating the violence, but he did know keeping the gemstone in his possession was the only chance he and his friends had of surviving.

Deep within the heart of the untamed Costa Rican wilderness, Kass, Jack, Olivia, Gab, Harlen, and Martin set out once again on their expedition. The humid air teemed with the calls and cries of wildlife and the vibrant jungle pulsed with activity. Their footsteps rustled through the undergrowth, each member of the group spellbound by the extraordinary sights and sounds of the natural world.

Then within their first mile of hiking, they stumbled upon a pack of raccoon-like animals, coatis, close to a dozen in number. The coatis, with their sleek, elongated bodies and distinctive long tails, turned their focus toward the group of teenagers, their beady eyes gleaming with curiosity.

The teens froze in their tracks with a tangible sense of foreboding. The coatis, displaying a high degree of synchrony akin to a well-drilled army, let out a high-pitched, eerie squeak, followed by a collective hiss that resonated through the jungle. The sound was a chilling symphony, a testament to the creatures' intent. The group of friends understood they had encroached upon the coatis' territory, and these creatures were not ready to back down.

Their sinuous bodies, moving with a hypnotic predatory agility, started to creep toward the teens. Their fur bristled with unbridled energy. Kass and the others backed away with slow deliberate steps. But the coatis kept closing the distance.

"Everybody, spears at the ready. Prepare to stand your ground," Jack commanded with authority.

"Stay calm. We're not easy prey," Gab added.

"We need a strategy," Harlen whispered to Kass.

The coatis advanced, their hisses growing louder, their glares more predatory.

"Let's form our defensive circle and keep the spears pointing out," Kass suggested.

"And don't forget to watch each other's backs. We're in this together," Olivia said.

"Stay focused, everyone. We've got this," Martin added.

The teens formed the circle, each watching a different direction and determined to protect one another from the advancing coatis. The battle was about to begin.

The first clash was swift and chaotic. One of the coatis lunged at Jack. With a quick, reactionary thrust, Jack impaled the creature on his spear. The coati let out a piercing cry, but its companions showed no fear. Instead, they retaliated with a coordinated attack.

"They're not backing down. Everyone, fight!" Gab shouted.

The battle raged on. Coatis lunged and hissed, their sharp claws slashing through the air. The teens, their adrenaline surging, successfully held their ground. After a grueling battle, the coatis finally realized they had met their match and began to retreat. They hissed and squeaked in frustration as they slinked back into the jungle, disappearing into the dense underbrush. The group's determination and teamwork had paid off.

"We did it!" Martin shouted.

"Well done, everyone. We stood our ground and defended ourselves," Jack said.

With the battle behind them and the mysteries of the jungle lying ahead, the teens could collectively breathe a sigh of relief as they pressed on, their hearts set on finding a way back home.

Chapter 23

Three hours later, the six friends entered a section of the forest with very unusual foliage. The area appeared to be once occupied by some form of web creature. There were webs everywhere. The trees weren't as vibrant and most of them were limp and frail.

The forest felt still and quiet, with small harmless insects crawling about and the occasional flying insect that only took a swat to stave off.

"You know I missed you, right?" Martin said in a melancholy moment, walking side by side with Kass, while the other four hiked ahead.

"Of course, how could you not miss all this?" Kass teased, waving his hand from his head to his lower body. "Joking aside, I missed you, too. A lot."

"We need to get the hell out of here and get back home," Martin exclaimed.

"We will. We'll figure it out. I promise," Kass said, but realizing, perhaps, he shouldn't have used the word *promise*. He wasn't confident at all. He was just as clueless as his five friends.

"The good news is that we've been here before, so there has to be an out," Martin added.

"True. We hope."

"Now, if we can only find some alone time like Gab and Jack had."

"Oh, Martin, you naughty little boy," Kass said, and they shared a laugh.

"Seriously though, if I die, I want you to tell my family how much I love them. Make sure you hug my sister a few times and tell her how special she is to me."

"Martin, come on, we'll be fine."

"No, *you'll* be fine. You have superpowers. We don't know what's going to happen to the rest of us," he expressed with gloom.

"Hey, I'm going to get everyone home to our families and friends. You'll see," said Kass, even more determined than ever to figure things out.

He felt the gravity of saving five other lives and knew the others didn't quite understand that he, too, was scared and unsure of their future.

"So, what did you learn about my friends? I mean, our friends?"

"Well, don't tell anyone I told you, but Harlen has a crush on Olivia."

"Ohhh...Martin can't keep a secret. Martin can't keep a secret," Kass teased in a sing-song taunt.

"Man, I shouldn't have said anything."

"I'm joking. Plus, I already knew that. He told you how he felt about Olivia?"

"Well, he didn't exactly tell me."

"You two have bonded. That's great. I'm surprised he shared that with you."

"I put two and two together and he came clean when I asked him. You know, I'm not a dumb jock after all," Martin said.

"I just thought the ball might have hit your head one too many times."

Martin and Kass enjoyed the playful friendly banter. They were both madly "in like" with each other and yearned to be home to finally enjoy having a normal relationship, something Kass had admired about Gab and Jack's relationship for so many years.

Martin spent half of his time thinking about what it would be like to tell his family, friends, and the coach that he's gay. He also considered that perhaps their opinion didn't matter, although that particular perspective was presently difficult for him. And as his friends had advised him, let no one matter except the two of them. He wanted to do that, yet he couldn't. He wasn't at that point yet. The fear of revealing his true self to everyone haunted him. He replayed worst-case scenarios in his head, with even thoughts of Jessica creeping in. "Oh, that explains everything," she might say in her disapproving way.

The teens ventured deeper into this unusual, web-infested section of the jungle and suddenly the energy around Kass took on an ominous quality. He could feel an invisible electrifying force, enveloping him with supernatural powers.

In a bid to find a moment of solitude to collect himself, Kass stepped off the trail. Within seconds, the fabric of reality shifted. His vision blurred and his physical form became secondary as his consciousness detached from his body. He floated above the forest floor, a mere observer of his own actions, a witness to an extraordinary out-of-body experience.

His physical self convulsed and twitched on the ground below, while Kass's metaphysical self floated above the jungle canopy in a mystical state.

It was during this out-of-body experience that he visualized a creature emerging from the shadows—a creature so nightmarish that it defied categorization. Its face was a ghastly shade of gray, featuring protruding jagged teeth beneath hollow glinting eyes. Covered in scales reminiscent of a serpent, its body bore long claw-like appendages resembling sharp twisted vines. A flowing black membrane cloaked the creature as it moved with an eerie unsettling fluidity, a ghastly manifestation of the jungle's darkest fears.

The cloaked creature nodded sagely. Though its mouth didn't move, Kass heard it loud and clear. "You seek the monolith," it said with a tired yet soothing voice that carried the weight of ages. "The monolith is a sacred artifact hidden deep within the heart of the ruins. It holds the key to unlocking the mysteries of this realm and the power to bridge the realms. The monolith also holds the key to unlocking your gateway home. But beware, for the path to the monolith is fraught with peril, and only those who are worthy may find it. Follow the setting of the sun, find the ruins, discover the monolith."

Kass felt grateful for this information and was about to express his appreciation when the creature uttered its final words in a loud, frightful, and malevolent tone. "But to be worthy of what I am telling you, and before you can seek the monolith, you must first defeat me in battle or die!"

Bolts of crackling energy erupted as Kass, in his spectral state, fiercely defended against this monstrous threat. The creature wielded the powers of the jungle itself, conjuring vines that snaked and struck like lightning.

Reality warped as the ethereal conflict unfolded—a terrifying clash between the sheer determination of a scared teenager and a creature seemingly born from the darkest nightmares of the jungle.

Summoning every ounce of his will, Kass's spectral form channeled immense electrical energy and pushed against the creature's grasp. The beast screeched in agony, its form recoiling. In a blinding flash of light, Kass's consciousness was violently thrust back into his physical body.

Gasping for oxygen and soaked in sweat, Kass returned to his corporeal form, left shaken and trembling from the harrowing battle that had transcended the realms of reality.

As he regained his bearings, the jungle's enigmatic secrets and the surreal battle he had experienced left him in a state of profound bewilderment. The air around him still crackled with an undulating energy, a reminder that this world's wilderness held mysteries far more complex and fantastic than anything he could have ever imagined.

"Kass?" Jack's voice cut through the fog of semi-consciousness, pulling Kass back to the present moment. His eyes fluttered open to discover himself surrounded by concerned faces, Jack's being the closest.

Still disoriented, Kass struggled to find his voice. "What happened?" he croaked. "Where's the creature?"

Jack frowned, clearly baffled. "What creature? We turned around and you had just collapsed or something. Your eyes were twitching like you were having a seizure."

Kass's heart raced as he tried to make sense of the bizarre experience. The memory of the battle with the creature was fresh in his mind, but it seemed to have occurred on a different plane of existence. The line was blurred between what had happened and what his friends were describing, leaving him feeling utterly confounded.

With a deep breath, he began to piece together the fragments of his out-of-body encounter and the ghostly battle that had unfolded. He then realized he had been granted a glimpse beyond the wall of scientific knowledge.

"I was floating in the air," Kass whispered, his voice trembling. "The creepiest of creatures appeared, its face all gray with these huge, sharp teeth, wearing this black cloak. I've never been so scared in my life."

His friends exchanged worried glances; the gravity of Kass's words sinking in.

"Well, we didn't see any creatures with cloaks. Maybe you're dehydrated or something," Harlen said.

Olivia extended a water bottle to Kass. "Here, take a drink. It's crucial to stay hydrated in this heat. Maybe it'll help you feel better."

"I think something terrible is happening to me." Kass's voice trembled with panic. "The creature told me to follow the setting of the sun to find the ruins and the monolith."

"A monolith!?"

"Yes, a monolith. We need to find some ancient ruins and the monolith is hidden within the ruins," Kass emphasized.

Kass then did his best to recall and share in detail the events of his out-of-body experience.

"Hey, you're okay now, Kass. We're here for you, and we'll keep a closer eye on you. We'll get through this together," Harlen said, wrapping his arm around Kass.

Kass leaned into his friend's comforting embrace, still shaken but reassured by the strength of the camaraderie. With the determination to press forward and put Kass's unsettling experience behind them, Olivia took the lead. She spoke with resolve, her practicality guiding their next steps. "We can't afford to linger. The sun sets in the west and that's the direction we've been trekking for days now, so let's keep going and find those ruins."

The group nodded in agreement, ready to face whatever challenges the jungle had in store for them.

***

Days slipped away as the teens forged west in pursuit of the ancient ruins and the rumored monolith. Kass's vision fueled their spirits and empowered them to endure new challenges daily: navigating uncharted lands, the constant search for food, and battles with fierce creatures. What didn't kill them strengthened their bonds as compadres.

Then, on one fateful day, their perseverance bore fruit. Within extremely dense foliage, they discovered a moss-covered stone structure, adorned with intricate carvings depicting mythical beings of yore. It was as if these carvings whispered tales of ages past, secrets hidden within the very heart of the jungle.

"Hey, guys, look!" Martin's voice echoed through the trees. "I think we've found it—the ruins we've been searching for!"

"You're right," Kass exclaimed, his eyes wide with excitement. "This *is* it!"

Fascinated, they approached the carvings and saw depictions of creatures with wings and tails—images that reminded them of their experiences but also stirred their imaginations.

"Maybe these markings are more than mere decorations or historical stories," suggested Olivia. "Perhaps they're a map, or something even greater."

"Whoa," Martin exclaimed, peering closer at the intricate carvings.

"Looks like we're already standing amid the ruins," Gab observed, squinting at the weathered engravings.

Intrigued by the possibility of this being a guide, they decided to trust the path suggested by the carvings. "Fascinating, isn't it?" Gab marveled. "But seriously, where on Earth—or maybe not on Earth—are we?" Her gaze was fixated on the curious markings.

Harlen added, "Yeah, fascinating, but creepy, too."

"We should explore with caution," Jack said, scanning the surroundings for any signs of danger.

"Agreed," Gab chimed in. "Who knows what mysteries lie within."

Olivia's eyes gleamed with curiosity. "I wonder what stories these carvings hold," she mused, stepping closer to examine the intricate details.

"'Let's stick together," Harlen suggested, getting nervous.

With a collective nod, the group ventured deeper into the ruins, eager to uncover its secrets.

Following the cryptic map, they reached a huge open courtyard. Towering stone walls surrounded the expansive space, each surface adorned with even more intricate carvings. An unspoken question of hope ignited within the group. Could Kass's vision be true? Could their discovery of this map, if it was a map, lead them back to their own world and home?

"It's not just a map; it's a narrative," Olivia said after spending significant time studying the walls. "These carvings tell the story of the people who lived here, their customs and their connection to this place. Perhaps they left clues that could help us understand this civilization and, with any luck, find our way home."

As they continued to explore the courtyard, they came upon rooms with murals depicting the culture's myths and legends. One mural depicted a majestic winged serpent, a revered deity, coiled around a massive tree. The creature's eyes seemed to gleam with ancient wisdom and its body was adorned with intricate patterns that suggested a connection between the spiritual and natural worlds.

They moved deeper into the ruins and entered a chamber dedicated to the civilization's understanding of the cosmos. The ceiling of this chamber was adorned with a dazzling depiction of the night sky, the stars and constellations meticulously rendered. The carvings on the walls revealed their advanced knowledge of astronomy, with references to lunar phases and celestial phenomena: cycles, eclipses, and supernatural events.

Another chamber further along unveiled the civilization's profound connection to the natural world. The walls featured intricate carvings depicting animals, plants, and complex ecosystems. The details were so finely wrought that one could almost sense the life pulsating within the stone. Clearly, this civilization revered nature's delicate balance and aimed to pay homage to it through their art.

The group then arrived at a stone altar in the middle of the chamber, crowned with a magnificent gemstone. Olivia studied the carvings encircling the altar and suggested, "This altar is pivotal, signifying something very significant. Perhaps it serves as a portal or gateway, with the gemstone acting as the key."

Kass noticed the gemstone was similar to the one in his backpack, only somewhat larger. As he approached it, its radiance intensified, casting a light over the courtyard. It pulsed with an energy that responded to Kass's presence.

Harlen reached out and grazed the gem's smooth surface with his fingers, setting off an intense rise in its glow. The stone then surged with heat, sending tiny shocks through Harlen before he instinctively withdrew his hand. Despite the sensation, his daring nature compelled him to reach out and make contact again. Suddenly, the ground beneath them quivered, resonating with the gem's heightened luminosity. It was as if the air itself crackled with an electrifying energy, pulsating with an unknown force, drawing them deeper into its captivating aura.

"Something is happening. This gemstone is more than we thought," Jack surmised.

"I don't think this is a good idea," Martin said. "We shouldn't be here."

"We need answers; this place might have them," Jack insisted.

"Yeah, but at what cost?" Gab asked.

Kass felt compelled to put his hand on the large stone as if he were palming a basketball.

In that very moment, the ground buckled and the ancient ruins transformed. The stone structures shifted and everything blurred as if the fabric of reality had been stretched and twisted.

The six teens were thrust into a foreign realm—a place of ethereal beauty and portentous uncertainty. The world they had known—the dense Costa Rican rainforest, the ancient ruins, and the Earth itself—had vanished. In its place was the floating island on which they stood, along with the strange creatures they saw flying around, most adorned with jewels. It was a new reality where the laws of physics seemed capricious. Serpents, pterodactyl-like creatures, griffins with majestic wings, and hippogriffs soared through the air. Everything circled in slow motion, as if time itself had slowed to accommodate the presence of these mythical beings.

Their initial sense of awe was quickly overshadowed by a feeling of disorientation. They exchanged bewildered glances, attempting to make sense of their unbelievable surroundings.

"Where are we? What just happened?" Kass asked, still holding the gemstone.

"This doesn't look good," Harlen quipped.

"No, it sure doesn't," Jack said.

The group struggled to grasp the gravity of their situation. They had been transported to a world that defied the laws of nature, and the gemstone from the altar their only connection to the world they knew.

The floating island, the creatures that roamed the skies, and the ever-shifting landscapes made it clear this world, this realm, was far removed from their own. They had been forced to embark on a new journey beyond their wildest imaginations, and the way back home was shrouded in even more mystery than before.

The gemstone Kass held continued to emit an eerie, enchanting glow with some kind of magnetic-like pull. It refused to release its grip on him.

"I can't take my hand off of it," Kass muttered, his voice trembling with fear yet fascination.

"What's happening, Kass?"

"Jack! I am trying to let go of it but it's like...glued," he explained, his voice urgent. "Help me!"

"Martin, grab the stone from the other side and pull!" Jack ordered. "I'll pull from this side."

Worried with determination, Martin quickly moved to Kass's far side.

Jack and Martin attempted to pry the gem free from Kass's hand. Instead, they became glued to it, as well, and their struggle to break free was in vain. Harlen, Gab, and Olivia then grabbed on to the boys' arms in an attempt to pull them free. Again, the gem's power of attraction resulted in all six teens super-glued together and levitating—suspended in mid-air by the inexplicable force of the gem from the ancient altar.

A surge of electrifying energy tore through them, intensifying in every atom. The gemstone suddenly unleashed a burst of blinding illumination and the floating island became awash in a supernatural radiance, reminiscent of an extravagant fireworks display. The gem's brilliance cascaded, causing the entire island to convulse as if seized by a seismic upheaval.

A collective hush draped over the teens as they bore witness to the gem's might and beauty, their senses overwhelmed by the extraordinary spectacle unraveling before them.

Their hands remained cupped around the gemstone or adhered to another's arm when a new peculiar sensation swept through them. Their eyes twitched from side-to-side in a disorienting manner then forced to shut as if lured into a trance-like state at the command of an invisible force. A force that sought to seize their essence and claim the core of their being.

But even as Kass and the others were levitating together, their souls being sucked away by the unfathomable force of the gemstone, a powerful sense of determination and will enveloped the friends as a unified whole. Just when it seemed they might be overwhelmed by the force within the gemstone, they found themselves back on solid ground in the ancient ruins of Costa Rica.

Their bodies landed with a heavy thud. The now-released gemstone still glowed brightly, its aura suggesting a will of its own.

Silence fell over the group. The teens slowly sat up, rubbed their temples, and took a deep breath. They gathered close to one another, their expressions a mix of astonishment and concern.

"Is everyone alright?" Jack asked.

"I think so. That gem, it was like...was trying to pull me into it." Kass's voice quivered.

"It was sucking the air out of me," Harlen said.

"Ya, and into another dimension," Olivia added.

"It's as if the gemstone has a consciousness of its own, not just an object; it's something more, something alive in a strange way," Martin said.

"We have no idea what we're dealing with," Gab concluded.

With the chamber having returned to its original state and the way made clear, the teens did not hesitate to attempt to exit. However, when they approached the door of the chamber, a deafening rumble echoed through the ruins. Massive stone walls materialized in front of them, rising rapidly and sealing off the exit.

Panic gripped the group. They were trapped with massive stone walls on all sides of them. Entombed.

Kass carefully retrieved his gemstone from the depths of his backpack and cradled it in his hands. The gem appeared to be alive, its light communicating in a way that transcended language and forging an unspoken connection with Kass.

Miraculously, a mysterious maze manifested where only stone walls could be seen. Towering walls like monolithic guardians loomed on the sides of a pathway, guiding the teens into the maze. The shadows on the walls seemed to dance with secrets.

Soon the winding passageways began to stretch out in all directions, their jagged, uneven contours creating a confusing labyrinthine puzzle. Each step the teens took was accompanied by the faint, rhythmic hum of the gemstone, a reassuring presence in an otherwise silent tomb. Its dazzling display of colors guided them with a mysterious synchronicity, always indicating the path they should take.

At one point, they entered a mammoth underground cavern where a subterranean river flowed silently, its waters as black as the night. The gemstone's luminosity revealed an ancient bridge that spanned the river, its construction an awe-inspiring testament to the skill of the civilization that had carved these depths.

They crossed the bridge and ventured further. The gemstone began pulsating with a sense of urgency, as if it were a living entity guiding them toward a specific destination.

They reached the climax of their underground odyssey when, in the heart of the labyrinth, the walls opened to unveil an immense chamber bathed in an iridescent light. In the center of the chamber stood a crystalline monolith, at least five-hundred feet tall with a massive base that seemed as if it could be anchored to the core of the Earth.

The gemstone's pulsations reached a crescendo, resonating in perfect harmony with the energy that emanated from the monolith. As the teens approached, they were overwhelmed by a rush of emotions and ancient memories. Holograms of a once-thriving civilization and advanced technology were displayed vividly on the face of the monolith above them.

"Are you seeing what I'm seeing?" Kass said.

"I am," Olivia marveled.

"This is absolutely fantastic!" Gab exclaimed, her eyes wide with wonder.

"Harlen, seriously, don't touch anything. Last time you did, we were all floating in the air with life being sucked out of us," Kass warned.

"Yeah, Harlen, hands in your pockets, please," Martin chimed in. The teens stood in amazement of the monolith before them, captivated by its mysterious presence and the holograms it projected.

"What do you think this is?" Harlen asked.

"Well, it's certainly not any ordinary monolith," Olivia said in the tone of an obvious understatement. "Let's keep our distance."

"Clearly, the gemstone has been guiding us here," Kass said.

The hologram "movie" or vision, showed the civilization's scientists and scholars toiling tirelessly, their eyes fixed on the night sky, charting the movements of stars and planets, and decoding the intricate languages of the cosmos. Their observatories and laboratories were filled with instruments and scrolls, each crafted for scientific investigation.

Then images of Kelowna, the teens' hometown, flickered like elusive constellations in the cosmic panorama. The monolith transformed into a conduit of detailed scenes, revealing emotional fragments of their past—school hallways, the laughter of siblings, the warmth of a parent's embrace. Yet, intertwined with these memories were moments of sorrow, where siblings and parents shared the sadness in the threads of their lives. A fleeting vision of a familiar street, bathed in the hues of a glorious sunset, lingered as a poignant reminder of a reality they yearned to reclaim.

The holographic scenes shifted, revealing the scientists after their discovery of the magical gemstones, and the extensive research-based journey to understand their magic. In vast laboratories, scholars worked to decode the enigmatic properties of the celestial stones.

The scientists sought to unravel the mystery of how these magical gems became intertwined with majestic creatures. The teens witnessed scenes of a dragon-like guardian absorbing the magic from the gems. Over time, these radiant jewels began to grow and fuse with the creature's very essence, integrating into its body.

The teens' realization echoed through the chamber like a resounding revelation. No longer were the gems mere objects of beauty and power; they had transcended into living, growing entities, like an invasive species using the rainforest's majestic creatures as hosts. This truth loomed over Kass and his friends, adding urgency to their quest to get home. They had every reason to be concerned about the transformation Kass's body had already undergone with the gems taking root within him, especially the growing personal connection he had with the gem in his backpack .

"Does this mean you'll have gems growing out of your body?" Harlen questioned Kass.

"I don't know, Harlen. But if you've noticed, many of the creatures we've encountered so far have had gemstones on them," Kass responded, acknowledging the unsettling possibility.

"We need answers. We've got to either find a way out of this hellhole or uncover some truths before things get worse," Jack asserted.

As the teens gazed upon the magnificent crystal mono-lith, the walls of the chamber, responding to an unseen force, began to shift once again. The friends were involun-tarily forced to move in the direction of the maze's opening. Finally, after a ninety-degree turn, they stepped into the rainforest and the ancient ruins behind them vanished.

They heaved a huge sigh of relief. But their sense of relief was short-lived as uncertainty again clung to them like a viscous mist. They still had no idea of their exact location nor the pathway home.

Jack, the first to break the silence, declared, "We made it out, but what in the world just happened? That felt like something out of a dream."

"I still can't wrap my head around it—from one reality to another and back again," Martin said.

Olivia nodded in agreement, adding, "We definitely strayed far from where we thought we were headed. That was like stepping into a realm of myths and legends."

Gab couldn't help but share her observations, "Did any-one else recognize that dragon-like creature? It gave me major déjà vu from our camping trip. I can't shake the feeling it holds some profound significance in this world."

Kass was silent but when his friends noticed he wasn't contributing to the conversation, he blurted, "I'm pissed off! The vision told me the monolith would unlock our pathway home. But did it? Does anyone see a key or have a clue?"

Finally, Jack, feeling empathy for his best friend said, "You never know, Kass. The vision led us to the ruins. The ruins led us to the monolith. And your gemstone led us through the maze. Let's put our trust in the vision and simply observe how our journey unfolds."

Kass nodded. "You're right, Jack. I need to let go of feeling like I should have all the answers. Instead, let's trust the answers will come to us when we need them."

"Wisdom, man, wisdom!" Harlen declared. "And the answer I need right now is when do we eat!"

After a much needed laugh, the group pressed on, their need for sustenance and shelter compelling them to continue their journey into the unknown.

Chapter 24

The group reached an open field overlooking a river a good three-hundred feet down. They could see flying creatures below, circling over the river.

"What do we do, Gab?" Jack asked.

"Me? Umm...I don't know. Kass, what do you think we should do?"

"Seriously guys, I don't know anything. I know I have some special powers, but it's not like my gemstone is whispering in my ear. So please don't think I know how to get us out of here. I, I mean, I just don't."

"I'm sorry, Kass," said Gab, looking serious. "I think we all assumed you would know, or should know. But, of course, that's ridiculous and I'm sorry if we've been putting that pressure on you. Please don't feel like you have to figure this out for us. We'll do that together, as a team."

"Thanks, Gab. I appreciate that. But I also understand. These powers are amazing. I just feel like I've reached my limit after seeing what we saw in the ruins. I can't do this on my own anymore. I need input from everyone," Kass shared.

"Okay, from here on, we will do this together," Gab announced. "You have the dominant strength, but we will all need to contribute."

"Agreed," Olivia seconded.

"Yes, from now on we'll make decisions together. Or as usual, I'll take charge," Jack said, laughing.

"Okay, Jacko, so what are we going to do?" Harlen asked.

"Well, for starters, you call me Jacko again and I'll throw you into that river."

"Olivia, you're good at this stuff. What do you think?" Gab asked.

"Well, a rule of thumb is to follow the human footprints or follow the water. Unfortunately, or fortunately, there aren't any footprints. We could try to find the hut, wherever that is, or continue heading down river and not look back unless we truly have to. So...I think we need to follow the water."

"There's nothing at the hut we really need and I have no idea where it is at this point," Kass admitted.

"I say we keep following the river since it's flowing west to the Pacific Coast. And we know Costa Rica has a populated west coast," Olivia concluded.

"And Kass, if you have another wild vision, will you please inform your friends?" requested Harlen.

"I can do that," Kass said smiling. "Okay, we follow the river."

Everyone agreed. They would leave the fort behind and carry on with their journey west. But first they had to find a safe descent from the bluff and away from the flying creatures they had observed circling below them.

"Man, what I would do for a burger!" Harlen expressed his craving after the teens had been walking nearly an hour.

"Oh my gosh, don't talk about food right now," responded Olivia. "I'd do anything to have something from Gab's dad's bakery."

"We are almost to the river. How about we take a break, eat, and regroup?" Jack suggested.

"When we get home, I am never eating fish again," Harlen added.

"Don't start talking like that, my friend. You might be eating fish for a long time to come," Jack admonished. "Let's just appreciate the fact we have food!"

The fire burned, the fish roasted, and the water boiled for sterilization. The journey down the hill had been creature-free and rather pleasant. They were able to gather enough bark, berries, and other edible items to last for several meals. By necessity, their foraging skills had developed, learning more in a week than they had over several years in science class. Olivia could identify and differentiate among the medicinal plants, helping them with the cuts and scratches they sustained while walking through the wilderness. She taught her friends how to determine if a plant was poisonous by rubbing it on their inner forearm or outer lip, and then waiting twenty minutes to see if there was any reaction. She was a walking wilderness wikipedia and her friends were grateful for her knowledge.

"Hey, we should build a raft to help us get downstream faster," Martin suggested.

"I thought about that," Kass said. "But all six of us on the open water probably wouldn't be the safest. Too many flying creatures and water monsters."

"Yeah, let's stay on land. Good idea, Martin, but I'd prefer to eat fish for dinner than *be* dinner for birds," Olivia said with a chuckle.

After giving their bodies time to digest their meal, they packed up in preparation for the next leg of the trek.

Harlen beatboxed his way down the river, performing familiar tunes the other teens had fun humming and singing along to. His voice and beatbox skills pleased his friends and kept them entertained.

"Where's Olivia?" Gab shouted when she noticed her missing.

"Olivia!" Kass shouted.

"She was right next to me a minute ago," Martin said.

"Olivia! Olivia! Olivia!" Harlen called out with urgency.

They fought a collective feeling of panic and backtracked a few minutes hoping to find her, but she was nowhere in sight. Her spear, however, was spotted on the ground.

"Here, her footprints are right here, but disappear over there," Gab noticed and pointed. "Wait, look. Look at these prints. And there are more headed in that direction toward those huge webs, which could mean..."

"No! We have to find her!" Harlen screamed.

"Martin! Where's Martin?" Kass said.

"What the hell is happening? Grab his spear and stay close together," Jack commanded.

"Here, this way," directed Gab, following the webs and imprints.

"Man, there are so many cobwebs," Harlen said, using his spear to brush them away from his path.

"These aren't cobwebs, they're spider webs," Gab said.

"Spider web, cobweb, same thing," Harlen said annoyed.

"No, Harlen, cobwebs are abandoned spider webs. These are still in use," Gab explained, knowing she was delivering gruesome news.

The four teens continued their search for their friends. And minutes later, they noticed a small enclosed, shoe-horn-shaped bluff about five yards high.

"Oh my gosh, that must be them," Gab bellowed, noticing human-shaped cocoon casings hanging from web lines at the top of the bluff.

"Shh...yeah, that's them," Kass said.

"Don't move. There's one huge fucker right over there," Jack noticed, pointing to a spider the size of a mid-size car about twenty yards away.

"There's another one," Harlen pointed.

The spiders' hairy heads looked as if they wore large afros, while orange pedipalps extended from their faces. Their small beady eyes moved rapidly from side to side. And their smooth shiny bodies were held up by long thin legs covered with erect minuscule thorns. The spiders appeared strong enough to carry a human or tear one apart.

"Can you distract them, Kass, while Jack and I sneak around and take them from behind?" Harlen suggested.

"Take them from behind?" Kass questioned.

"Hey, leave the jokes to me," Harlen said, smiling.

"We have to get them separated," Gab added.

"Okay, here's the plan," Jack said. "Harlen and I will scale that little hill, jeweled spears in hand, and leap onto their backs. You take the one on the right, Harlen, and I'll handle the left. Kass, lead the distraction to catch them off guard."

"Risky, but it just might work," Gab concurred.

Kass added, "Gab and I will charge straight at them with two other spears. Gab, you take the left one with Jack, while I'll handle the other with Harlen."

The atmosphere filled with anticipation as Jack and Harlen successfully ascended the hill undetected. They then positioned themselves for optimal execution of the plan.

However, a guttural clicking noise froze the group in their tracks. Their gaze turned toward the silhouette of a third, much larger spider. Its dark hairy legs gripped the hillside with unnerving speed, closing in on Harlen and Jack.

The gargantuan spider towered menacingly over the landscape, its six malevolent eyes gleaming in the shadows. Upon reaching the hill's summit, it paused, calculating the situation with unsettling intelligence. In a sudden burst of speed, it lunged at Jack, venomous fangs glistening. Jack fell backward, hitting the ground. Harlen, desperate to shield his friend, launched his spear at the massive arachnid. It was in this very moment that Harlen realized he possessed some kind of superhuman power—probably as a result of his experience with the altar's gemstone. Harlen's spear traveled at breakneck speed, alarming and seriously wounding the giant beast. Seizing the opportunity to act, Kass ascended the hill with great speed and positioned himself behind the spider.

"I got this one. Go!" Kass shouted to Harlen and Jack.

Harlen retrieved his spear with lightning speed and left Kass to grapple with the enormous spider. Harlen then leaped off the bluff and landed on his initially targeted spider, riding it like a wild horse in need of taming.

With inexhaustible determination and pumped with adrenaline, Jack also sprang off the bluff, landing on two feet before rolling to break his fall. "Ouch, my ankle," he exclaimed, then stood and balanced his body to avoid falling over again. Masking his pain, he walked several feet and marveled that the pain was already subsiding. Within seconds, it was as if there was never an injury. He too then realized he possessed some form of superhuman power.

Gab and Jack's designated spider, now in rapid pursuit of Jack, intensified the urgency of the confrontation.

Gab's newfound strength from the altar gemstone surged as she ambushed the spider with gusto. Her spear found its mark in the spider's fanged mouth. She then quickly extracted it in preparation of her next strike. Gab impressed herself with how effortlessly her enhanced powers allowed her to navigate the battlefield.

The spider, frustrated by its failed attempts to bite Gab, hissed and lunged in desperation. Gab sidestepped the attack with finesse and, with a burst of energy, delivered a fatal strike to a vulnerable spot in the spider's exoskeleton.

The once-menacing creature convulsed in defeat. Gab stood observing the spider's demise, catching her breath and grinning in amazement.

Kass successfully grappled with the largest spider. Recognizing its impending defeat, the ugly arachnid attempted a hasty retreat down the hill. Jack cornered it and in a single powerful swipe of his spear, lanced multiple eyes. Blue blood sprayed from the spider's eyes and halted its menacing advance.

United in purpose, Jack, Kass, and Gab then joined forces to inflict well-placed strikes to the spider's legs and underbelly. Kass struck one final blow to its back and neutralized the creature.

Meanwhile, Harlen continued his battle with his own tenacious adversary. Despite the spider's agile leaps to dislodge Harlen from its back, Harlen clung tightly to the spear he had thrust into the creature. With each tumultuous movement, Harlen was able to drive the spear deeper into the spider's body. He then yanked out the spear and launched a series of rapid strikes, targeting the spider's neck and head. "Ahhhhh! Die, you miserable son of an eight-legged webber!" Harlen shouted with a brutal stab into the spider's head, dispatching the last of the three spiders.

"Harlen, Harlen! It's done. You killed it," Jack said, pulling Harlen away from the spider.

Harlen collapsed and cried profusely, as if he had gone into a psychotic state of rage. He then lifted his head, looked to the skies, and let out a primal scream.

"Harlen, it's okay. It's over now," Jack said, pulling him up and hugging him.

"Hey guys, up here," Kass shouted, after he and Gab had reached the top of the small hill where they had access to the webs holding the human cocoons.

"I'm going to cut them down, but you have to catch them. Ready? Go."

Kass cut the first cocoon, which dropped about twenty feet and landed in Jack and Harlen's arms. Gently, they set the cocoon on the ground. Kass and Gab quickly moved to the next cocoon, cutting it from its hanging web and watching it also land safely in the boys' arms.

"How are they? Are they okay?" Kass yelled as he and Gab scampered down the hill.

Jack, Harlen, Gab, and Kass carefully cut the web casings that shrouded Martin and Olivia, uncovering their faces first.

Kass carefully cradled Martin's frail body in his arms, his worried expression mirroring the concern engraved on Harlen's face as he held onto Olivia. Both victims were unconscious but alive.

Gab, ever resourceful, reached into a backpack and retrieved a carrion flower root that she and Olivia had prepared earlier for emergencies. She placed some under Olivia's nose and handed some of the root to Kass so he could do the same for Martin. They hoped the aroma would help rouse their friends from unconsciousness.

As the sweet but pungent scent of the carrion flower root wafted through the air, they anxiously waited, hoping to see any sign of movement or awareness from their friends. Olivia's eyes fluttered open. Regaining consciousness, she let out a gasp. A look of disgust crossed her face when she caught a whiff of the carrion flower root. However, her vision quickly cleared and she found herself looking directly into Harlen's eyes. Without hesitation, she reached for his face and pulled him into a passionate, unexpected kiss that left him breathless. After a moment, Harlen reciprocated, wrapping Olivia in his arms and pouring all the love he had harbored for her into that embrace. When they finally broke from the kiss, they exchanged smiles.

Meanwhile, Jack, who had been watching this unexpected display of affection with wide eyes, could only manage a surprised "Whoa."

Martin, still recovering from his unconsciousness, finally regained some composure. He coughed several times before his eyes blinked open. When he saw Kass, a warm smile spread across his face. Kass returned the smile, and in that moment, their unspoken affection for each other was stronger than ever.

"I'm not Harlen, you'll have to wash this crap off of your face before I kiss you," Kass said.

"Wait...what?" Martin raised his head and looked around, trying to understand Kass's obscure comment.

Jack and Kass helped Martin stand, peeling off the excess layers of web residue from his body.

"Come here," Kass said, pulling Martin into a firm embrace. "You had me scared. Don't leave my side again."

"How's your ankle, Jack?" Gab asked.

"Remarkably good, actually. Either it wasn't as bad as I thought or it healed at an extraordinary rate," Jack replied.

"That's fantastic," Kass said.

"But why would it heal so fast?" Olivia inquired.

Gab, Jack, Harlen, and Kass exchanged glances. There was crucial information to share with the two cocoon dwellers.

"Well, it turns out we've all gained some superhuman abilities. We believe it happened inside the ruins when we were connected to the gem on the altar," Jack revealed.

"Wait, you mean Olivia and I have powers, too?" Martin exclaimed.

"That's the theory. Jack, Gab, and Harlen all have them. So, we're assuming you two do, too," Kass explained.

"Wow, that's incredible!" Martin exclaimed.

"Yes, this means we'll be much stronger if we need to fend off any more nasty creatures," Olivia remarked.

"But considering what we saw inside the ruins, with the monolith and everything, I hope our powers don't come with any harmful consequences," Jack added.

The teens were thrilled about their newfound powers, especially having already witnessed Kass's abilities. But they also knew the gems were not just objects of power but living, growing entities. There was reason for concern and Kass began to question whether he needed to cling onto the gemstone in his backpack solely for its powers or if it had become an integral, perhaps dangerous, part of who he was.

The six friends retrieved their weapons and bags and headed back to the trail that would hopefully lead them to civilization. But first, they needed baths to cleanse themselves of the sticky, repulsive residue left by the webs.

Chapter 25

The group resumed their journey through the forest walking in pairs and holding hands to ensure no one else mysteriously disappeared. Martin and Kass were paired up, as were Gab and Olivia, and Jack and Harlen.

While Harlen had hoped that his passionate kiss from Olivia indicated a deeper connection between them, he sensed an awkwardness in their interactions during the walk back to the river. He became lost in thought, wondering if perhaps the kiss had meant more to him than it did to her. Maybe Olivia had simply acted on impulse, overwhelmed with relief at being alive and reunited with her friends.

"Hey man, is everything alright?" Jack asked. "I've never seen you this quiet. I mean, we can talk about how sweaty your hands are."

"Uh, I'm okay."

"I know, you're thinking about Olivia and that kiss she laid on you," Jack said.

"Man, what if she's regretting it?"

"Harlen, so what, don't overthink it. You two are friends and might always be just friends. She loves you. Heck, I'd kiss you too if you were the first person I saw after that horrific cocoon experience."

"True. But what if she changes? What if she feels so awkward she doesn't want to be around me anymore?"

"Maybe have a chat with her later when you two are together. Again, you're the closest of friends. And Harlen, if she's not into you, she's just not into you. You'll have to move on and find someone else when we get home." Jack's big brother approach always played a positive role in their friendship. "Just let it go for now. We need to keep our eyes and ears open."

"So, you want to talk about that kiss?" Gab asked, nudging Olivia as they walked.

"Not really," Olivia replied, seeming curt.

"Hey, I think you do want to talk about it and you should, but only when you're ready. You two have been besties since you were seven. You know he's had a crush on you for years, and I actually think you've been crushin' on him, too."

"I'm sorry, I didn't mean to be rude. I do like Harlen. I love him, but I don't know if I love him like *that*," Olivia said, struggling to express her true feelings. "I have other fluid thoughts and if I start something with Harlen, there's no going back. It could ruin us."

"I get it. It's a delicate situation," Gab said.

"I don't even know how to process it. You and Jack are coupled. Kass and Martin are together. What if we never make it home? What if we are stuck here forever?"

"Then you marry Harlen and you have a bunch of awesome babies," Gab said, trying to lighten the mood. "Hey, relax about it for now. Just have a conversation with Harlen when you two are alone. I'm sure nothing is more important to him than his friendship with you."

"Okay, so what did I miss, Kass? Did Olivia and Harlen actually kiss?" Martin inquired, walking side by side.

"Ha, they sure did. It was amazing. It was straight out of a movie."

"So, do you think sparks will fly between them?" Martin asked.

"It's a bit of a mystery. Being out here for so long, they might hook up, but as for a full-blown relationship, that remains uncertain. Olivia's into girls as well, you know."

Martin's eyes widened with surprise, the revelation catching him off guard. "Oh, I had no idea about that. Fascinating," he said, his curiosity piqued.

***

The sun was setting and a cool breeze arrived. It came time to build a shelter to protect themselves through the night.

Kass and Olivia, being the shelter-building experts, directed everyone to gather branches and rocks of various sizes. They then efficiently orchestrated the building of the overnight lean-to. It was nothing elaborate like Kass's compound, but it was safe and sufficient.

The somnolent friends ached for rest. Jack pressed himself to Gab's back and they, once again, immediately relaxed, closed their eyes, and fell fast asleep.

"Come here," Harlen, who had laid himself down in the shelter, whispered to Olivia. "Let's not be awkward about this. That kiss was great, but our friendship is even better. Come on...come lay next to me." Harlen patted the ground and looked at Olivia with soft eyes.

"Okay," she whispered with a little smile.

"What do you want? Spoon? Head on my chest? My head on your chest?" he asked, again trying to erase any tension.

"Well, I'm not spooning with you," she said and they chuckled together in hushed tones.

"Yeah, you kinda got me all worked up earlier. Here," he said, tapping his chest on which she laid her head. Harlen wrapped his arms around her and they too fell fast asleep.

Kass and Martin sat in front of the fort having volunteered to be the lookouts for the first three hours of the night. They held their spears and engaged in quiet conversation to keep each other awake. "I wonder what my sister, mom, and dad are doing right now," Kass shared in a quiet voice.

"Yeah, I wonder about my family, too, especially my sister," Martin said.

"I've watched so many movies where someone goes missing and the search ends," Kass added.

"Hey, no one is ending their search for us just yet. Still too early in the game. I just can't believe we're in a situation like this. Who would have thought? We should be goofy teens getting into other kinds of trouble, not disappearing in Costa Rica," said Martin with a sigh. "You know, like getting drunk and arrested at a park. Spray painting something. Being in the wrong place at the wrong time. Stupid teen stuff."

"Yeah, knowing me, I'll probably avoid all of that stupid stuff during my adolescent years," Kass said.

"Yeah, you do seem like a good boy."

"Hey, I never said I was a good boy," Kass teased in a sexy voice, raising his eyebrows and giving Martin a quick wink.

Martin smiled and took Kass's hand while they continued to hold their spears in their opposite hands. They sat silently together under a canopy of stars, hearing only the burbling flow of the nearby river.

"Alright, show me some of your bad boy skills," Martin said, leaning in closer. Their lips were mere breaths away from a tantalizing connection when the nearby sound of rustling leaves shattered the moment. Twigs snapped and a mysterious trickling noise was heard in the nearby trees, forcing Martin and Kass to spring to their feet.

"What was that?"

"Keep your spear out," Kass said.

They again heard only the soothing sounds of the river. But this made the boys even more alarmed, knowing predators are often quiet just before pouncing on their prey.

"Not on my watch," Kass hissed.

Minutes passed. All remained silent. Martin and Kass slowly returned to their relaxed positions, but this time, both hands gripped their spears. Their romantic moment was over and they stayed ready for the pounce, should one come.

"I still think we should build a raft," Martin said, bringing up an old idea that was shot down earlier. "Even though there's some added risk, we'll be able to cover more territory faster if we float downstream."

"Funny you should mention that, Martin. I heard you had some type of hallucination with me on a raft."

"Haha...I guess I did. I really don't remember much of that experience," Martin blushed. "I suppose you also heard about me dancing in my underwear with the tree branch?"

"Oh, what I would have done to see that!" Kass laughed.

Martin waited a beat then thrust his lips against Kass's, giving Kass a surprised jolt.

"Sorry, I needed to do that."

"I liked it," smiled Kass with dreamy eyes.

"Woah!" Martin flinched.

"Is that okay?" Kass asked. He had taken a hand off his spear and was softly rubbing Martin's crotch.

"For sure!" Martin replied.

Kass continued massaging the outside of Martin's jeans. His flaccid penis slowly enlarged. Soon it was fully erect, pulsating through his jeans.

"Wow, nice," Kass smiled.

With his heart beating so fast he couldn't breathe properly, Martin took his hand and reciprocated Kass's gesture. They both enjoyed the fondling play while kissing.

When they broke their kiss, they gazed at each other in the low light. It was a gaze that spoke emotional volumes—passion, affection, and a promise for what lay ahead. The dark forest, with its secrets and stillness, became a backdrop to their private moment, allowing the night to guard the intimacy that had unfolded beneath its cover.

"Man, I wish I could take your clothes off," Martin whispered.

"I know, me too," Kass said.

"I'm sure they're asleep," Martin hinted.

"No way, there's too much going on out there. I don't want to be caught off guard with my pants down. Plus, we should wait until we have more privacy," Kass said.

"We need to get out of here, Kass. We need to build a raft. Give it a roof. Put spikes on it. And constantly be on the lookout for flying creatures," Martin reiterated.

"I'm still concerned it will make us more visible, and more vulnerable to attack. And the current could do damage, especially not knowing how turbulent the water will be. There could be rapids or even waterfalls. Look, I want to get out of here just as bad as everyone else, but I don't think being on a raft is a good idea. We can continue on foot, hidden, and near the water where it has proven to be a little safer," insisted Kass.

"Alright, I trust you."

The boys carried on with their conversation, partly to ward off sleep, but also because they realized they had much more to discover about each other. They discussed what life might hold for them upon their return to Kelowna, often substituting "if" for "when" in their dialogue, acknowledging the unpredictability of their future.

After Kass and Martin's guard shift, Gab and Olivia took over for three hours, beginning and ending their shift in an incident-free calm forest with only the musical songs of croaking frogs and the meditative sound of the flowing river. Jack and Harlen were on duty as the sun rose, making the canopy glint. A cool gentle breeze rustled the leaves in the trees overhead and refreshed the boys as it brushed over them.

"This is nice," Harlen whispered.

"Yeah, it sure is," Jack whispered back. "But it also feels like the calm before the storm."

"Yeah. I'm afraid you could be correct."

"You and Olivia looked cozied up. Things are cool between you two, then?"

"I hope so, Jack. Weird for a minute, but I think we're cool. Right now, we don't have anyone but each other."

"Hey, you got me, man," Jack exclaimed.

"Ha, you know what I mean. I can't imagine being stuck here for months or even years without someone—not being able to have someone the way you have Gab, and Kass has Martin."

"Dude, we are getting out of here. We are!"

***

"Good morning," Kass said, wiping his eyes and patting Harlen and Jack on their backs as he exited the shelter.

"Good morning," both boys replied.

"Good morning, guys," Martin said, exiting the lean-to a few moments later.

"Good morning," Olivia followed, awake and jovial.

"Where's my eggs and pancakes?" Gab asked as she entered the sunlit campsite. "And one of my dad's donuts, please."

"Hey, I thought we weren't going to do that!" Harlen announced.

"I'm sorry, I couldn't help myself."

The six teens sat relaxed on the side of the river, each relishing the fresh morning air. While rubbing lemon grass over their arms, necks, and faces to help repel the dawn mosquitos, they discussed preparations for their day.

"So, I think we should get started on a raft," Kass announced.

"Wait, what?" Martin's happy surprise caught the attention of the other four.

"Martin's been right all along and my lucid dream last night confirms it. It was more of an 'intuition hit' than a vision, but the message was strong. We will cover more territory with better time on a raft. We'll build it with safeguards, knowing the added risk of being more visible. By my estimations, with us all having special powers now, it will only take one full day to build the base, the walls, the roof, multiple oars, and all."

Martin and Kass shared a sweet but serious look of mutual respect. With a nod and furrowed brow, Kass conveyed, *I got you. I'm listening.*

After a brief discussion of the pros and cons, the group was on board with the new plan and quite excited about the possibilities. They collaborated on the construction design, with Kass taking the lead in assigning duties to ensure everyone executed the plan effectively. Empowered by their newfound abilities, the teens moved with an agility and speed beyond their usual limits.

Hours passed and the raft was coming along smoothly with Kass mastering the craftsmanship and Gab and the others brainstorming the technical aspects of creating a reliable and protective sailing vessel. It was built with a variety of natural floating products: matted clumps of vegetation, wood, bark, and bamboo. The design was like a cage with side-by-side vertical posts serving as the walls. The roof featured sharp spikes protruding outward and upward in all directions. The front entrance was narrow and a mere three feet high to keep out large creatures, while the supporting base of the raft was a hefty eight square feet.

The sun watched over and entertained them as they worked, then descended and disappeared beyond the trees. They had used a full day constructing a raft that would hopefully sail them safely to their freedom.

Chapter 26

The giant, century-old trees of the Costa Rican rainforest guarded the darkness. And soon, the slow flow of the river reflected the moonlight.

It was another peaceful night's sleep without any creature attacks, which allowed the friends to relax and recharge. As the morning sun began to warm the land, the temperature stayed pleasant for the first few hours. Birds chirped and the dew-covered leaves emitted a fresh earthy scent.

It was an ideal morning for the friends to embark on the tranquil river, giving them hope for a productive day navigating the unfamiliar waters on their makeshift raft. They quickly maintained a steady flow after experimenting with their oar strokes to coordinate the raft's movement. Despite the pleasant and surprisingly enjoyable journey, all six teens remained vigilant while also wearing smiles and feeling confident.

"Hey, this is more fun than I thought it would be," Gab said, standing next to Olivia.

"Yeah, this *is* fun. But I have a feeling something is about to change. This is just too good to be true."

"Don't think like that. We have to believe, have faith, and hope."

"I know, it's hard sometimes, but you're right, I'll chill. I'll enjoy this with you for as long as we can," Olivia concluded.

"See that?" Martin said, pointing to a large bird, soaring about a thousand feet up.

"Yeah, I see it," Jack acknowledged.

"Keep an eye on it, boys and girls. I have a feeling she's not flying alone."

"See, I told you. Too good to be true," exclaimed Olivia.

"We're good for now, gang. Just stay alert," Kass directed. "Martin, track that one up there and everyone else keep your eyes open for its feathered friends."

An hour passed with no further action in the sky. The bird that had been hovering above had vanished beyond the trees. Its sudden disappearance left the group feeling grateful but still uneasy. Had the bird retreated to gather its comrades with the intention of launching an attack? The friends remained on high alert for any sign of enemies in the sky or on shore.

It was late in the afternoon before they beached their raft with care and securely tied it to a sturdy tree with a rope made from braided vines. With the remaining daylight, the teens caught fish for dinner, gathered berries, and foraged for other edibles in the forest. The simple act of working together to prepare a meal brought a sense of normalcy to their otherwise abnormal situation.

As evening descended upon them, they enjoyed a relaxing dinner together, grateful for the calmness and companionship that had helped them navigate the challenges of the wilderness. Their common bond had grown ever stronger through adversity, and they were determined to face whatever lay ahead as a united front.

The moonless night cloaked the group in darkness as they sat in a circle around their campfire. Their voices broke the silence of the night along with the calming white noise of the river and the quaint chirps of crickets and croaks of frogs. They talked about their day and shared their thoughts about what lay ahead.

"Guys, we're getting close," Kass said. "I know it. But close to what, I'm not yet clear."

The hopeful mood of the moment shifted abruptly when Olivia, seemingly out of the blue and with odd timing, made a heartfelt revelation. "Hey, I think I want to change my pronouns to they/them/their."

Surprised by Olivia's unexpected announcement, everyone turned to look at her, their curiosity piqued. Harlen was the first to speak. "Okay, I'll start. What the heck? Where's this coming from?"

Olivia took a deep breath before explaining. "Well, I've been thinking about it a lot over the past few months, and honestly, for the past two years, as well. It's really been on my mind more recently. I don't always feel like a girl or a boy. I believe that identifying as non-binary is a way for me to explore gender non-conformity and embrace the full spectrum of gender within myself. I just don't feel comfortable with 'she' and 'her' pronouns anymore. The expectations and limitations that come with being identified as a girl are exhausting. I'm tired of people labeling me as a tomboy or expecting me to fit into certain gender roles, whether in clothing or behavior. Being non-binary means I can always be my most authentic self. It means it doesn't matter whether I'm perceived as a boy or a girl because I'm neither. I was never meant to fit into the mold because the mold doesn't fit me."

As Olivia shared their personal journey and the decision to embrace their non-binary identity, the group sat in contemplative silence, absorbing their words and offering support for their self-discovery and the journey of self-acceptance they had embarked upon.

"Well, wow. That was a mouthful," Harlen said, feeling uncomfortable and somewhat rejected.

"I like the way you dress," Jack said.

"It isn't only the way I dress."

"No, I know, I was just giving you a compliment. Take the compliment; I don't give out too many." Jack laughed.

"Thanks. I just don't want to be judged by what I wear or what I look like, or by my genitalia."

"I think that's great, Olivia," Jack said. "I'll support you with whatever decision you make or whatever identification you feel is right for you."

"Yeah, you do you," Kass followed. "I support you, too."

"It makes sense to me. I'm on board with your happiness," added Gab.

"Me too," Martin said.

"Wait, still not making sense to me," Harlen said, confused and frustrated, his body perched and inquisitive. "Are you lesbian?"

"No, she's...*they're* not saying that, Harlen," Kass jumped in.

"It's okay, Kass," said Olivia. "I'm still learning, too." Then, turning to Harlen, they explained calmly, "No, it doesn't mean I am a lesbian or straight, or bisexual, or whatever. It just means I am free to be who I want to be without any stereotypical labels or expectations. I don't always feel like a girl, so why do I have to be called a girl, or she, or her? I'm attracted to boys and girls, but that's my sexuality, not my gender. Harlen, my choices have nothing to do with you. This is about me and how I feel about myself."

"Nah, I get it. You're right. Sorry if I came across as a dick."

"Not a dick, but maybe a prick," Olivia said with a smile.

"Ya, I do have a penis," Harlen cracked. "Wanna see it?"

"No thanks, you weirdo," Olivia said dryly.

"Have you shared this with your parents?" asked Jack.

"No, not anyone until now," Olivia answered. "Well, do you know Elaine? They are someone who I've been hanging out with lately."

"Okay, *they*...got it. *They* are non-binary as well?" Harlen snarked, obviously feeling threatened by the mention of Elaine.

"Yes, and you're not allowed to ask me any more questions or make comments if you can't be cool about this," Olivia said, sharp as a jewel-laden dagger.

"Damn, I'm sorry. I'm just so confused."

Olivia ignored Harlen's excuse for his immature response and continued with their sharing. They explained they had met Elaine through the LGBTQIA+ group at a downtown community center.

"They're nice. I like them."

"That's great, Olivia. I want to meet them when we get back," Gab said.

"Me too. We all do," Jack said, narrowing his sight on Harlen who sat quietly until he noticed Jack's scowl.

"Yeah, me too," Harlen added while thinking, *Did I just hear my chance of ever being with Olivia has expired?*

Kass and Harlen took the first lookout shift for the night. Harlen was quiet, unusually so for him. Kass understood where his thoughts were and gave Harlen the space to reflect and process his feelings. It was a good half-hour before Kass spoke. "I hope you take my advice, Harlen."

"And your advice is to sit back and wait until she's no longer interested in Elaine?"

"Nope, that's not it. My advice is to let them follow their own path to happiness, and for you to love Olivia without strings or conditions. If it so happens their relationship ends, then maybe you'll have another chance. But I don't think you should wait around for anyone. You've had a crush on your best friend since you were seven. Time to detach, man, and find other interests. Seek someone who wants you the way you want them," Kass shared.

"Look, I know you're right. It's just hard."

"And one day it won't be," added Kass.

"You're right. What am I doing? Olivia's my best friend, not my girlfriend. I should stop this. Wait, did I say that right? Is it they-friend or girlfriend?"

Both boys laughed. "We can ask Olivia in the morning," Kass said.

Behind them, Olivia, who had lain awake listening to the conversation, smiled and let their eyes drift shut. Olivia savored the moment, reassured that everything would turn out just fine between them, Harlen, their friends, and their family.

***

The next morning, the six teens geared up for another day of adventure on the raft. Pushing off from the shore, they immediately faced the whitewater choppiness of a new section of the river, which added an extra layer of challenge to their rafting skills. The swift, shallow stretches of water pulled the raft downriver faster than before, requiring them to steer with agility to keep from crashing into the rocks—rocks large enough to smash their craft. They often had to hold on with one arm and occasionally use their oars to push away from the boulders. The steep gradient was alarming, pulling them ever faster.

"Hold on! Brace yourselves!" Jack shouted. The raft tilted and almost toppled over, but fortunately, the wisely-designed, heavy base of the raft slammed back onto the surface of the water.

"Here we go again," shouted Gab, as another set of rapids pulled them even faster downstream. "Hold on!" she bellowed.

Unaware of the intricacies behind their newfound strength, Kass's friends rallied to maneuver the raft, their movements surprisingly synchronized and more powerful than they had previously realized. Were their powers and abilities increasing over time as had been Kass's experience?

Kass employed his super strength to guide the raft through the cataracts and prevent a major collision with some huge rocks. However, he couldn't evade the fallen tree sprawled across the river's path.

The raft's collision with the tree severely jolted them, knocking Jack into the water. As if with one voice the teens screamed, calling for Jack to grab on to something.

Kass observed Jack being pulled downstream while the raft was still snagged on the fallen tree. He leaped into the river to rescue his best friend and deftly navigated the rapids, using the forceful pull of the current to approach Jack, who had clung to a log lodged between rocks. However, Jack's grip on the log slipped and he was carried further downstream and further away from Kass.

The raft finally broke free from the tree and sped downriver.

"Hold out your hand!" Kass yelled, continuing to swim while using the river's current to get close enough to grab onto Jack's arm. "Don't worry miss, I've got you," Kass said, in his best superhero voice.

"If you've got me...then who's got you?" Jack laughed, quoting their favorite line from the 1978 *Superman* movie the friends had watched together countless times.

"Yeah, I wish this was Metropolis," Kass returned the reference. "Hold on. Whatever you do, don't let go, Jack."

"I won't."

"He's got him!" Olivia screamed out.

Kass and Jack managed to grasp a lodged branch hoping to hold on long enough for the raft to get close. Harlen, Olivia, Martin, and Gab then attempted to slow the raft with the oars so Jack and Kass could manage to grab hold. When they did, Martin and Harlen pulled them up onto the raft. The water-logged Jack choked and coughed, feeling exhausted. After a few minutes, he regained his composure.

"I may have new powers," Jack said smiling, "but swimming is not one of them! Thanks, Kass. You're my hero!" Jack faked a Lois Lane swoon.

"Enough with the drama, boys!" yelled Olivia, "We could use your help here!"

Jack stood erect, looking determined. He took the oar from Olivia and instructed them and the others to find seats inside the raft's secure "cage" to catch their breath.

Soon after Jack and Kass navigated through another short series of challenging rapids, they arrived at a more tame section of the river, an open expanse of water that allowed direct sunlight onto the raft and exposed the teens to the intense heat. Rivulets of sweat ran down their backs.

"Everyone okay?" Harlen asked, looking around at his five friends, who nodded and inhaled deeply, then exhaled with audible sighs. They released their tight grips on the oars and let their bodies relax.

Chapter 27

"No, no, no!" Olivia shouted, pointing up to the sky. The mid-day sun beamed, causing a glare that prevented them from seeing details, but they felt the shade of darkness in the shape of flying creatures above.

"Ah, hell! This is not going to be good," said Harlen.

Their brief respite on the tranquil, open waters had abruptly ended, signaling the need to prepare for another possible ordeal. They placed the paddles inside the shelter-cage area of the raft then stationed themselves, spears in hand, around the perimeter to cover all sides.

The presence of the five bird-like creatures above was reminiscent of the day the lost friends were reunited with Kass. On that day, one giant bird had summoned dozens of smaller yet vicious birds. And like the giant bird, these five creatures were similar in size and adorned with gemstones intricately embedded in their features, giving them a futuristic appearance. Each gemstone emitted a soft shimmer that changed colors in the movement of flight. Their sharp, dagger-like beaks glistened with deadly intent, while their talons were indicative of their predatory prowess.

The creatures hovered in the windless sky, their shadows mirrored on the water's surface, circling, their wings flapping in a methodical clockwise motion. It was a strange and disturbing sight.

"Everyone ready?"

"No, Jack, I don't think any of us is actually ready," Martin said. "But, uhh...yeah, let's do this."

The group stood guard while allowing the raft to drift with the river's gentle current.

In one simultaneous motion, the five creatures lowered their big bodies and spiraled closer to the water, closer to the raft.

"Everyone, spread out, stand close to a wall. I'll take the front. Grab onto a pole with one hand, spear in the other!" Kass yelled.

Within a moment, the first bird left the band and plunged straight down with a second creature piercing the sky close behind. Then the third and fourth followed while the fifth remained in the air, maintaining its circular flight pattern.

"Here they come," Kass alerted.

"Get ready," said Jack.

"Spears out!" Harlen shouted.

Kass intentionally chose the most visible location on the front deck of the raft, which bristled with spears sticking out in all directions.

The first bird flew very close to him but abruptly changed direction, pulling off a sharp swoop then soared back up high. The other three creatures quickly followed suit, copying the lead creature's evasive move. This display of synchronized aerial maneuvers left Kass and his companions both impressed and on edge as they tried to make sense of the creatures' intentions and prepare for their next move.

"They're fucking with us," Harlen declared.

The creatures resumed their perfectly spaced circle in the sky, hovering directly above the raft which was still drifting with the current. One by one, the birds again took nose dives toward the raft, getting closer with each swoop.

Kass, seizing the moment, thrust his spear, hoping to strike one of them down. But the creatures were cunning and skillfully dodged his spear while maintaining a cautious distance.

"They're not dumb, are they?" Gab commented.

"Apparently not. They seem to be calculating," said Kass.

Suddenly, instead of swooping down from the sky, they transformed into aquatic projectiles, plunging into the water like cannonballs, one by one. The impact reverberated with a series of deafening booms from all sides of the raft, creating a chaotic ripple effect that sent the vessel undulating and spiraling out of control.

The teens braced themselves against the unexpected and terrifying tactic. They continued to cling to the sturdy posts of the raft while also clutching their spears. In the midst of the chaotic onslaught, Olivia's head violently collided with the raft's sharp unforgiving corner, resulting in a substantial wound. The impact was brutal and blood poured alarmingly from the gash. Because they had stationed themself on the back corner of the raft, the others did not notice Olivia was wounded.

Overwhelmed by dizziness, Olivia fought to stay conscious. They clung tenaciously to the raft, determined not to succumb to the disorienting sensation. Blood continued to flow from the wound, coating one of their eyebrows and trickling down over their eyelids. With a trembling hand, Olivia attempted to wipe away the blood, only to smear it further across their face. It was then Olivia truly grasped the gravity of their injury.

Above the group, the creatures resumed their threatening aerial dance, orchestrating the next assault. One by one the bird-like creatures again plummeted from the sky, mimicking their previous cannonball strategy. But, as they emerged from beneath the water's surface, they fully extended their huge wings to amplify the tsunami effect.

The raft teetered perilously, tilting almost ninety degrees until Kass threw his weight over the elevated edge of the raft's base and utilized his formidable strength to prevent the vessel from capsizing. It was then he noticed Olivia in distress.

"Gab, grab Olivia," Kass shouted, drawing everyone's attention to their limp body laying on the base of the raft, an arm wrapped around a pole but their legs dangling over the edge. Motionless. Bleeding.

The raft stabilized enough to allow Gab to get to Olivia and pull them tight against the outside wall of the raft. Gab then splashed water on Olivia's face, followed by several small slaps in hope of reviving them. It did the trick. Olivia gradually regained consciousness and appeared at least semi-coherent.

"Are you okay?" Gab asked with urgency.

"Yeah, um, did you just slap me?" they laughed, trying to shake off the dizziness.

Olivia, looking a bit off balance, clumsily grabbed the spear. "I'm alright, guys. I've got this," they said.

But Olivia's attempt to keep it together failed as they staggered, clearly disoriented. Blood continued to seep from their wound. "Guys, something's wrong with Olivia!" Gab cried out in rising panic.

Kass left his station and steadied himself as he made his way to Olivia. Olivia's eyes had closed and their body had gone limp, unconscious from the trauma. Gab was holding them from falling in the river.

"Get me something to stop the bleeding!" Kass said to Gab. He then held onto Olivia and waited for Gab to tear a piece of fabric from her shirt sleeve. Intuitively, Kass pressed his hand firmly against Olivia's forehead. A sudden surge of power and tiny, sparkling lights shot from Kass's hand, surrounding Olivia's wound. In an unbelievable turn, the blood clotted and the wound healed within moments.

Olivia regained consciousness and their eyes flickered open.

"Wait, did you just heal Olivia with your hand?" Jack gasped.

"Shut the hell up!" Harlen blurted out. "Who are you?" he added, his eyes wide with shock.

Olivia, with regained composure and perfect health, re-claimed their spear and assumed a battle-ready stance, poised to face the challenge once more.

"Alright everyone, we need a different strategy," Jack announced.

"We're going to have to throw our spears at them," Harlen suggested.

"Nah, then we'll be without weapons if we miss," said Martin.

"I'll climb to the roof of the raft and if a bird cannonballs into the river again, I'll jump onto it," Kass informed his friends.

"That actually sounds like a pretty good plan," Harlen agreed. "You'll need to cower and appear non-threatening so they don't suspect anything."

"Right."

Within a few minutes, the five flying creatures plummeted into the river one by one. Kass prepared, ready to act. Before the last bird hit the water, he leaped, landing on top of it and thrust his spear into the back of the creature's feathered frame. The river turned red at the point of contact before the creature's lifeless body surfaced and floated away.

Moments later, Kass pulled himself out of the water and back onto the raft, spear in hand.

"You did it!" his friends shouted.

"One down, four more to go!" shouted Martin.

The creatures elevated and resumed their rotating circular formation high in the sky. Kass returned to the roof of the raft and knelt down, waiting and witnessing the creatures accelerate the flapping of their wings. Instead of diving, however, they flew in all four directions then U-turned and, like jets, flew at high speed directly toward the raft.

"Everyone, two people together on each side. Someone join me up front!" Kass ordered.

"Let's go!" Martin shouted to Harlen.

The creatures came close to the raft before sweeping upward. Their intense flapping created a wind gust that forced the teens to their knees.

"Get up! They're coming back," Kass yelled.

And once more, the teens were forced down by the strong wind created by the creatures' dive-bombing.

"Everyone take cover!" They followed Kass's command without delay and huddled inside the cage.

"When I say jab, you jab through the open spaces between posts or beams. Hard! And don't let go of your spear."

The creatures, sensing the change in the teens' tactics, abandoned their current assault strategy. Instead, they took to the skies, circling ominously for several heart-pounding minutes before launching a renewed attack. Two of them swooped in close while the other two landed gracefully on the roof of the cage, cunningly avoiding the menacing spikes that shielded the raft.

Kass's five friends waited for his command.

"Jab!"

And with that resounding battle cry they acted as one, thrusting their spears between the raft's sturdy support beams with fortunate precision. Two of the menacing beings were vanquished in the teens' collective effort.

However, their triumph was marred by the gruesome aftermath. Blood sprayed from the creatures' bodies, drenching the roof of the raft and dripping through the open spaces onto the teens. It was a shocking and visceral spectacle. This horrifying sight stirred a mix of emotions within them—disgust at the gruesome outcome but also the deep-seated satisfaction of a hard-fought victory.

As the fatally wounded bodies of the defeated creatures tumbled into the water, they released one final, spine-tingling screech, marking their demise. All of the teens screamed in celebration.

The two remaining creatures continued to circle above, their once perfect formation shattered by the loss of their comrades. They maintained their aerial vigil for nearly twenty agonizing minutes, leaving the teens to ponder: What were they up to? Were they waiting for reinforcements? Or were they plotting their final, merciless assault?

Their questions were answered when the two creatures began their descent. They seemed more ferocious, even more determined. Their collaborators had been defeated and they were clearly out for vengeance.

"This doesn't look good, guys," Harlen said.

"No, this sure doesn't. Get back inside!" Jack shouted. "Now!"

The creatures closed in and all six of the teens scrambled toward the small entrance, reentering just in time. As if on a suicide mission, the birds violently collided with the sides of the raft. Again and again, they nose-dived and body-slammed into it, severely jolting the raft and causing the teens to tumble around, piling up on each other in the small area. It was painful and chaotic.

To compound the situation, the river had narrowed and grown turbulent, propelling the raft downstream at a rapid, unsafe, and uncontrollable speed.

In a daring move, Martin exited the cage and sprinted toward a dive-bombing bird. He nearly lost his balance, but ultimately managed to fatally stab the fourth creature.

"Got it!" Martin shouted, pulling his spear out of the foul flying bird.

The last surviving beast, angry, intelligent, and resistant, hovered above. It soon dove and targeted the raft's structural weaknesses. With calculated precision it used its sharp talons to slash through the less substantial branches in the raft's walls, shredding the once-sturdy frame. Its massive wings thrashed violently during the demolition, creating a tempest of wind and debris. Repeating this tactic, each strike like the blow of a sledgehammer, threatened to reduce the makeshift vessel to nothing more than kindling and driftwood.

The bird proved to be more calculating than the other four. Surprisingly, it was too fast even for Kass to conquer.

The teens looked up to witness the dark gray clouds turn as black as spilled ink. Strong winds arrived and thrust the raft forward, moving it rapidly along with the current while also pitching it to and fro. Although the violent storm had forced the final flying creature to retire, it also required the teens to hold on for their lives. They flailed about, their legs dancing uncontrollably.

"Umm...this doesn't look good!" Harlen yelled.

"Please stop saying that!" Olivia hollered.

They suddenly realized a perilous fork looming ahead. The wind had become an unrelenting adversary, ruthlessly pushing the raft to the right and veering them away from the river's intended course. The raft was yanked deeper into the foreboding channel, an undeniable omen of evil.

"Brace yourselves!" Jack commanded, as a tempestuous derecho storm loomed on the horizon.

In an instant, the storm seized the raft, spinning it through the air like a ragdoll caught in the grips of a cyclone. The vessel, or what was left of it, passed through a black veil of mystery then entered a maelstrom of doom.

The teens had been thrust into a nightmarish realm where the world was erupting in a deafening symphony of chaos. Thunder clashes melded with volcanic eruptions, while streaks of lightning illuminated the obsidian sky in a horrific yet dazzling display.

Then, as suddenly as it began, the tumult ceased, plunging them into a haunting silence that enveloped them like a shroud.

Chapter 28

"**A**h damn, damn...damn!" Harlen said, lifting his head off the pristine, white sand beach where he and the others lay stranded.

"Wait, let me guess, this doesn't look good?" Olivia stammered, with the right side of their face depressed in the grit.

"Nope. Not at all," he replied.

Hearing this, Jack, Gab, Olivia, Martin, and Kass also lifted their heads to witness almost two dozen women warriors staring fiercely at them with piercing gray eyes, spears pointed in their direction.

The teens discovered themselves enclosed in a cove, a place where nature's grandeur took center stage. Towering sheer cliffs formed imposing walls that embraced the warriors from behind. The rugged surfaces of the cliffs were etched with the scars of time and adorned with resilient trees, roots tenaciously clinging to narrow crevices and providing splashes of greenery against the stark stone canvas.

The female warriors had strong physiques and skin of glistening russet tones. They wore meticulously crafted leather breastplates, intricately inscribed with tribal designs, to offer protection and convey a fierce aesthetic.

Their knee-high boots, forged for resilience, featured reinforced soles, ensuring the necessary durability for combat across diverse terrains. Fitted skirts made from natural materials like leather, woven vines, and leaves allowed unrestricted movement through dense vegetation while safeguarding them from the underbrush. Cinching leafy belts around their waists completed their attire, adding tribal motifs for a touch of cultural significance.

The warriors stood united in silence. A tapestry of intricate tattoos adorned their arms, stretching from their shoulders to their wrists. Their spears, gleaming with the brilliance of precious jewels and compressed metals, stood at the ready, proclaiming their martial prowess. With vigilant eyes, they observed the gathering of adolescents.

"Please tell me these are the Agojie and they're taking us to the Woman King," Harlen whispered.

"Yeah, let's hope so," Gab softly replied.

"Om-a-ka!" the women simultaneously sounded. "Om-a-ka!" they said again, while stepping forward and stomping down. The ground vibrated and their force inflicted fear within the teens. While chanting, the women formed two tight columns. They then stepped apart, meticulously crafting a ceremonial pathway that unfurled before their leader. With hushed reverence, each woman lowered her head and, with a resounding thump, slammed the blunt end of her spear onto the ground, signifying deference for the esteemed leader.

A powerful final thump echoed. "Stand!" demanded a woman in the front of the pack, glaring at the teens.

They slowly rose to their feet, staring at the woman who spoke while also glancing at the other fierce warriors.

"Wakanda forever!" Harlen said, folding his arms across his chest.

"Harlen, don't piss them off!" Olivia whispered in a firm voice.

The leader glared at Harlen with confusion and annoyance. Then, assuming Jack was the leader of the group, pointed a finger at him and spoke with an assertive tone and clear confidence.

"I am Bekae. You? Speak to me. How did you land here?"

"Wait, did she just say Becky?" Harlen whispered.

"No, she said Begay," Martin joked.

"No, she said Bucky," Olivia said.

"Silence!" commanded the lead warrior, as all of the women again stomped the blunt ends of their spears to the ground.

"We mean no harm" Jack babbled, hoping to explain. "We are just trying to get out of here and get back home. We don't even know how we got here in the first place."

"You arrived armed with weapons," Bekae said, pointing to her warriors who held the teens' spears. "And you're carrying the stones of Enkarius on these weapons," she added.

"Enkarius? We aren't sure who that is," Harlen said, "and we don't understand what's been happening to us. You see, it all started when we went camping with our classmates. A huge creature attacked a creepy creature who was attacking us and Kass found a...a..."

"And we got lost," Kass interrupted, worried Harlen was about to divulge information about the gemstone he still carried in his backpack. "And just a few minutes ago we were on a river being attacked by flying creatures. We used the weapons to protect ourselves."

The warrior-in-command wore a puzzled and suspicious expression, showing no signs of amusement. Her gaze fell upon Kass's backpack, and in that moment, a sense of impending danger crept over him. He mentally began formulating a plan for a potential counter-attack, ready for any hostile move.

"And who is your leader?" she demanded..

The teens exchanged glances, uncertain of how to respond. Gab pointed at Olivia, Harlen gestured toward Jack, and Martin singled out Kass. In a surprising twist, Kass deflected the question, opening both his palms toward his five friends, indicating a collective leadership within their tightly-knit group.

"Umm...we don't have a leader," Olivia admitted. "We're just friends trying to figure out how to get out of here."

"Yeah, we just want to get home. How do we get out of here?" Harlen asked.

"Where are we?" Gab followed.

Bekae waited a beat before sternly declaring, "There's no way."

"What do you mean, there's no way? There's a way!" Gab snapped back.

"No, you can't leave," Bekae exclaimed in a tone that signaled the other warriors to raise their weapons and assume a defensive posture.

The teens looked at each other with panicky expressions. Jack and Kass began to visually scour the area for an escape route. The others noticed and did the same.

"We cannot let you leave. Our land is sacred. Only one human from the outside world has ever arrived here. And that human was killed one-hundred-thirty years ago," Bekae added, continuing to hold her face stern and fierce.

"So, let me understand what you are saying," Jack said with a calm voice. "We accidently passed through some horrible black veil of chaos and now you're not going to let us leave? Meaning, you're going to imprison us, enslave us, or kill us?"

Jack stood strong. His t-shirt and jeans gripped his physique, displaying his muscular body. Even though his clothes were stained, dirty, and ripped in various places, his six-foot-five stature remained impressive—not to be easily dominated, even by a tribe of fierce warriors. Kass stood next to his friend, counting on his powers from the gemstone to equalize any battle. The boys clearly indicated they were prepared to fight should one be required.

Soon, the other four teens stood strong, too. They weren't as ready without their weapons. Instead, they were burdened with added fear and doubt knowing the odds were against them. Battling jungle creatures was one thing, but combat with trained and conditioned human warriors was a different level of fear. Nevertheless, the teens also knew they had acquired special powers and were not going to bow down without a fight. They appeared ready to die rather than be taken as prisoners.

Bekae signaled her troop to take attack positions. They spread out around the cove to prevent the teens from escaping.

"We mean you no harm. We just want to get home. Help us," Kass pleaded.

"No! You cannot leave and we do not want prisoners who might escape and signal others to our sacred lands." Bekae said firmly.

"Signal others? What does she think we have—telepathic powers?" Harlen said.

Bekae moved forward. Her troop followed her lead.

All the teens, except Kass, stepped back. His friends noticed an odd aura coming over him and sensed his superpowers were kicking in. The women again stepped forward, assuming a more hostile stance.

Kass threw out his arm and opened his hand, extending his fingers to emit a powerful electrical force that summoned his spear from the possessor's grip.

Swoosh!

He caught the spear and twirled it a half-dozen times before gripping it with both hands and taking a very serious warrior's stance. The eyes of the women warriors opened wide as they witnessed this remarkable feat.

"What the heck was that?" Martin said.

"I've had time to perfect some of my skills, remember?" Kass glanced at Martin and winked.

Bekae held out her arm and fist to command her troop to stop.

Kass began to spin his spear, faster and faster, creating a wind powerful enough to force the women warriors to retreat, eventually backing them up against the rockwall of the cove. Several of the women attempted to throw their spears, but none could break through Kass's wind-propelled shield.

With a deft and mesmerizing display of skill, Kass brought the spinning vortex of his spear to a sudden stop, yet held it in a masterful manner in a single hand. His command over the weapon was nothing short of awe-inspiring. Then, with a swift gesture, he summoned the other five spears from the warrior women and skillfully distributed them to his friends. In no time, all six teens were armed and presented a formidable front.

The women warriors were in awe, intrigued by Kass's powers. And while Kass and his friends held their defensive positions, waiting for Bekae and her troops' next move, Bekae contemplated the situation. She weighed the unexpected display of combat-readiness by the young teens, considering how to address their skill level while also ensuring the safety of her warriors.

"Look, we mean no harm." Jack yelled. "We just want out of this place. You have our word we won't mention any of this to anyone; wherever this place might be."

Bekae and her team stood in tense silence. The teens anticipated a possible violent and fatal confrontation and held their spears upright.

"Okay, are we going to stand here all day, or can we leave?" Harlen whispered from the side of his mouth.

"Yeah, really. This is scary and way too intense. I wish they would say something already," Olivia added.

"Let's slowly move in that direction," Kass said, nodding his head to the left, the opposite direction from where he believed the group of warrior women had emanated. Taking slow and small side-steps the teens retreated to the left.

"Om-a-ka," the women suddenly chanted, but without moving a muscle or changing their solemn facial expressions. "Om-a-ka! Om-a-ka!" they repeated.

"Alright, let's not keep waiting for these people to attack us," Harlen whispered.

Kass, observing the still stoic position of the women warriors, said, "Okay, pick up the pace a little, but if they attack, get behind me so I can take out as many as possible."

"Take out? What? Kass, these are human beings. We can't just start killing people," Martin squirmed.

"Just keep moving, Martin. If they attack, it's either kill or be killed. And there's a lot of things I want to do with you before I die." Kass smiled, lightening the tension of the moment.

"Okay, since you put it that way," grinned Martin.

The teens continued to side-step toward the forest and away from the warriors as they gave each other pep-talks, preparing for what they feared might happen.

"We have to think of them as creatures so we don't back down," Gab reasoned. "This is a matter of survival."

"Okay, you're right. Think of them as creatures," Olivia stammered.

"Agreed," Harlen said.

"I can't believe we're having this conversation. I can't do it. I can't kill anyone," Olivia announced.

"Olivia, get your vegan don't-kill-animals head out of your ass!" Harlen hissed. "We don't have a choice. One thing I learned in science, we are all animals."

"Okay...okay..." Olivia said with resignation in their voice.

"Alright, so we're doing this but only if they attack," Jack said with confidence.

The teens looked at each other with growing intensity. They intentionally festered more rage and built more courage with each side-step left. They knew if Bekae issued the command, her troop would obey with no hesitation.

While the women warriors continued to exude an aggressive demeanor, their faces also revealed a subtle shift that reflected both a heightened focus and rabid anticipation. Beads of sweat, like glistening pearls, dripped from the sinews of their shoulders, accentuating the rippling muscles beneath. With each tense movement, their veins protruded, pulsing with raw power and determination.

Kass moved a step closer to the women but signaled his friends to not follow. Again, he twirled his spear several times before gripping it with both hands. Bekae signaled for a group of women to attack. Kass ran swiftly toward his attackers and leaped into the air, exhibiting a perfect flying side-kick as if he had had many years of Taekwondo training. He didn't. In a flurry of violence, Kass's foot struck one of the women, hurling her ruthlessly to the ground. He wielded his spear with savage precision, each merciless blow leaving several other women incapacitated in its brutal aftermath.

Other women joined the battle. One, propelled by frenzied aggression, lunged at Jack with blinding speed. His deft evasion was marred only by a guttural grunt of exertion. In a swift and retaliatory maneuver, he unleashed a ferocious right kick, immediately followed by a cold-blooded stab to her leg.

The battle's relentless intensity offered no respite. Another woman, her determination steadfast, delivered a flying side-kick into Jack's exposed back. Caught off guard, he faltered and stumbled to the ground.

The woman then stood over Jack, about to stab her spear into his chest when, instead, Gab's spear was thrust deep into the side of the warrior's rib cage. The woman fell to the ground, dead. Jack leaped up, quickly pulled the spear out of the woman's body, and handed it back to Gab.

Jack stepped forward again and leapt into the air, spinning around as his next opponent's guard went up. He struck her with his spear, and several other nearby adversaries.

Bekae threw her spear at Kass, braising his thigh. Kass screamed and fell to the ground.

Harlen and Martin joined forces and held their own against a skilled warrior who swung her spear, striking Martin's face. Blood splattered from his nose. He flew backwards and landed on the ground.

In the midst of the chaos, Gab, Jack, and Olivia were ambushed by two soldiers. Armed with spears and their recently honed strength, the teens swiftly shifted from defense to a potent offense, repelling the attackers with remarkable skill.

Kass was able to raise his wounded body from the ground but stumbled forward and fell again. Bekae retrieved her spear to resume her attack. Kass quickly rose and, this time, remained on his feet. He twirled his spear around several times as Bekae approached. They took turns forcefully clanking spears, trying to overpower the other. Kass swung his spear around his body in a crisscross motion, mysteriously forming a hoop and some kind of shield, enabling him to slice a chunk of skin from Bekae's hip. She gasped, put one hand over her bleeding wound, then began viciously attacking Kass like a one-armed crazed and wounded animal, kicking and swinging her spear to push Kass further back until he tripped over a large rock and tumbled to the ground.

Bekae leaped over Kass's body, intent on lunging her spear through his heart. But in that moment, a loud piercing screech halted everyone abruptly. The screech, the same terrifying screech the teens had heard during their camping trip, was repeated several times.

Bekae gasped and looked in the direction of the haunting noise, giving Kass the opportunity he needed to roll away from the pride of the spear's arrowhead before it could be thrust into his chest.

The sand on the beach began to vibrate and shift. The tranquil river became turbulent. Bekae plunged her spear into the ground and flattened her body onto the sand. Her warriors did the same. Kass and his friends all watched as three enormous creatures protruded in flight through the same black mystical veil that Kass, Olivia, Jack, Martin, Gab, and Harlen had previously burst through.

"Everyone, over here," Jack said, directing his crew to run for cover behind some substantial boulders and weathered, sun-bleached tree trunks strewn on the farside of the cove's windswept beach.

The boulders, rugged and massive, stood like ancient sentinels along the shoreline. Eroded and smoothed by centuries of ceaseless tides, they provided substantial protection.

The air echoed with deafening roars as the three massive, shadowy creatures swooped perilously close to the humans occupying the cove before soaring upwards. Fear gripped the women warriors, causing some of them to stumble and fall. With determined resolve, they regained their footing and joined the others who had hastily scattered to relative safety on the other side of the cove, away from the teens. A series of ear-splitting roars echoed through the cove as the dragon-like creatures circled above. Their cries pierced the sky, creating a constant and jarring noise that left no doubt about the threat they presented.

They bore a predatory physique, designed for ruthless aerial mastery like a pterodactyl. Their vast, leathery wings sliced through the air with a sinister elegance, casting shadows upon the scene below.

Each creature featured a serpentine neck, with a ghastly set of jagged, obsidian-hued fangs protruding menacingly from its mouth, gleaming with deadly intent. They had fiery eyes, burning with an insatiable hunger. Their bodies, encased in scales as black as an abyss, seemed to consume all light along with all hope of surviving their attack.

As the teens cautiously peeked from their concealed spots, they observed the creatures circling above. Minutes felt like hours as the monstrous beings continued their aerial patrol. Then, with a final pass at low altitude, they swooped up and disappeared beyond the mountain's peak. The warming sun reclaimed the sky.

"We really need to get the hell out of here," Martin urged, casting a concerned look at his friends.

"Absolutely, let's run before things get messy again," Harlen chimed in. "Those women will definitely plot another assault any minute now."

"Okay, what's the plan, Kass?" Olivia asked, as they wiped the sweat from their forehead.

"Jack?" Kass said, looking over at him. Jack's face looked sorrowful, exhausted, and afraid. He stared over at the women on the other side of the cove, who were also crouched behind boulders and driftwood.

The women stepped away from their hiding places while continuing to monitor the whereabouts of the flying creatures. Gripping their spears, they crept slowly toward the center of the cove.

The teens, watching discreetly from their hiding spots, noticed Bekae engaged in conversation. It was clear she was coordinating a fresh strategy for their upcoming attack.

The teens remained concealed yet trapped with the rocky cliff of the cove behind them and the warriors too close for comfort. "Get ready, everyone," Harlen said, pumped for battle. Despite his personal fear of death, he was even more deeply concerned that none of his friends would survive a battle against Bekae and her army of formidable warriors.

"This is our last chance. We have to fight for our lives and walk away from this unscathed," Jack said, to ready the others.

Suddenly, a loud rumbling roar violently shook the land on which they were standing. Once again the sand began to pulsate and the tranquil water became choppy.

"What now?" Harlen exclaimed. "I'm getting sick of surprise guest appearances."

Another roar was heard. Louder and closer. The women warriors held their position. They remained composed and delayed any plan to resume battle.

The three earlier prehistoric-like creatures that had flown over the mountain's summit were still absent. But these new hair-raising cries of an as-yet-unknown creature were deafening and terrifying .

All of a sudden, the black illusory veil that continued to hang over the water began to shake, and an airborne creature of enormous size, ferocious and angry, appeared.

It tore through the sky with awe-inspiring intensity and savage power. Each beat of its wings sent shockwaves rippling outward. Its massive form was a breathtaking combination of speed and agility. Every dive, every ascent, and every sharp turn exhibited its fierce purpose. Its eyes burned with a wild, primal fire as it pressed forward, epitomizing the spirit of unstoppable determination.

"Enkarius!" the women shouted.

Chapter 29

After taking shelter, the women and the teens marveled at the creature's sheer power, an entity more massive than an elephant and boasting a neck rivaling the length of a brachiosaurus. The creature's pointy ears appeared minuscule in comparison to its enormous head, while its narrow nose featured an oddly thin septum and downward-facing nostrils, adding to its odd appearance.

The teens gazed upon the creature's impressive spine and noticed a curious pattern: a sequence of jewels adorning its back, starting as small and gleaming gems near the creature's tail then gradually growing in size as they ascended toward its head. Amid this dazzling display, one detail stood out: a conspicuous absence, a precious jewel missing, leaving a gap in the otherwise resplendent array.

Enkarius was the same creature from their horrific first encounter, a haunting memory that had come full circle. Their initial moments with the beast had occurred in the dead of night, bathed only in the moon's feeble glow and concealing the details of the creature's formidable presence. In the daylight, they could now fully appreciate its intricate features and horrific magnificence. It loomed before them, a specter of darkness and dread that seemed to swallow the very light around the teens.

"Is it here for the gemstone?" Kass's voice quivered, barely above a whisper. "Or is it here for me!?"

"It just might be here for both," Jack said, telling his best friend the terrifying truth.

"But should I try to return it? What should we do?"

"I have a feeling it's going to try to kill you either way," Harlen interjected, his tone grave. "It looks pissed."

"Thanks, Harlen. That makes me feel *a lot* better."

"You lose that gemstone, you might lose your powers, and maybe we'll all lose ours, too."

"You're right Gab. I'm not giving it back!" Kass declared, a note of defiance cutting through the fear that threatened to overwhelm them all.

The group fell into a tense silence, the gravity of their predicament bearing down on them.

The abominable beast continued to circle above, unleashing a barrage of roars. It then descended, coming to rest on the elevated terrain of the cliff that served as the cove's backdrop. The terrified humans all remained concealed.

Enkarius perched there, its impressive wings wrapped around its body to resemble a protective cocoon. It stood utterly motionless with its gaze penetrating down upon its prey.

"Oh great, another stand-off," Martin said.

"What do we do now?" Olivia asked, looking panicked.

"Well, the good news is we probably don't have to fight Bekae and her troops...at least for now," Gab offered.

"Always seeing the brighter side of things," Jack remarked, sharing a smile with Gab. "I love you," he whispered softly, a heartfelt farewell in his words.

"I love you too," Gab replied, her voice quivering.

To make matters worse, the three dragon-like creatures that had previously flown off reappeared over the mountain's summit, soaring near Enkarius as though summoned to create chaos and flush out the prey so Enkarius could complete the grim task of eradicating the humans.

The dragon-like creatures swarmed over the teens and the tribe of women warriors, drawing nearer and nearer in synchronized dives. Then, because the warriors were the more visible and less protected, they were the first to be attacked. Spears flew through the air, some hitting and puncturing the thick skin of the monstrous beings. But, two by two, women were snatched by vicious talons and carried high into the air, then dropped to their death. One woman, in the grasp of a dive-bombing creature, was submerged underwater. The creature then resurfaced with a lifeless body that it then dropped back into the water. The teens, in shock by the extermination they were witnessing, cried silent tears, knowing they were next.

Bekae was one of the last warriors standing. She persisted in an intense fight with one of the creatures, who was able to take hold of her and throw her a great distance. Fierce with rage, Bekae grabbed a second spear and ran with great speed up the tail of the creature and onto its spine. She simultaneously thrust both spears deep into its body. The creature released a loud wail and plummeted to the ground.

Bekae tumbled down with the beast but quickly righted herself, realizing the two remaining creatures were advancing her way. Kass ran from behind the boulder and over to Bekae. He jumped in front of her and the other surviving warriors that stood nearby. Like before, he twirled his spear, then held it with both hands before looking down at a fallen spear near his feet. He picked it up and, with ruthless intensity, launched it at one of the incoming creatures, puncturing its eye. When it fell to the ground, Kass fatally trounced on its neck, severing the spinal cord.

The last dragon-like creature picked up a large rock in its talons and flung it at the women, hitting two and crushing their bodies. It returned and grasped Bekae, lifting her from the ground and swooping her high into the air. She stabbed the creature's foot and was released from its talon but she kept from falling by clinging to the small feathers on the bottom of the creature's foot. Bekae then climbed up its leg, onto its back, and finally to the neck area where she repeatedly thrust her knife into the creature's face. It released a loud screech.

A spurt of bright red blood sprayed from the creature's body, staining the sand on the beach in a macabre display. Bekae's descent was as sudden as it was brutal; her body crashed to the ground and remained eerily still.

In parallel, the creature faced a no less dramatic fate, smashing into the beach then rolling into the water. There was no triumphant ascent for the beast; it simply vanished, its destiny hidden below.

The scene was traumatic to watch and the teens felt intense empathy for all who survived along with deep compassion for those who lost their lives.

Enkarius unfolded its wings and let out a loud screech before diving toward Kass. Kass ran, separating from the group to deter the beast and protect his friends, still standing as their guardian even though they now possessed their own unique strengths.

At first, Enkarius pursued Kass, but then reversed course and beelined it to the others who were hiding behind the giant boulders.

The five vulnerable teens witnessed Enkarius heading their way with murder in its eyes. Kass ran back at super-hero speed and leaped on top of the tallest boulder that shielded his friends. Enkarius rerouted again to dive down and, using only its lower set of wings, picked up a boulder the size of a car tire. Its upper set of wings still enabled it to stay aloft.

It flung the rock it was carrying at the boulder where Kass stood and the others hid. Startled, Kass jumped six feet vertically and hurled his spear another twenty feet, narrowly missing Enkarius, who had veered away.

However, the thrown projectile hit its mark and the boulder burst apart, shattering into a hundred pieces. Fragments from the exploded rock hit the teens, wounding them. All five fell to the ground, stunned, bruised, and bleeding.

Kass ran in front of his friends, shielding them from Enkarius, who, in preparation for its next attack, had ramped up its speed. Sand flew in all directions from the turbulence.

Kass's friends managed to stand and gather ranks close behind Kass who shouted, "Hold on to each other!"

They pulled into a tight group hug with Kass standing alone, determined to keep them alive.

Enkarius showed no mercy. The beast flapped all four wings. Its long protruding snout pointed directly at its prey.

While Kass's friends closed their eyes, fearing the worst, Kass only crossed his arms in front of his head and stared directly into the evil eyes of the monstrous Enkarius.

"No!" Kass commanded in a voice so resolute and loud it echoed around the stone walls of the cove.

The teens could feel a powerful force vibrate throughout their bodies. The sensation was painful but, at the same time, mystically surreal, as if a million volts of electricity were passing through them, separating their cells, and vaporizing them into nothingness.

Chapter 30

T he darkness slowly receded and a profound silence painted over the six teens who lay outstretched on a grassy field, their bodies still, their hearts pounding with adrenaline. Then, one by one, their eyes opened and the reality of their return to the Kelowna school grounds settled upon them like a delightful wave crashing against the shore.

Harlen's voice, shaky with emotion, broke the silence. "Now, this looks good," he said, looking around, with a tear of joy and relief escaping his eye.

"Wait, are we home?" Olivia asked in awe as their eyes scanned the familiar surroundings.

"We're home!" Jack's exclamation echoed through the field of Cypress High. Tears welled up knowing he could finally let down his guard and relax.

Instead of rushing to their feet, the teens remained lying on the freshly mowed field, their hands reaching out to one another, fingers connecting in silent solidarity. They held on tight, not wanting to let go of the support and strength they found in each other.

Tears streamed down Gab's face. She couldn't contain her elation as she cried out with a voice that cracked with emotion, "We made it!"

With a concerned furrow in his brow, Jack asked the pivotal question, "Is everyone okay?"

His five friends responded in unison, their voices filled with reassurance and euphoria, confirming their safety. Miraculously, even their wounds from the battle had healed, making the moment all the more special.

"We actually made it," said Martin, his voice quivering and laden with the significance of the journey they had undertaken.

"I've never been so happy!" Olivia said.

In that emotional moment, Kass, who had remained quiet, spoke up with tears in his eyes, too. "I want to thank all of you. I didn't think we were going to live to see this place again."

The six teens then stood and embraced tightly, celebrating their triumph over the impossible. They were not just friends, they were a family forged in the fires of adversity.

Amid their elation, Olivia asked, "What now?"

The gravity of the question hung heavy.

Harlen's response carried a sense of urgency. "I need a burger!"

After laughing with emotional relief, the others chimed in.

Olivia exclaimed, "I need to relax in my bed and binge-watch talk shows." They stretched their arms out dramatically, as if envisioning the luxury ahead.

"I'm going to give my dads the biggest kiss and eat one of their cakes all by myself," Gab said and pretended to gobble up an imaginary cake. Her infectious laugh projected.

"I'll join you," Jack added with a grin. "Well, maybe not the kissing your dads part," he teased, earning a playful shove from his girlfriend and more laughter from the group.

"And I am going to shower for an hour, then sleep for a week," Harlen deadpanned, causing the others to burst into laughter once again.

"I need to hug my sister, mom, and dad!" Kass said, his eyes reflecting the deep love he felt for his family.

The group of friends knew their hearts were forever intertwined, bound by a shared experience that had tested their limits, revealed their strengths, and taught them the true value of friendship and love. They were ready to face the future, hand-in-hand, forever grateful for the extraordinary moments that had shaped their lives.

As they sat together on the field, discussing the aftermath of their incredible journey, a swirl of fear and uncertainty remained. They knew that explaining their extraordinary experiences to others would be an uphill battle, one filled with skepticism and disbelief.

Olivia voiced their concerns, "Who will believe us? We were transported to another world, faced mythical creatures, and experienced things beyond imagination. People will think we've lost our minds."

Gab nodded, "And the media? They'll twist our story into some sensationalized headline like, '*Missing Canadians Abducted by Wild Monkeys!*' We'll become the talk of the town and our lives will be under constant scrutiny."

"But keeping it a secret feels like lying to our loved ones. They deserve to know the truth, even if it's hard for them to believe," Jack said.

"But what about the authorities? Shouldn't we report what happened? It might help them understand all the strange occurrences in Kelowna," Martin added.

"We can't deny that this journey has changed us, and it's a part of who we are now. But we need to weigh the pros and cons carefully. Sharing the truth will undoubtedly lead to ridicule and judgment," Kass said.

"Hey, maybe we could start a secret society and only reveal our incredible adventure to those who prove worthy," Harlen joked.

Despite the lighthearted remark, the group knew their decision was not to be taken lightly. The decision to keep their adventures secret or share their story was of the utmost significance.

"You're right, Kass. We would be interrogated, probed, poked at, and accused of lying," Gab said.

"Then let's just tell everyone that..." Kass paused, head down in thought and frustration. "Actually, I don't know how we can do this."

"Well, we need to think fast before we're spotted," Jack advised. "Maybe we hide somewhere while we think about it."

"Jack's right. We need to figure this out fast," Gab said.

Martin was sprawled on his back with Kass's head resting on his lap. The moment felt intimate as the soft green grass gave them comfort. Jack and Harlen sat next to each other with their legs crisscrossed. Olivia's back faced Gab, relaxing as Gab re-braided their hair.

"I got it!" Jack shouted. "We tell everyone we were blindfolded, taken to an unknown location, and then released this morning. Just dropped off."

"Okay, I think Jack has the beginning of a good idea," Kass agreed.

"But we would have to say we were blindfolded the whole time," Olivia said, not convinced.

"Hmm...they took the blindfolds off and the room was..." Martin began.

"This isn't going to work," Kass interrupted. "One elaborate lie kept secret among six teenagers just isn't going to cut it. They'll know we're lying and things will get worse."

"Why don't we just tell them we don't remember anything? Nothing. The monkeys took us somewhere in the forest and then we reappeared here days later. That's it. We just don't remember anything," Olivia suggested.

"I can't lie to my dads," Gab said.

"You're right. I can't tell my mom and dad something so fabricated and outlandish," Kass agreed.

"Actually, we need our parents to help us figure this out. We need to tell them all at the same time and give them the truth. Then they can help us figure the rest out," Jack said.

"You're right," Kass added.

"I agree," Martin said.

"Me too," Olivia said.

"Then it's unanimous. We will talk to our parents first. They'll help us for sure," Harlen said.

"Now, how do we get from here to our homes without being seen?" Harlen asked.

"Good question," Jack said.

"Minivan!" Kass shouted. "One of us goes to my house or Gab's house, since we are the only ones with minivans. We get the parents to come pick us up then drive us into the garage so we won't be seen."

"Yes!" Harlen shouted.

"Okay, who?" Olivia questioned.

"Me," said Kass. "I look less like myself than any of you. The whiskers on my face, my hair's a mess, my shoes are dirty, and my clothes make me look like a homeless boy living in a box. No offense to homeless people," Kass said.

"You're right. No one will recognize you dressed like that."

"I'll explain to my mom and dad, and then we'll come pick you up. I'll tell them to call your parents right away and have them meet at our house."

"Okay, Kass, it sounds like the best option. We'll hide over by the bleachers. Go, and good luck. And please go as fast as you can...well, maybe not superhero fast," Jack chuckled. "That might draw some unwanted attention."

"Ya, I'll just jog, but if any of us gets noticed before I return, don't say anything to anyone without our parents present," Kass advised.

"Yes, just go mute on their ass," Harlen said.

The friends stood and embraced, forming a domed huddle by wrapping their arms around each other's back and putting their heads together. They inhaled, then exhaled.

Kass saw himself as a powerful and influential individual, burdened with the responsibility that came with it. These realizations bore down with great force as he carried the backpack containing the mystical gemstone. He turned to the west, ready for the last leg of his journey home as the sun dipped below the horizon and painted the sky with fiery shades of glorious reds and oranges.

After Kass walked only a few feet, he abruptly stopped. Seemingly dormant after their harrowing teleportation home, the gemstone in Kass's backpack began to hum with eerie vibrations. The odd occurrence chilled Kass to his bones while at the same time set his nerves on fire. His heart raced as he reached into the backpack, his trembling fingers closed around the gemstone and discovered it pulsating with vibrant energy.

Vivid visions of past and future adventures exploded within the minds and before the eyes of all six teens in that very same moment. Heart-pounding peril, glorious triumphs, enigmatic encounters, and long-buried ancient secrets clawed their way into their collective consciousness.

The vision continued with the six friends glimpsing back at the horrors that had transpired during their recent journey; the experiences that had carved indelible marks of sorrow and terror into their memories.

Then emerging from the shadows within the group's vision, the ghastly creature Kass had seen during his out-of-body experience came into their view. It moved with an eerie, unnatural grace, its black cloak flowing around it. "Wanderers," the creature's bass voice boomed with haunting resonance, "beyond the veil of reality, you've had but a fleeting glance at the matrix of destiny. The gemstone has cast its mystical gaze upon you and your fate is forever interwoven with the cryptic strands that bind the essence of time. Secrets unfold in whispers and mysteries deepen with each step you take. Beware, for shadows stir, and ancient forces have taken notice. They will come for you."

The stunned teens absorbed the creature's every word.

"Enkarius, the crystalline being, was once a ruler among its kind. Long ago, it sought to amplify its powers, merging its essence with the monolith stone."

The ghastly creature then gestured toward a holographic map that had materialized before them.

"This crystalline labyrinth is both your destination and your greatest trial."

Lines of light crisscrossed the map, creating a dazzling ever-shifting lattice that seemed to pulse with life. These weren't ordinary lines; they functioned as pathways and routes infused with a celestial energy that cast an other-worldly glow on the faces of Kass and his friends. The holographic map was a beacon to provide guidance through the vast unknown. It embodied their purpose, beckoning them.

The ghastly beast continued. "The gemstone you carry evolved and became your guide on your perilous journey into the depths of Enkarius' realm. The gem is now your key to unlocking the mysteries of the future. It is your compass, pointing the way to your destiny."

As the sun dipped below the horizon, fear shivered down the spines of Kass, Gab, Harlen, Jack, Olivia, and Martin. The tension in the air was palpable, gripping their souls. Yet, beneath their fear, determination flickered like a burning ember, casting defiant shadows across their faces.

Gratitude weaves through every page. To my editors, whose unwavering dedication chiseled this work into its finest form. Special kudos to author Gary Tubbs, whose wisdom, humor, and inspiration sparked life in every chapter. Please forgive the bear; its tale was an indispensable part of the journey.

To all who've joined this journey through my story, thank you sincerely. Writing it brought me joy, and your connection to its pages is incredibly meaningful—it's what makes sharing stories so rewarding.

Within the everyday lies the extraordinary. Embrace your quirks and differences, for they hold the key to turning the ordinary into something truly remarkable.

Shawn Thorn, a seasoned child therapist and dedicated educator, has blended his passion for storytelling with decades of commitment to shaping young minds. Having emerged as a luminary in children's literature, Shawn is the creative force behind two cherished picture books: *Don't Tease Mr. Beeze* and *First of Many*.

Inspired by the enchanting landscapes of Shawn's home, nestled amid forested mountains, North Vancouver, British Columbia, serves as a canvas painted with the beauty of nature. Shawn and his family, including his loving scientist husband, their flourishing five-year-old son, a cherished honorary teen daughter, and the ever-faithful vizsla companion named Ridley, embrace the joys of life in this scenic haven. Surrounded by the frequent presence of bears as hungry neighbors, Shawn's daily life becomes a harmonious blend of the wild and the familial.